BETTER THAN SUNSHINE

BETTER *than* SUNSHINE

BETTER THAN SUNSHINE

Sunset Siesta Series

ERIN BROCKUS

GREEN SAGE PRESS

Chapter One

AUSTIN

A MAN DESERVED to hear the whisper of the ocean breeze with his first cup of coffee, not the battle cry of a demolition crew attacking the derelict mansion next door. This was a truth I held self-evident, right up there with never trusting a politician who claimed to understand the tides.

My careful universe, rebuilt shard by shard over thirteen years, had developed a significant, ear-splitting crack. Its name was Heron House. More accurately, its new and apparently noise-immune owner.

I cradled my ceramic mug, its familiar weight a small comfort as I leaned against the porch railing of my conch house. The coffee was strong and black, the way I liked it. No frills, no nonsense. Just like my life.

Or how my life used to be.

The meticulous order of my home—every plank of clapboard siding painted a crisp white, each rich green shutter aligned with military precision—reflected the internal calm I fought to maintain. The house was my sanctuary, a fortress against the world's unpredictable turmoil. Now, that fortress had a thunderous siege engine parked on its border.

For the past two weeks, since the arrival of one Iris Holloway from somewhere up north, my days had become a relentless assault. Sunrise, which once painted the Gulf in silent strokes of apricot and rose, was now heralded by the guttural roar of a rented generator, followed swiftly by the echoing thud of hammers against ancient, protesting wood. Today's special included an off-key rendition of some pop song by Sutton Vale I vaguely recognized from my brother Eli's dive shop radio, punctuated by an occasional yelp. Whether of frustration or accidental self-injury, I couldn't tell.

And didn't want to.

Heron House itself had always been a fixture, a grand, decaying Victorian lady sighing her slow surrender to the salt and sun next to my property. Three sprawling stories of off-white, peeling paint like sunburnt skin, porch railings sagging like weary shoulders, and gardens so overgrown they probably hosted species unknown to science. But old Lady Lawson had possessed the good grace to let it crumble in peace. Until she passed away and left the entire thing to this Holloway woman, some sort of relative. The new owner, however, seemed to believe resurrection required a full-blown rock concert. Starring herself.

A particularly violent screech, like a pterodactyl being put through a woodchipper, rattled my coffee cup against the railing. My gaze moved to rest on the tropical crimson of my hibiscus hedge that separated our properties. I closed my eyes and inhaled a slow, deliberate breath, counting the seconds like prayer beads.

One... two... The ghosts of the past were always

quieter in the early morning, before the world woke up and reminded you of all the ways it could go wrong.

Three… four… This stillness, this order, wasn't just a preference. It was a necessity. A way to keep the edges from fraying, to keep the memories locked tight where they couldn't do any more damage.

Five… six… And now this. This cheerful, oblivious destruction of my carefully curated peace. Today even the gorgeous red blooms couldn't soothe me.

She had no understanding of the delicate balance of a place like Dove Key, where the hush was as much a part of the landscape as the mangroves. Holloway thought she could just waltz in, all bright ideas and Home Depot enthusiasm, and bend a hundred years of history to her will without ruffling a feather. As it happened, my feathers were thoroughly ruffled.

And then some.

The screeching stopped, replaced by a series of resonant thwacks. I pictured her, a vague image culled from glimpses through the hedge I kept trimmed to perfection— a flash of long, sun-streaked blonde hair escaping a messy ponytail, the surprisingly determined set of a dirt-smudged jaw. A whirlwind of limbs usually covered in some new form of construction debris. But limbs that were undeniably female.

That thought made me scowl. She probably wore flip-flops to operate heavy machinery. Her crew wasn't much better. The whole damn enterprise reeked of amateur hour.

Enough. I couldn't sit here and let my blood pressure rise with the sun. It was time for escape.

Line Dancer was waiting.

I drained my coffee, the last dregs mirroring the gritty mood that had settled over me. Inside, my kitchen—with

its natural maple Shaker cabinets, honed granite counter-
tops, and the stainless-steel section I'd installed for cleaning
fish—was a practical haven. I grabbed my gear bag, the
worn canvas familiar in my hand.

The drive to Sunset Siesta Resort was short, but long
enough for me to attempt a mental reset. My home was
one of several conch houses, plus the monstrosity next
door, that anchored the northern shore of the residential
district on the island's northwest quadrant. My mood had
improved enough that I tapped my truck door shut in the
parking lot instead of slamming it. As I passed the open-
form pool area, the resort was already stirring. A few early
risers headed for the beach, the scent of breakfast from
Driftwood Grill mingling with the salt air. It was a different
kind of noise here. The hum of a working place. Of
family.

My family.

Their lives were all moving forward in a steady current
of engagements, weddings, and babies. Sometimes I was a
stone in that current, unmoving, watching the water flow
around me.

Prepping *Line Dancer* was therapy. The familiar rituals
of checking fuel and oil, stowing bait, wiping down the
already spotless fiberglass deck. The rhythmic clink of ice
into the cooler. My charter for the day was a family of four
from Ohio: an eager dad, a slightly apprehensive mom,
and two kids, a boy and a girl, practically vibrating with
excitement. The boy, maybe ten, with eyes like saucers, hit
me with the inevitable question before we'd even cleared
the no-wake zone.

"You think we'll catch a shark, Captain Austin?"

I managed a noncommittal grunt that I hoped sounded
encouraging. "Sorry, kid. We don't hunt sharks here. Other
outfits do, but the ecosystem has plenty of challenges

without depleting its apex predators." I smiled to soften the news. "But we'll likely catch plenty of snapper, maybe a dorado if we're lucky. The sea's got its own ideas about what it wants to give up."

I didn't voice my hope that the Gulf would give up a sudden, localized waterspout aimed directly at Heron House. Purely for noise abatement, of course.

Once we were out on the open water, the familiar sense of rightness settled over me. Dove Key became a low, green smudge on the horizon, the only sounds the thrum of the diesel, the cry of a distant tern, and the slap of the hull against the chop. The ocean didn't judge. It didn't demand. It just was. Honest. Mostly predictable, if you knew its language. And I spoke it fluently.

I guided the family, showed the dad the subtle flick of the wrist needed to cast into the mangroves for snook. The girl had a surprising knack for it, and I helped her reel in a respectable red snapper, her face a mask of fierce concentration and then pure joy. I answered their questions about tides, currents, and the best way to cook their catch with the practiced ease of a thousand charters.

"What a day!" the dad, Drake, exclaimed several hours later, his face ruddy with sun and excitement as he landed a feisty jack crevalle. He tossed it in the ice cooler. They'd caught as many fish as they could handle and learned the importance of returning the ones they didn't plan to have the restaurant cook for them. "You run a tight ship. Best charter we've been on in years."

I just nodded with a slight smile, accepting the compliment with my usual economy of expression. It wasn't about running a tight ship. It was about respect for the process, for the environment. You read the water, you found the fish. Simple. Clean.

As I guided *Line Dancer* into her spot at the Sunset

Siesta dock, the familiar resort spread out before me, a sprawling collection of buildings that had been the backdrop to my entire life. More history than hotel, as my sister Harper often joked, though it was currently undergoing its own metamorphosis.

An hour later, hosing down the deck where the scent of salt and fish created a familiar, almost comforting perfume, Harper stepped onto the boat. Even six months pregnant with twins—God help her and her husband, Chase—she moved with a brisk, purposeful energy. Her chestnut hair was pulled back in a practical ponytail, but wisps had escaped to frame a face that looked both tired and determined. A file folder was tucked under her arm.

"Good trip, Austin?" She paused at the edge of the slip, her hand resting on her prominent belly.

"Yeah. Ohio folks. They were happy." I turned off the hose. "How are you? You're looking more… uh… expanded."

Smooth, Coleridge. Real smooth.

A weary smile touched her lips. "Feeling like I'm smuggling a pair of particularly active bowling balls. But otherwise, yes, expanded is the word."

"Expanded? Harper, you look like you're about to launch your own little fleet." Braden's cheerful voice preceded him as he sauntered up and hopped on board. Our youngest brother was all easy grins and restless ambition, his light-brown hair already escaping the baseball cap he wore. He ran Tidal Hops, the brewpub at the resort, and had an opinion or a joke ready for any occasion. Though we were very different personalities, he was the sibling I tended to gravitate to.

He bent over and peered at Harper's belly. "Seriously, sis, are you sure there are only two in there?"

She laughed. "Pretty sure, little brother, unless Chase

managed to sneak in a third when I wasn't looking. And perish that thought. He's currently designing Nursery Wing Alpha and Bravo." She turned back to me. "And yes, Austin, I'm on light duty, which apparently means juggling seventeen crises instead of twenty. Chase and I should finish moving into Mom's place this week."

"Good timing," Braden chimed in, leaning against the rail. "That guest cottage was getting a bit snug for Team Bowling Ball, I imagine. Mom's got to be thrilled to have an excuse to extend her *Eat, Pray, Love* world tour."

I smiled. Braden could lighten even my moods, and Mom deserved her escape. She'd come up with the idea of moving into the two-bedroom guest cottage Harper and her young son, Finn, had occupied for years, letting the growing family have the house we had all grown up in. Then she'd announced she was off on an extended holiday, giving them plenty of time for the big move.

"She sent a postcard from Juneau," Harper added, dropping onto the padded bench seat. "Apparently, she's an expert on glacier calving now and is off to Italy next. Says she'll be back after the twins arrive, then who knows where she'll jet off to."

"Good for her," I said. "And the main house has more room for… all that." I gestured vaguely at her midsection.

"Tell me about it." Harper's gaze swept over the resort grounds, a familiar worry line creasing her brow. "The resort reno is chugging along without too much drama at the moment. Lobby demo starts next week, which is going to be fun."

Braden winced. "Maybe not so much for the guests trying to check in alongside a cloud of hundred-year-old plaster dust. But hey, progress, right?" He nodded toward the end of the beach where four bungalows stretched along the sand. "Those things have been a hit."

"The bungalows are an absolute gold mine," Harper agreed, her eyes lighting up. "Booked solid for months. Chase, for all his occasionally terrifying focus on minute design details, knows his stuff."

"He usually does," I agreed.

Chase was a good man, and I was glad Harper had him. She'd earned some peace and reliability in her life. As she talked about spending more time off her feet, I was the familiar observer to all this forward momentum washing over me. It wasn't a bad feeling. Just… separate. The thought of more little humans running around, more noise, more chaos, brought a faint, strange pang. More noise, I told myself. That's all it was. Couldn't be envy.

Braden's face had soured. "Yuck. Too damn much domesticity going on around here."

"Well, you're safe. What I have isn't contagious." Harper patted the folder. "Thanks for the break, but I'd better get back to it. Just wanted to give you a heads-up about the lobby demolition traffic, Austin."

"Noted."

Braden pushed off the rail. "And I've got a new shipment of hops calling my name. Don't work too hard, you two." He gave us a wave and headed toward Tidal Hops.

As I gave Harper a hand up, she gave me a look with a familiar flicker of sisterly concern in her eyes. "Heron House still sounding like a war zone?"

The question brought the morning's irritation roaring back. I rubbed my dark scruff. "You have no idea. It's a violation of the Geneva Convention on noise pollution."

She smiled and winced sympathetically. "Oof. Good luck with that. And try to get some actual rest. You look like you're running on fumes and black coffee."

"I'll try."

Then she was walking away, her focus already on the

next item on her to-do list. She was right. I was tired. Tired of the noise, the disruption, and this low-grade, simmering anticipation for a confrontation with a woman I hadn't even officially met.

I finished securing *Line Dancer*. On the other side of the pier, the resort dive boat, *Sunset Diver*, was tied up. As I walked the length of the wooden structure toward my truck, the thought of my tranquil house and the crumbling mansion next door loomed like a gathering squall.

A reckoning was coming, whether I wanted it or not.

And it sure as hell wouldn't be quiet.

Chapter Two

IRIS

THE OLD BRASS DEADBOLT, its surface mottled with rust, was a stiff, reluctant thing. My exit from Heron House's front door was a daily wrestling match, a test of will against ancient, stubborn metal. Of course, I could use the easier kitchen door, but I had to teach this thing who was boss.

"Oh, come on, you ornery old beast."

My fingers stung as I gave the tarnished thumb-turn another heave, putting my shoulder into it. For a terrifying moment, nothing happened. Then, with a groan, the bolt slid back. The monstrously heavy, nearly black door shuddered open begrudgingly with a horrifying, protracted creak that sounded like the dying moan of a forgotten sea monster. A sound rapidly becoming the official soundtrack to my life.

At last, I escaped into the Dove Key morning. Stepping onto the wide, dilapidated front porch, I shook out my shoulders, trying to dispel the dread that came over me every time that damn door shrieked.

I really needed to replace the awful, shitty door.

That thought made me frown as my gaze swept around the grand old manor. I was forming a new identity here in Dove Key: Iris Holloway, proprietress. It had a nice ring to it. A certain gravitas. And proprietresses in charming seaside communities likely didn't punctuate their sentences with words that would make future guests blush.

"Note to self, Iris," I said, making a mental list. "Item one—learn advanced carpentry. Item two—cultivate a vocabulary more befitting a gracious hostess than a frustrated longshoreman. More tea party, less dockside brawl."

Pleased with my decision, I filled my lungs with the possibilities of the morning. The air still held a hint of the night's coolness, rich with the sweet perfume of hibiscus from my neighbor's yard. Definitely not from mine, which currently smelled more of centuries of compost and neglect. The warm air felt like a minor parole after two weeks of sleeping in Aunt Constance Lawson's old bedroom, the only habitable space in the house. My only changes there had been a new mattress and box springs for the antique bed I'd found on Main Street.

The tropical sun was already climbing, promising another day of balmy heat and humidity. It wasn't the gentle, hazy light of Abingdon, Virginia, which I'd recently left. This sun was a bold, unapologetic glare that, once it fully hit Heron House, illuminated every speck of dust, cobweb, and daunting shadow within its crumbling walls.

I still couldn't quite believe it was all mine. This grand, decaying Victorian lady. Ancient, dilapidated rooms, gardens so overgrown they probably hosted species unknown to science. Aunt Constance must have possessed a unique sense of humor. Or perhaps an overly optimistic view of her distant great-niece's renovation skills.

I didn't truly understand why she'd left me this enormous, beautiful, terrifying, money-eating behemoth. Or her shockingly substantial bank account. The lawyer's letter had been brief and formal. No family anecdotes, no hazily remembered shared memories. With my mom gone eight years now, Aunt Constance had been my only remaining family, even if we were practically strangers. I never expected to hear from her, let alone inherit her entire world. The news had landed in my quiet life like a meteorite, displacing everything.

But I refused to dwell on the obstacles. My gaze caught on the tiny, resilient details—a patch of original stained glass in a grimy transom window winking in the sun, the elegant, though listing, line of the roof against the vibrant sky. My dream, the one that had been a low, persistent hum for years, surged again and chased away the tendrils of panic. That dream was on its way to becoming a reality.

A bed & breakfast.

Heron House Bed & Breakfast.

I could see it, clear as the cloudless sky above. This porch, not ramshackle and peeling, but restored, with comfortable rocking chairs filled with happy guests sipping iced tea. Or something stronger if they preferred. I didn't judge. The gardens a fragrant sanctuary instead of a jungle. The house itself not groaning, but singing. Maybe my sociology degree would find its true purpose here— understanding people, creating community, fostering connection. This wasn't just a building. It was a calling. At least that's what I kept telling myself every time I smashed a spider.

I'd turned thirty a few months ago.

The number still echoed in my head with the faint

clang of unmet expectations. My married friends back home were buying sensible minivans. I'd just inherited a house that might require an exorcism before an inspection. But Heron House wasn't just an inheritance. It was a dare from the universe. A chance to stop drifting through receptionist duties and part-time winery tasting-room jobs and build something real, something lasting.

Something I would actually finish.

The memory of the half-renovated space in Abingdon was a sour taste in my mouth. The one with the perfect five-year business plan and the lease I'd broken after six months when it got too overwhelming. My pottery studio that was never to be. This time had to be different.

"Okay, house." I propped my hands on my hips and surveyed the uneven floorboards and peeling shutters. "You and me. We're going to make some magic."

The sheer scale of the work, however, was enough to send my potent optimism into a temporary coma. I had a construction crew for the heavy stuff, but they were off on weekends. This morning, all was serene at the old mansion. Today, I needed a win. Something manageable. Something that involved fresh air and didn't require battling a century of accumulated grime with a tiny sponge and a giant prayer.

My gaze fell upon the overgrown disaster of the side yard, the part that abutted my mysterious and aloof neighbor's property. Specifically, the ancient, erratic sprinkler head that had been giving me the evil eye since my arrival. It was technically on my property, near the invisible line where Heron House's jungle met his unnervingly perfect hibiscus hedge with its riot of red.

The sprinkler had a habit of sputtering to life at random, usually when I was trying to wrestle something large out of my car, and it had a distinct, almost vindictive tendency to overwater one specific patch of weeds while drenching a section of my neighbor's immaculate hibiscus hedge.

I'd caught glimpses of him.

My construction foreman had told me his name, Austin Coleridge, though he'd said it with a sour look toward my neighbor's beautifully restored house. Tall with dark hair and stubble, Austin was all lean, quiet economy of movement. The faded denim of his jeans stretched taut over powerful thighs, his bare arms corded with muscle when he crossed them over a chest carved from oak. A younger Clint Eastwood, maybe. Distractingly attractive, even if he'd never so much as glanced my way. Not a hello, not a welcome, just an occasional scowl thrown in my general direction. All of which had left me uncharacteristically unsure of how to introduce myself.

Now, peering through a gap in my overgrown foliage, I glimpsed him. He was on his covered back patio, relaxing in a rocking chair with a coffee cup in hand as he stared out at the sea. He looked peaceful. Undisturbed.

"Good neighbor points, Iris, good neighbor points," I muttered, grabbing a pair of pliers from my new, yet already rusting, toolkit. "This will show him I'm a considerate, capable individual, not just the lady wrestling a haunted house into submission." And might even lead to a friendly meeting.

The sprinkler head, up close, was a relic of a bygone era, probably installed when Bush was in office. Either Bush. It was caked with rust and mineral deposits.

"How hard can it be to adjust a sprinkler?" I muttered, recalling a YouTube video I'd half-watched while munching on Oreos last night. "It's just a nozzle. Twist it a bit. Thump it once or twice. Simple."

I gripped the pliers around what I assumed was the adjustable part and gave it an optimistic, firm twist.

Nothing.

Dropping to my knees, I grunted and applied more pressure. I grinned when the metal started to give. The old metal groaned, then, with a sickening snap, the entire head broke clean off in my hand. For a split second, I stared at the offending part in almost comical silence. Then, like a miniature Old Faithful, a powerful, uncontrolled geyser of water erupted from the pipe, spraying everywhere.

But especially shooting like a cannon with pinpoint, vengeful accuracy directly at my neighbor's perfect, vibrant red hibiscus hedge.

"Oh no!" I shrieked, dropping the pliers. "Oh, holy hibiscus, NO! Not his flowers!"

Cold panic clawed at my throat. This wasn't a gentle misting. This was a full-scale aquatic assault. The beautiful crimson blooms were being battered, petals flying like scarlet confetti. Branches snapped. The manicured ground around them was quickly turning into a swamp. I lunged, trying to stuff my hand over the break. The water pressure nearly knocked me over, soaking me in an instant. Mud splattered my jeans and my face, and my hair dripped.

"He's going to call the garden police!" I hissed, looking wildly around. "He's going to sue me for emotional distress to a shrub! He already looks like he could wrestle a shark and win. What's he going to do to me?"

And why, oh why, did he have to be so unfairly, distractingly handsome? This was not how I'd wanted to introduce myself.

"Holloway!"

The voice was controlled thunder, each syllable laced with disbelief and a gathering storm of annoyance. It sliced through the gushing water, and I swore the air grew colder. I froze, still on my knees, water careening off my arm to destroy more blossoms.

Slowly, dreadfully, I turned my head.

Austin stood at the edge of his lawn, where the swamp began. His short, dark hair was slightly messed up, as if he'd run a hand through it in sheer exasperation. His gray eyes, narrowed to slits, were fixed on his hibiscus, then on me, then back to the hibiscus, as if trying to decide which was the more offensive sight.

"Is that," he began, his voice dangerously calm, the stillness before a Category Five hurricane, "some newfangled form of DIY plumbing you've invented, or are you actively attempting to hydro-blast my award-winning hibiscus into the Gulf of Mexico?"

My mouth opened, but only a pathetic squeak came out. I was dripping, muddy, and still holding the broken piece of plumbing like a particularly unconvincing scepter. "Oh! Mr. Coleridge! Austin! I am so, so incredibly sorry! It just… it was aiming a little wild, and I thought I could redirect it a tiny bit. An attempt at experimental irrigation that, uh, went slightly sideways. It seemed like such a simple adjustment." I tried for a smile. It likely looked like a grimace of terror. "Guess it really wanted to water your side today? Extra thoroughly."

His expression did not soften. If anything, the thunderclouds in his eyes gathered. He didn't say a word. He just started walking toward me. Not fast, but with a deliberate, ground-eating stride that made my insides clench. He didn't stop at the property line. He stalked along an overgrown path right into my yard, into the watery, muddy mess I had created, his bare feet squelching slightly.

"I'm really sorry!" I rose to my feet, my dark-blonde hair darker as it dripped into my eyes.

With a string of muttered curses that involved "amateurs," "delicate root systems," and something I thought might be "assault on private property values," he stopped near the hedge. Propping both hands on his hips, he took in the damage.

I braced myself. For yelling. For a lecture on proper plumbing etiquette. For him to maybe just pick me up and toss me into the nearest man-eating shrub.

Instead, he moved several feet down the hedge and bent at the waist. His large, calloused, and surprisingly nimble hands found the buried shut-off valve—a valve I hadn't known existed—and gave it a sharp, decisive twist. The geyser choked and sputtered before finally dying.

Leaving behind a pathetic gurgle and a scene of utter horticultural devastation.

He straightened slowly, wiping a muddy hand on his equally muddy shorts. His jaw was tight, a muscle twitching just beneath his stubble. I could practically feel the waves of condemnation rolling off him.

"It doesn't look so bad now," I squeaked.

"Holloway." He said my name like it was a piece of garbage he'd just found on his can. "My hibiscus. My day off." He paused, and for a terrifying second, I thought he might spontaneously combust. "Try to confine your renovation disasters to your goddamn property before you declare war on the entire neighborhood's landscaping. And for God's sake, next time you feel the urge to fix something that involves water pressure, call a plumber. Or a landscaper." He took a huge, long breath that didn't seem to steady him. "Or better yet, just… don't."

He didn't wait for a reply, which was wise, since I was incapable of forming one. He turned on his heel, his bare feet making squishing sounds as he retreated across his now partially swampy backyard and disappeared through his back door without a backward glance.

I was left drenched and caked in mud, clutching a broken piece of sprinkler head, surrounded by a watery chaos of my own making. The silence he left behind was almost as deafening as the geyser. My face was hotter than the sun. My grand plan to impress him had backfired in the most spectacularly wet fashion possible.

The scary front door of Heron House, with its horrifying creak and aura of ancient disapproval, now loomed like a welcoming retreat from the righteous, hibiscus-fueled fury of Austin Coleridge. My determination to win him over hadn't exactly vanished, but it was currently taking a serious, mud-caked, and very damp beating.

Still, as I trudged back toward the house, leaving a trail of muddy footprints, a tiny, irrepressible thought sparked.

Well, at least he knows I exist now.

And despite the ruined hibiscus and the ruined Saturday, despite the almost certain knowledge that my disconcertingly hot and snarly neighbor considered me a certifiable menace, the smallest of smiles touched my lips.

This was going to be interesting.

Chapter Three

AUSTIN

THE WATER WAS SCALDING, or as close as I could stand without peeling skin. Thick, suffocating steam filled the shower, but it did nothing to soften the jagged knot of anger lodged in my chest. I scrubbed at my hair, raking my scalp with my fingertips, then moved to my skin with a pressure that bordered on punitive, as if I could physically wash away the mud, the floral damage, and the sheer, unbelievable gall of the woman next door.

Iris Holloway.

Even her name sounded like a whimsical, fluttery disaster waiting to happen, a pastel-fragranced bomb set to detonate in the middle of my monochrome existence.

"Experimental irrigation," I muttered under the drumming spray. "Sweet Jesus."

I leaned my forehead against the cool, white subway tile, the porcelain a soothing contrast to the water sluicing over my back. Four years. Four damn years I'd nursed that hibiscus hedge from scrawny, hopeful transplants into a vibrant wall of crimson. A living shield. In less than four minutes, she'd nearly blasted it into the ocean with the misguided enthusiasm of a toddler wielding a firehose.

Holloway was a scourge. A genuine, grade-A, property-value-lowering, peace-shattering scourge.

Dressed in clean cargo shorts and a plain white T-shirt blessedly dry against my skin, I stalked into the kitchen. The rich, dark scent of coffee did little to soothe my mood. I poured a cup before automatically reaching for the box of Wheaties from the pantry. Routine. Order. The corner-stones of a life that made sense.

I sat at the wooden table I'd salvaged from a junk shop and refinished myself, its surface scarred yet beautifully smooth beneath my fingertips. My gaze drifted to the window, the one specifically placed to offer an uninter-rupted view of my little kingdom—my yard and, further out, the sea grapes that bowed gracefully in the breeze.

And my hibiscus hedge.

Even from this distance, the damage was brutally obvi-ous. Gaps in the lush green like missing teeth in a once-perfect smile. A noticeable, drooping section that had borne the brunt of the assault. It looked wounded.

"Can't even have a goddamn bowl of cereal in peace," I grumbled to the empty room.

I ate, my jaw working overtime. My Saturday morning, usually an expanse of solitary productivity or restorative ocean time, had been utterly hijacked.

Maybe I'd been a dick about it. The thought flickered, unwelcome as a sand fly at a picnic. Her face, when I'd confronted her, had been a mask of sheer dread. Those wide blue eyes—eyes I had to admit were rather striking. And she'd been soaked, the thin cotton of her floral blouse doing nothing to hide the curves underneath. But then the image of my drowned flowers resurfaced.

No.

I hadn't yelled.

I'd been firm. Direct.

Controlled, even, considering the provocation. She needed to understand this wasn't some community-garden free-for-all where whimsical destruction was chalked up to artistic expression. This was my goddamn property. My peace. She caused the problem, not me. That was the simple, unvarnished truth.

The cereal bowl was empty, my stomach churning with stale Wheaties and fresh resentment. I couldn't sit here. Couldn't just look at the damage and let it fester.

My gardening shears were solid and familiar in my hand. I strode to the hedge, the earth still squishy and dark beneath my boots where the Holloway-generated deluge had lingered. Up close, the carnage was worse. Broken stems hung limply, their vibrant green insides exposed like fresh wounds. Perfect, intensely red blossoms were torn and mud-splattered, their delicate, papery beauty ruined.

"Damn it, Holloway," I muttered, the words a low, frustrated growl that did nothing to alleviate the pressure in my chest.

I started work with methodical, almost surgical precision. *Snip.* The shears bit cleanly through a hopelessly damaged branch, the sound crisp in the humid air. *Pluck.* A ruined flower, its life cut short by horticultural waterboarding, dropped into the bucket at my feet with a soft, mournful thud. *Wipe.* I gently swiped my thumb across a mud-caked leaf, trying to restore some of its dignity, to let it breathe again.

This hedge wasn't just a row of plants. It was a statement. A living symbol of patience, care, and the stubborn satisfaction of nurturing something beautiful in a world that often felt relentlessly chaotic.

I'd never intended to enter the damn thing in any competition. Braden, with his usual uncanny talent for goading me into things I'd rather avoid, was the sole culprit behind that particular foray into public horticulture.

I'd won the whole damn shooting match.

And Holloway, with her good intentions that paved the road to hibiscus hell, had nearly drowned that accomplishment.

I worked for over an hour, pruning, cleaning, assessing the extent of the damage. The sun climbed higher, beating down on my neck, but I barely noticed. This was a ritual, almost a penance. For what, I wasn't sure. For thinking this small patch of the world could remain untouched?

Thankfully, the damage wasn't as terminal as I'd first feared. The roots were still strong, anchored deep in the soil. The hedge would recover. But it would bear the scars of this morning for a while.

Just like my goddamn peace of mind.

I gathered the bucket of floral casualties and dumped them into the trash can. The clang of the metal lid sounded definitive. Another piece of chaos, however temporarily, wrestled back into place.

But the edginess remained, a low, persistent thrum beneath my skin like an engine idling. I pulled out my phone, my thumb hovering over Eli's name. He was probably underwater with a dive class or, more likely, blissfully entangled with Jules in that honeymoon bubble that rendered him impervious to the outside world. They had married on the resort beach last month, and Eli settled into newlywed life like a fish taking to, well, water. Another sibling lost to domesticity. Still, the urge to connect, to hear a familiar voice, was strong. I hit dial.

It rang three times before he picked up, his voice predictably cheerful. "Captain Grinch! To what do I owe the honor? Did you run out of brooding material and need to bounce some new ideas off me?"

"Very funny, Eli. You got a minute? Or is Jules making you color-coordinate your socks now?"

A hearty laugh crackled through the phone, and a smile touched my lips. "Hey, a little order never hurt anyone. Besides, she says the sock routine brings out the blue in my eyes. What's up? You sound tenser than usual. Which is saying something."

"Neighbor issues," I said, keeping it vague. No need to rehash the whole sordid Sprinklergate. "Got an itch to get wet. You free for a dive?"

A pause. "Aw, Austin, you know I'd love to, but I've got an open-water class starting in about an hour. And Jules wants to unpack those last wedding gift boxes."

"Right. The joys of domestic bliss."

"Hey, don't knock it 'til you try it, brother," Eli said, his voice still cheerful. "Though I don't see you rushing to the altar anytime soon. Tell you what, though. I could swing a night dive if you're up for it. Just us. We could dive right off the beach at the resort."

The thought was tempting. The ocean at night was a different world. Secretive, alien. But the disquiet was a coiled spring in my gut now. "Nah. Tonight's no good. Got to get my beauty sleep."

Eli snorted. "Beauty sleep? Austin, you need a damn beauty coma. But hey, your loss. Don't want you scaring the nocturnal critters with that mug of yours anyway."

That finally drew a laugh from me. "Yeah, yeah. Hilarious. Another time, then."

"You got it. Hey, seriously… you okay?"

"Peachy," I lied. "Just peachy."

"Uh-huh. Well, if peachy involves needing to blow off

steam when I'm not otherwise occupied, give me another ring. See you later."

"Thanks. Later, Eli."

I hung up, the brief exchange leaving me feeling both slightly better and oddly more adrift. Even my usual escape routes were temporarily blocked. Meeting Braden for a beer at Tidal Hops was too much effort.

Too much explaining.

Too much people.

I found myself walking along the strip of sand and pebble beach that fronted this northern edge of the island. The rhythmic sigh of waves breaking on the shore, a sound that usually soothed the tight, familiar knot in my gut, offered little comfort. Today, even the ocean couldn't quite unravel the tangle of irritation Holloway had introduced.

I walked west, toward where my carefully tended property gave way to something wilder—the untamed, overgrown jungle of Heron House's grounds. It looked like nature had thrown a drunken, years-long party and forgotten to clean up. The sprawling mess of tangled vines and invasive Brazilian pepper trees sagged under the weight of neglect.

"And what fresh hell will be next?" I asked a passing crab, which wisely scuttled away.

The possibilities, given my brief but memorable introduction to Holloway's capabilities, seemed depressingly, creatively endless. Weariness settled deep in my bones, a feeling far older than my thirty-four years. A weariness of fighting for meaning, for order, in a world that seemed determined to conspire against both.

Sunday morning dawned almost suspiciously serene.

I sat on my back patio, the wood of the rocking chair

creaking faintly as I cradled my first cup of coffee. The air was still and heavy with the promise of another hot day, the only sounds the birds in the trees and the gentle, rhythmic lapping of the tide against the shore.

No generators coughed to life. No off-key singing assaulted the sanctity of the sunrise. Just calm. In the forgiving morning light, my hibiscus hedge looked less traumatized. The gaps were still there, the bruises on the leaves, but a few brave, unopened buds hinted at a future.

I finished my coffee, the last dregs bitter on my tongue. The silence from next door was like the hush in the eye of a storm, not a lasting, dependable truce. But today I had an escape chute.

The thought of getting to Sunset Siesta and taking *Line Dancer* out on today's charter was a lifeline. Out on the ocean, things made sense. The wind, the tides, the subtle, almost imperceptible signs of fish moving beneath the surface. Hard work and tangible results. No unpredictable neighbors. No flood-inducing repairs threatening prize-winning flora.

Just the vast, honest, unforgiving welcome of the sea.

As I pulled my truck out of the driveway, I glanced involuntarily at Heron House. Still. Silent. Looming like a sleeping giant, its windows dark and watchful. I pressed down on the accelerator, leaving my complicated, unfortunately attractive, and undeniably disruptive new neighbor behind.

For now.

Chapter Four

IRIS

SUNDAY MORNING GREETED me with bright sunshine and dry, heavy eyes. The image of Austin Coleridge's furious face—his gray eyes narrowed into stormy slits as he surveyed the watery carnage of his hibiscus hedge—was seared onto the inside of my eyelids. It had replayed on a loop all night, a silent horror film starring me as the hapless, mud-caked villain, complete with a soundtrack of gushing water and my pathetic, squeaked apologies.

"Experimental irrigation," I groaned into my pillow. "Why did I say that?"

When I dragged myself into the kitchen's echoing expanse, it did little to dispel the gloom. Dust motes danced in weak shafts of sunlight struggling through salt-crusted windowpanes. The ancient percolator sputtered and hissed like a dying dragon before reluctantly producing coffee that tasted faintly of rust, regret, and possibly nineteenth-century despair. After putting up with this relic for two weeks, I needed a real coffee maker. STAT.

From the window, I could see it.

The scene of the crime. His hibiscus hedge.

Even through the distorting haze of ancient glass, it looked sad. Accusatory. Yesterday afternoon, I'd caught a glimpse of Austin back out there, his tall, lean frame bent over the damaged plants. He'd moved with focused, almost tender precision, assessing the destruction I'd wrought and gently snipping broken stems, his dark head bowed.

I'd wanted to run over then, to babble a fresh torrent of apologies. To offer to personally hand-pollinate every remaining bud with a tiny paintbrush if it would help. But my feet had remained rooted to the dusty floorboards, my courage shriveling under the imagined weight of his disapproval. My optimistic smile from yesterday was long gone.

As I sipped my questionable coffee, the guilt gnawed at me, a persistent, uncomfortable itch right between my shoulder blades. When my world spun out of control, one thing always centered me.

Baking.

The familiar ritual was a tangible act of creation in the face of my recent act of destruction. I rummaged through boxes stacked haphazardly in what I hoped would one day be a charming butler's pantry, but which currently resembled a cardboard-box shantytown. I unearthed my mixing bowls, a half-empty bag of flour, a canister of sugar that felt depressingly light, and one precious bag of semisweet chocolate chips I'd bought for just such an emotional emergency.

"Chocolate chip cookies," I announced to the chipped Formica countertop. "The universal peace treaty. The culinary white flag. No one can stay furious at someone who brings them warm, homemade chocolate chip cookies. Right?"

But as I assembled my meager supplies, another truth

emerged. I had exactly zero vanilla or eggs. Operation Apology Cookie was already hitting a logistical snag.

"Okay, Iris," I coached myself. "Nothing a quick trip to the Island Market can't fix. Plus, I can pick up a new coffee maker." I spun around and trotted to my room to change.

Island Market on a Sunday morning was a cheerful mix of locals stocking up for the week and bewildered tourists searching for sunscreen and Key lime pie. I navigated the bustling aisles with focused determination, grabbing flour, sugar, a carton of eggs, and a brand-new, generously sized bottle of pure vanilla extract. Then I triumphed by adding a glorious new coffee machine to my cart. Mission accomplished.

Driving back down Dove Key's charming, sun-drenched Main Street, a sense of cautious optimism filled me. Then a storefront caught my eye—a splash of cheerful paint and a whimsical, hand-painted sign that read *Bookshop in Paradise*. On an impulse born of a desperate need for a temporary escape from my head and the looming specter of Austin Coleridge, I pulled over.

The bell over the door chimed a welcoming, melodic greeting as I stepped inside. The air was cool and enveloped me in the immediate, comforting aroma of old paper, binding glue, and freshly brewed coffee. Bookshelves lined every wall, crammed with colorful spines that promised adventure, romance, and mystery.

"This place feels like a hug," I murmured, my shoulders relaxing.

"Good morning!" a warm, friendly voice called out. I looked up to see a woman with long, auburn hair and kind, intelligent green eyes smiling at me from behind a counter laden with new releases. She looked to be about my age, with an open, welcoming face. "Can I help you find anything?"

"Oh, just browsing. This place is absolutely lovely."

"Thank you." Her smile widened. "I'm Brenna. I own the place."

"Iris Holloway," I replied, returning the smile. "I'm new in town."

"Welcome to Dove Key!" Brenna's green eyes widened.

"Thanks." I took a fortifying breath. "I just inherited Heron House. Over on Frigate Lane?" I braced myself, expecting the polite but wary look I'd started to recognize.

To my surprise, Brenna laughed, a warm, sympathetic sound. "Oh, Heron House! Wow, that's quite an undertaking. You're brave. My brother Austin lives right next door."

My stomach performed a spectacular dive into my shoes. "Austin Coleridge? He's your brother?"

Amusement twinkled in Brenna's eyes, a knowing, almost conspiratorial look. "That's him. Don't worry, his bark is usually worse than his bite. Mostly." She gave a tiny wink that somehow made me feel both better and marginally more terrified. "I'm Brenna Coleridge-Markham. So you're tackling Heron House? What are your plans for it?"

"Likely unrealistic," I admitted with a rueful smile. "But I'm turning it into a Bed & Breakfast."

"That's fantastic!" Brenna's enthusiasm was infectious. "Dove Key could absolutely use another charming B&B."

"And I'm trying really hard," I added, a self-deprecating grimace twisting my lips, "not to accidentally destroy the neighborhood in the process."

Brenna raised an eyebrow, a flicker of understanding in her green eyes. Thankfully, she didn't press for details. "Well, if you're looking to meet people, we have a book club called Sips and Pages. We read books and drink plenty of wine." Her smile grew as she smoothed a hand over the slight rounding of her belly. "But no wine for me for a while."

I clapped my hands. "Congratulations!"

"Thanks. My husband, Hunter, and I are pretty ecstatic. And it's even more special because my sister is pregnant too. With twins! It's going to be a decidedly busy year for the Coleridge baby department."

"You guys will need a babysitter on speed dial." I smiled at her obvious happiness, unable to deny the sad twist in my stomach at yet another life stage I had missed with my thirtieth birthday.

"Enough baby talk, though," Brenna said with a casual wave. "Our book club meets next week. We're reading…" She scanned a nearby shelf, plucked a brightly colored paperback, and handed it to me. "*Love on the Tide*. Perfect beach read. You should come."

The invitation, so unexpected and warm, was a lifeline. "Oh! I'd love that. Thank you so much."

"Consider it your official Dove Key welcome packet," Brenna said with another easy smile.

I bought *Love on the Tide*, and as the bell chimed my departure, the warmth of the sun outside felt less oppressive, more welcoming. That hadn't been so bad. Brenna hadn't run screaming when she heard the words *Heron House*. She didn't even seem to think Austin was a fire-breathing ogre, just a typically grouchy older brother. A brother with shoulders wider than a zip code.

Maybe there was hope for me in this quirky little town yet.

Back in the Heron House kitchen, armed with my new baking supplies, coffee maker, and a fragile, Brenna-inspired sense of optimism, I dove into Operation Apology Cookie with renewed vigor. The familiar, rhythmic process of measuring flour, creaming butter and sugar until light and fluffy, and stirring in generous handfuls of chocolate chips worked its usual magic. As I placed dough on my cookie sheets, I sang my own version of "Neon Heart", which I'd heard recently on the radio. I crossed my fingers when I turned on the not-exactly-chic, avocado-green wall oven, but it heated up just fine.

The warm, comforting scent of baking cookies gradually overpowered the kitchen's lingering mustiness, a fragrant symbol of hope and profound regret. Soon they emerged from the oven, golden-brown and ready for their diplomatic mission. A wicker basket, rescued from the yawning walk-in pantry, became their vessel. I lined it with faded floral napkins and nestled a dozen of the most perfect ones inside, like precious jewels. Finally, I tied a faded blue ribbon around the handle, fashioning a slightly lopsided but undeniably cheerful bow.

"Okay," I said, holding up the basket for inspection. It looked presentable. Friendly. Hopefully not too desperate. "Just a neighborly gesture. An extremely apologetic neighborly gesture."

Basket clutched in a hand that was only slightly trembling, I took a deep, fortifying breath and headed for Austin's front door. The walk felt a little less like trudging toward my own execution this time, thanks in no small part to Brenna's kindness. Knowing he had a nice, normal sister somehow made him marginally less terrifying. After all, I was the one who had screwed up.

His yard was a picture of serene, almost severe, order. The white clapboard siding of his house gleamed in the afternoon sun, and the dark-green shutters aligned with a precision that made my haphazard renovation efforts feel vaguely criminal. Even the shells bordering his walkway were arranged in perfect rows.

My courage wavered as I stepped onto his porch. No clutter. No fuss. I raised my hand, took another shaky breath, and knocked on the dark-green wooden door. The sound was a loud, definitive thud in the otherwise profound silence. I waited, the basket growing heavier in my hand, the scent of the cookies suddenly, overwhelmingly cheerful.

No answer.

I knocked again, a little louder. Still nothing. I craned my neck, trying to peer through a nearby window, but the glass reflected the bright sky, revealing only dim, orderly shadows within.

"He's not home," I whispered, a strange mixture of profound relief and sharp disappointment washing over me. I'd psyched myself up for this confrontation, rehearsed my lines, and braced for the impact of his disapproval.

And… nothing.

Defeated for now, I turned and walked back home. The book club with Brenna was next week, so I sat at the kitchen table with a dang good cookie and settled in to read.

The rest of the afternoon passed in a restless, cookie-scented limbo. After several chapters, I tried to focus on unpacking more boxes, sketching out preliminary plans for the B&B guest rooms, wrestling with the ancient, terrifying fuse box. My attention kept drifting to the window and Austin's house, watching for any sign of his return.

Late in the afternoon, as the sun began its slow, spectacular descent toward the ocean, I heard the distinct, welcome rumble of an engine, followed by the crunch of tires on his shell driveway.

"He's back!"

I rushed to the window, my heart thumping a nervous, erratic rhythm against my ribs—a mix of dread and something suspiciously like anticipation.

Unfolding his tall, lean frame from a dark-blue pickup truck, Austin moved with an efficient, practiced grace. He reached into the truck bed and began to unload gear—several long, serious-looking fishing rods, a battered cooler that no doubt held the day's catch, and a worn canvas gear bag slung over one broad shoulder. I stood on my tiptoes to inspect the words embossed on his truck door more closely.

Sunset Siesta Fishing Charters.

"Fishing charters?" I breathed, pressing my nose closer to the grimy windowpane.

So that's what he did. If he was driving a work truck, he was likely the captain. It explained the aura of reserved competence, the way he seemed so at home in the elements. It also made my idiotic blunder with the sprinkler even more pathetically amateurish. He probably spent his days wrangling actual sea monsters and recalcitrant, nauseated tourists, dealing with all sorts of unpredictable, dangerous situations. And on his day off, he discovered me attempting to drown his meticulously tended garden with the finesse of a bewildered, landlocked walrus.

But also… a captain.

There was something undeniably romantic about that, wasn't there? The man of the sea, at the lonely helm of his ship, wrestling with the elements, bringing home the bounty of the deep…

Focus, Iris! I admonished myself sternly. *Apology! Not composing seafaring fantasies about your aggravated neighbor.*

A fresh wave of determination, admittedly shaky around the edges, surged through me. Austin was a fishing captain. He dealt with unpredictable things all the time. Surely, he could handle one profoundly apologetic neighbor armed with a peace offering of homemade chocolate chip cookies.

I grabbed the cookie basket from the counter, its ribbon still jauntily tied, and gave myself a stern nod in the dusty hall mirror. My hair was still a bit wild, but my eyes held a new, steely resolve—or possibly just terror masquerading as resolve.

"Okay, Captain Coleridge," I said to my reflection, squaring my shoulders. "Prepare to be apologized to. Vigorously."

My stomach did a nervous flip-flop, but I ignored it. I marched out the back door of Heron House. This was not the time to wrestle with the possessed front door. The basket was clutched in my hand like a shield or, perhaps, a fragile, crumbly olive branch. I set off purposefully, my sensible canvas sneakers making determined crunching sounds on the shell path, heading directly toward Austin Coleridge's front door for the second, and hopefully final, time today.

Chapter Five

AUSTIN

I STOWED my gear near the cleaning station I'd built in the kitchen. My rods leaned in the corner, the black snapper still encased in ice inside the cooler. It could wait. After a long day, I was ready for a cold beer.

Then a sharp, determined knock echoed from the front door, and my head snapped up. Who the hell was that? My siblings usually texted or, in Braden's case, just materialized on the porch with a couple of beers.

"Shit." If it was some door-to-door salesman trying to peddle solar panels or salvation, they were about to have a very short conversation.

I strode to the door, my expression anything but welcoming, and pulled it open. And stared.

Holloway.

Son of a bitch. She stood on my porch, clutching a wicker basket covered with a brightly colored cloth napkin. Her blonde hair, the shade of sun-bleached driftwood, was pulled back in a loose, messy ponytail, but rebellious strands had escaped to frame a face scrubbed clean of makeup. It made her look younger, softer. And her wide blue eyes, the color of a clear summer sky over the flats, were fixed on me with an expression of acute, almost painful, nervousness. She shifted her weight from one foot to the other like a sandpiper testing the tide.

I braced myself. What now? A petition to have my hibiscus formally declared a public nuisance? Then I registered the anxiety radiating off her. The way her knuckles were white where she gripped the basket handle, the slight tremor in her hands. It was a marked contrast to the determined, if spectacularly disastrous, amateur plumber I'd encountered yesterday. This version looked vulnerable.

And it threw me completely off balance.

An uncomfortable feeling squirmed in my gut. Not guilt. Definitely not guilt. More like acute social discomfort.

"Holloway," I muttered, the single word sounding more like a reluctant acknowledgment of an unavoidable natural phenomenon than a greeting.

Her eyes widened further, if that was possible. "Mr. Coleridge. Austin." Her voice was a little shaky, a little breathless. "Um. Hi. Can I… I mean, I wanted to…"

She gestured awkwardly with the basket, as if it held the secrets of the universe. The faint, sweet, unmistakable scent of baked goods wafted from beneath the napkin. Chocolate chip, if I wasn't mistaken.

Cookies? She baked cookies? After yesterday? I'd expected a complaint, an argument, maybe even a demand for me to fix the damn sprinkler she broke. This was disarming. And, as much as I didn't want to admit it, thoughtful. She'd likely spent hours on this, psyching herself up for another encounter with the neighborhood monster.

Me.

"I am so, so incredibly sorry about yesterday," she rushed out, the words tumbling over each other. "About your hibiscus. And your day off. It was completely my fault. I was an absolute idiot with the sprinkler, and I just wanted to… well, I baked these." She thrust the basket forward, a hopeful, desperate offering. "As an apology."

I stared at the basket, then at her earnest, anxious face. My mind, usually so quick to retreat into grumpy solitude, seemed to have short-circuited.

"Right. Cookies." The words sounded flat, even to my ears. I cleared my throat. "Well, thank you. Uh, come in."

The invitation was out before I could stop it.

Holloway stepped hesitantly into my living room, her eyes darting around as if she'd just entered an alien space-craft. Which, compared to the chaotic jungle of Heron House, my home probably was. She looked so out of place, a brightly colored, slightly disheveled tropical bird that had somehow flown into a minimalist art gallery. Her presence, her nervous energy, and the sweet scent of her damn cookies filled my carefully ordered space.

Without comment, I turned and led her into the kitchen. Cookies belonged in the kitchen.

Her eyes darted around the room, taking in the clean counters, the gleaming maple Shaker cabinets, the lack of clutter, the restored Dade County pine floors that shone with a hand-rubbed luster. Probably comparing it to the disaster zone she was inhabiting next door. A strange, inexplicable urge to apologize for its neatness rose in me. Which made zero sense.

"You can, uh, put that there." Gesturing vaguely toward the kitchen table, I was still off-kilter, like the deck of *Line Dancer* in a sudden squall.

"Oh. Right. Thank you."

She placed the basket down with an almost reverent care, as if it contained fragile, priceless artifacts. An awkward silence descended, thick and heavy as pre-hurricane air. I leaned against the counter, arms crossed, trying to project an aura of unconcerned detachment I was far from feeling.

She stood by the table, fidgeting with the ribbon on the basket. Her gaze landed on the cluster of fishing rods propped in the corner. Tools of my trade, symbols of my escape, an integral part of my identity. To her, they were probably just sticks.

"Fishing rods, huh?" she asked, her voice still a little breathless. "You fish a lot?" She was clearly grasping at conversational straws.

"It's my job," I said, my tone brief. "I run charters out of Sunset Siesta. It's our family's resort on the western edge of Dove Key."

"Oh! You are a captain. That's… that's really something." She paused, then rushed on, a delicate pink flush rising in her cheeks. "I've been fishing! At summer camp as a kid. Caught a trout, or maybe it was a bass. It was very small."

She finished with an earnest nod, then blinked rapidly as she apparently realized how that sounded to a man who caught marlin for a living. She gestured with her hands, indicating something the size of a minnow, and shot me a fleeting smile.

I almost snorted. It was clueless yet somehow utterly, disarmingly sincere. The way she was blushing now, a deep crimson spreading from her neck to her hairline, like she'd just confessed a heinous crime instead of a minor fishing inadequacy. It was…

Endearing?

No. That was absolutely not the word.

Just less actively annoying than the sprinkler incident. Yeah, that was better. The color in her face reminded me of dawn on the water. Dammit, I was staring.

"Oh, shucks and sticks. I'm sure that sounded really stupid." Her voice came out hushed, her gaze fixed on the floorboards. "Comparing my… my trout… to what you do."

A beat of silence stretched. Then, I heard myself say, "No. It's just different, Iris."

The use of her first name hung in the air, a small but significant shift, like the tide turning. Her head snapped up, and our eyes held.

"Deep-sea fishing is a bit more involved than pulling a trout out of a lake, but it's the same principle." I almost smiled. The corner of my mouth might have twitched. It was hard to tell.

The blush on her cheeks softened, replaced by a hesitant, shy smile that did strange, unwelcome things to my insides. "I can imagine."

The tension in the kitchen eased a fraction. The air was still charged, but the immediate threat of open warfare —or at least a stern lecture on property boundaries— seemed to have receded.

"Oh! I went to Bookshop in Paradise today and met Brenna," she offered, as if trying to establish common ground. "She mentioned you. That you were her brother."

"Brenna talks too much," I said, but there was no real heat in it.

"She was very nice." Warmth filled her voice. "She invited me to her book club. To get to know people."

"That sounds like her."

The book club. Of course. Next, Iris would be organizing neighborhood potlucks and trying to get me to participate in a group singalong. The thought was horrifying. I leaned back against the counter to ground myself in reality.

"Well…" Iris glanced toward the door as if suddenly remembering she was in enemy territory. "I should let you get back to whatever it is sea captains do when their hibiscus hasn't been destroyed." She gave a self-deprecating grimace. "Thank you for letting me apologize. Properly this time."

Thick, awkward silence stretched for a beat. I just watched her, this whirlwind of earnest apology and accidental destruction. My default setting was a curt nod and a retreat into monosyllables. But instead, unbidden words emerged.

"The hedge will recover." My voice came out rough, like an engine that hadn't been run in a while. I cleared my throat. "Yesterday, I might have been… abrupt." Abrupt was an understatement. "You, uh, caught me off guard."

Her head, which had started to droop, lifted slightly. A flicker of surprise, maybe even hope, sparked in those wide blue eyes.

God help me, I continued, "Hibiscus are surprisingly hardy." Finally, I got ahold of myself and added gruffly, "Just aim away from it next time."

A shaky smile touched her full lips, relief softening the anxiety in her eyes. "Deal. No more rogue water features, I promise."

My eyes darted to the basket on the table. "Thanks for the gesture."

What on earth made me say that?

I was saved from further distress when she moved toward the back door. She paused, her hand on the knob. "The cookies are chocolate chip. My mom always said they could solve most of life's minor catastrophes. Enjoy." Her smile was fleeting, a little sad around the edges. Then she was gone, the door closing behind her with a soft click, leaving an Iris-shaped hole in the silence of my kitchen.

I stared at the closed door. The silence she left behind was somehow different than the silence before. More thoughtful. Agitated. I ran a hand through my hair, feeling strangely drained and wired at the same time. She was a complication I didn't need.

And yet…

My gaze fell on the basket of cookies on my table, the colorful napkin slightly askew. A Trojan horse, filled with sugar and good intentions. I eyed it suspiciously. Then, with a sigh that sounded like surrender, I lifted the napkin.

They were golden-brown, generously studded with chocolate chips. I inhaled deeply, unable to help it.

"I bet they taste like sawdust and desperation," I muttered, just to maintain my internal equilibrium.

I picked one up. A perfect ratio of cookie to chocolate chip. I examined it critically, as if searching for hidden flaws, for evidence of shoddy workmanship. Then, I took a bite.

And another.

Shit.

They were good. Really good. The edges were perfectly crisp, the center delightfully chewy, the chocolate rich and plentiful. Not too sweet.

A minute later, I was pouring a tall glass of cold milk from the fridge, an accompaniment I hadn't indulged in for years. I ate another cookie. And another. Before I knew it, I was sitting at the table, and half a dozen were gone.

"Okay," I conceded to the empty milk glass. "There's at least one thing the woman can do right. She can bake a decent goddamn cookie."

I wiped the lingering crumbs from my mouth with the back of my hand, staring out the window toward Heron

House. The late-afternoon sun slanted through the trees, casting long shadows across her overgrown yard. I could just make out her silhouette moving inside, a blur of motion behind the dirty windows.

A fleeting, unwelcome, and entirely inappropriate image flashed through my mind: that same messy blonde hair, not tangled with leaves but wild and windblown from the salty spray of the ocean. Her face flushed with excitement, maybe even a bright, unrestrained smile directed at me, out on the deck of *Line Dancer*, the vast blue of the Gulf stretching behind her.

I pushed the thought away, hard, annoyed at its sudden intrusion.

Nope. Not going there.

She was trouble. End of story.

But the cookies had been infuriatingly good. I put the milk glass in the sink with more force than necessary, the clatter loud in the suddenly too-quiet kitchen. I was unsettled. Deeply. The order of my world had been disturbed, and not just by a broken sprinkler.

Iris Holloway, with her disastrous DIY skills, her wide, anxious blue eyes, and her dangerously good cookies, was proving to be a complication I hadn't anticipated.

And as much as it pissed me off, one I couldn't entirely dismiss.

Chapter Six

IRIS

THE BASKET SAT on my kitchen counter, a wicker trophy from my recent and non-catastrophic encounter with Austin Coleridge. It was empty. Gloriously, wholly, not-a-single-crumb-left empty. A smug smile played on my lips every time I'd looked at it over the past couple of days.

He'd eaten them.

All twelve of my apology chocolate chip cookies.

He'd returned the basket yesterday, a brief, almost gruff transaction on my porch that had nonetheless been a monumental victory. He thrust it at me, his gaze fixed somewhere over my left shoulder, and muttered something that sounded suspiciously like, "You're a better baker than you are a landscaper."

It wasn't exactly a Shakespearean sonnet, nor did it erase the memory of his earlier, thunderous disapproval. But from Captain Grumpy, the man who communicated primarily in minimal sentences and intimidating scowls, it was practically a declaration of undying admiration. My heart had done a ridiculous little flutter kick.

Sipping coffee—real coffee, brewed in my brand-new, extra-fancy coffee maker—I replayed the brief interaction in his kitchen. The way he'd looked so utterly uncomfortable having me there, like a bear who'd discovered a determined, slightly manic raccoon hosting an impromptu tea party in its den.

The way his voice, usually so controlled, had been rough, almost hesitant, when he'd admitted to being "*abrupt*." The almost imperceptible twitch at the corner of his mouth when I'd babbled about my less-than-epic summer-camp trout-catching adventures. It was amusing. And, if I was honest with myself, oddly appealing. Austin was so buttoned-up, so fiercely guarded. My cookies, my humble peace offering, had clearly managed to short-circuit at least a few of his grumpy defenses.

My thoughts drifted to his dark, thick hair, slightly messy from the sea wind or from running his strong-looking hands through it in exasperation. The dark scruff shadowing his admittedly fine jawline gave him an air that was both ruggedly handsome and a little dangerous. It made his intense gray eyes, the color of a storm-swept ocean, even more striking.

There was no denying it. The man was distractingly attractive, even when scowling at me like I was a persistent barnacle he was trying to scrape off the hull of his life. I could just picture him, tall at the helm, standing firm against an ocean storm.

"Whoa there, girl." I gave my head a little shake to dislodge the image of Austin Coleridge looking windswept and heroic. "You have more important things to think about. Bed & Breakfast. Renovations. Not brooding, handsome, probably-still-annoyed sea captains."

I set my coffee cup down and turned my attention to the mountain of tasks Heron House presented. The small victory of the cookie mission, and the unexpected crack in Austin's grumpy facade, had left me feeling lighter, more hopeful. But the reality of this enormous, crumbling, glorious old house was a constant, sobering reminder of the marathon ahead.

I did a mental walkthrough, a familiar ritual of assessing the battlefield. The first floor was a symbol of a grander time, built for entertaining. A wide, sweeping staircase dominated the foyer, its newel post scarred but its bones still strong. To one side, the formal parlor with its massive, soot-caked fireplace would be combined with the living room to make a more modern space. A dining room that could seat twenty lay on the opposite side. In the back stood the cavernous kitchen, with its avocado-green appliances, which was currently my command center and chief source of despair.

The real heart of the B&B was upstairs. The second and third floors held nine bedrooms, a sprawling maze of rooms in various states of dusty neglect. Each had good bones—high ceilings, large windows that promised stunning views once the grime was scraped away. The real challenge was the bathrooms.

Or rather, the lack thereof.

My grand plan involved a bit of architectural thievery —stealing space from oversized linen closets, repurposing forgotten nooks, even sacrificing one small, sad room entirely—to create modern, luxurious en-suites for each guest room. It was ambitious, maybe even overreaching, but it was the only way to turn this grand old dame into a place modern guests would pay to stay.

For today, I'd tackle a built-in set of drawers in the living room, tucked beneath an old window seat that overlooked the enormous magnolia tree in the back yard. Cleaned up, the little nook could be stunning, a focal point. I envisioned guests perched there with morning coffee. Or me, curled up with a good book, the window open to the scent of those huge, creamy blossoms.

The bottom left drawer slid open with a surprisingly smooth, quiet sigh, as if it had been waiting. It was lined with faded, rose-patterned paper that smelled faintly of old lavender.

A single, cream-colored envelope lay nestled in the center. Beside it, arranged with care, was a sprig of what had once been magnolia blossoms, now dried and brittle, their petals the color of old ivory. A deliberate, poignant arrangement.

My heart gave a little jump. My fingers trembled slightly as I picked up the envelope. It was thick, the luxurious paper slightly brittle with age, addressed simply to *Iris* in an elegant, slightly shaky, old-fashioned cursive.

"Aunt Constance?"

The air in the living room grew thick, expectant. I hadn't received anything personal from my great-aunt, just the stark pronouncements of her will. This was different. Intimate.

I had no proof the writing was hers, but who else could it be?

Pushing to my feet, I sank onto the dusty cushion of the window seat. The mayhem of renovation momentarily forgotten, I carefully slit open the envelope. Several folded sheets of matching stationery lay inside, crinkling softly as I unfolded them.

My Dearest Iris,

If this inheritance, and indeed this letter, comes as a surprise, I can only imagine it is due to the unfortunate distance that has long existed between our branches of the family. I confess, old woman that I am, I held onto certain rigid ideas of propriety regarding your mother's choices so many years ago when she found herself expecting you.

It was a different time, or perhaps I simply used that as an excuse for my narrowness. My disapproval, I see now with the clarity that often arrives too late, was a wall I built, not a bridge. For any coldness you may have perceived from me over the years, child, I am truly, deeply sorry. It was never a reflection on you, nor on the bright spirit I always sensed you possessed, even from afar.

My eyes stung, and I had to pause.

My niece Caroline and I were two sides of a stubborn, complicated coin, each convinced of our own unassailable rightness. It made for a difficult love, often overshadowed by pride and misunderstanding. And distance. Then she was gone, along with any chance for me to make amends. Until now. My hope was always for your happiness, Iris, for your security, even if my methods were clumsy and born of my limited, and perhaps judgmental, views.

A wave of sadness washed over me, a poignant ache for the lost years, for the connections never properly forged between my mother and her aunt. And what I had missed out on too.

This old pile of wood and memories, Heron House, has seen a lot of life, Iris. It has weathered storms both literal and figurative. It needs a strong hand now, and a warm, determined heart to coax it back to its former glory. I've watched you from afar, more than you know. I always saw in you a stubborn sort of light, a creative, restless spirit that reminded me so much of my grandmother, Clara, who scandalized everyone by eloping with a lighthouse keeper. Perhaps this house, with all its daunting flaws and forgotten beauty, along with my accompanying financial estate, can be the canvas for your own unique masterpiece.

MY BREATH CAUGHT. She saw something in me. Aunt Constance, the distant, formidable great-aunt I barely knew, had seen a spark.

DOVE Key has a way of testing you, child. It demands resilience, a certain comfortable relationship with the unpredictable. Don't let the naysayers or the occasional hurricane of a problem deter you. The salt air here has a way of scouring away pretense and revealing what's true, what's lasting.

Iris, I leave Heron House to you not as a burden, though I know it will feel like one at times, but as a beginning. An opportunity. A place to put down roots, I hope. Make it your own. Fill its empty rooms with life and laughter and the scent of baking bread again. That, my dear girl, would be the greatest gift you could give this old woman.

WITH MY ENDURING, if perhaps poorly expressed, affection and love,

Your Great-Aunt, Constance Lawson.

I FINISHED THE LETTER, tears now openly tracing paths through the dust on my cheeks. I carefully folded the fragile sheets and held them to my chest, the faint, dry scent filling my senses. For the first time, Heron House felt less like an overwhelming project and more like a gift. A sacred trust.

A story I was meant to continue.

Aunt Constance wasn't just a distant, disapproving relative whose lawyer had sent a shocking letter. She was a woman with her own complexities, regrets, and unexpressed hopes.

"Thank you, Aunt Constance," I whispered to the silent, dusty room. "I'll try my best."

I tucked the letter back into the drawer, arranging the magnolia sprig on top, a profound shift settling within me. My determination to succeed with the B&B, already strong, was now fortified by a sense of legacy, a desire to honor the complex, ultimately kindhearted woman who had chosen me.

With a new surge of purpose, I wiped my face dry. I padded into the grand foyer and stopped at the base of the sweeping staircase. Its elegant lines were obscured by dust, but the potential was breathtaking. The hand-carved newel post was worn by over a century of passing hands, its former glory waiting to be coaxed back to life. I ran my fingers over the cool, solid wood, then arched a brow as my gaze swept up the curved risers.

"I'll have to warn guests to use care," I murmured to the empty hall. "It'll be something else when it's refinished, but one misstep on a staircase this grand could ruin a vacation in a hurry."

Shaking the sobering thought away, I focused instead on the promise of it all. Aunt Constance saw a stubborn sort of light in me, not a girl who abandoned a half-finished pottery studio when the logistics got messy. She saw the potential. And for the first time, I felt a desperate need to live up to it.

THURSDAY AFTERNOON, armed with my copy of *Love on the Tide* and a healthy dose of nervous anticipation, I walked the few blocks from Heron House to a bungalow in the residential district for my first Sips and Pages book club meeting. Pam, a friendly woman with a neat brown bob and a welcoming smile, was the de facto den mother of this literary coven.

The door to her charming, brightly lit bungalow was already open, cheerful voices and laughter spilling out into the warm air. The scent was wonderful as I stepped inside —a mix of paper, wine, and something deliciously sweet and spicy.

"Iris! You made it!" Brenna's voice, warm and familiar, cut through the happy din. She emerged from a cluster of women, her auburn hair gleaming under the light. She moved with an easy grace, something I suspected wouldn't be too deterred as her pregnancy progressed.

"I wouldn't miss it." A smile spread across my face. A friendly face could dispel lingering anxieties.

Brenna drew me into a cozy living room packed with comfortable furniture, overflowing bookshelves, and about a dozen women of various ages, all chatting animatedly, wine glasses in hand. The atmosphere was instantly inclusive, a far cry from the stuffier book clubs I'd tentatively tried back in Abingdon.

"Everyone, this is Iris Holloway," Brenna announced, her voice carrying easily. "She's new to Dove Key and is bravely taking on the resurrection of Heron House! Dove Key will have a new B&B soon."

A welcoming chorus went around the room. A blush crept up my neck, but it was a pleasant, warm feeling, not the mortified heat I associated with, say, creating a swamp in my neighbor's yard.

Brenna guided me toward a plush armchair, then leaned in conspiratorially. "I want you to meet someone. Liv! Over here!"

A woman with a cascade of long, brown curly hair and a smile that could light up a lighthouse detached herself from a group near a platter of what looked like miniature cheesecakes. She was curvy and vibrant, her eyes glinting with infectious energy. Her stylish sundress had a sprinkling of flour dusting it.

"Iris, this is Liv Markham," Brenna said. "Liv owns Sweet Dreams Bakery on Main Street. You absolutely must try her Key lime macarons. And she's also my sister-in-law."

Liv's handshake was firm and warm, her grin wide. "Welcome! Wow, tackling Heron House is ambition with a capital A! Any friend of Brenna's, and anyone brave enough for that glorious place, is a friend of mine."

An instant connection sparked. "I'm a huge admirer of professional bakers. Your shop always looks so wonderful when I drive by. It smells incredible even from the street."

"Aw, thanks!" Liv beamed. "I moved here myself not so many years ago and opened the bakery from scratch. I totally get the whole new-in-town, slightly terrified, trying-to-build-a-dream vibe. It's a wild ride, but worth it."

The book discussion got underway, fueled by more wine and Liv's amazing miniature cinnamon-apple cheesecakes. But my attention, and later my conversation, drifted back to Liv.

"So, a bed and breakfast," she said during a lull when Pam was refilling wine glasses. "That means a whole lot of breakfast baking. You a baker yourself?"

"Enthusiastic amateur," I admitted. "I love it, but

scaling up for guests and doing it consistently well… that's the part that keeps me up at night. That, and the plumbing in Heron House, which I suspect is possessed."

Liv laughed, a rich, throaty sound. "Oh, honey, possessed plumbing is practically a prerequisite for owning an old Keys house. Listen," her expression grew earnest, her eyes sparkling, "any time you want to talk shop, troubleshoot a recipe, or just vent about contractors, you give me a call. We small-business gals, especially in the hospitality game, need to stick together. I can teach you a few tricks for high-volume scones that'll knock your guests' socks off."

My heart swelled. "That is so incredibly generous of you, Liv. I'd love that."

"Don't mention it." She pulled a pen from her pocket, grabbed a napkin, and scribbled down her number. "Call me. We'll do coffee. Or taste-test experimental batches of muffins. My customers are always up for being guinea pigs."

The book club wrapped up with hugs, laughter, and the announcement of next month's selection, a historical romance set in Key West during the Depression.

Brenna handed me a copy. "See? Painless, right?"

"More than painless," I replied. "It was wonderful."

I walked back to Heron House with the new book tucked under my arm and Liv's number safe in my contacts. The air was soft, fragrant with tropical flowers. Dove Key, which had felt so daunting just a few days ago, was starting to feel different.

Smaller. Friendlier.

Like a place where a thirty-year-old woman with a dream about a rambling old house and a love of baking might actually find her footing. Aunt Constance's letter felt like a quiet blessing, and Liv's offer of friendship and mentorship a practical lifeline.

Maybe I could pull this off.

And maybe the pastry offensive needed to continue. I could bake something else for my grumpy, handsome sea-captain neighbor. Just to see if I could make him almost smile again. Surprisingly, the thought didn't fill me with terror. It filled me with a curious, hopeful, and possibly inappropriate little flutter.

Chapter Seven

AUSTIN

MY SURF ROD bent in a familiar, satisfying arc, the braided line hissing through the guides as the lure sailed out over the breakers. I worked the shoreline behind my house, the wet sand cold and firm beneath my bare feet, my movements a practiced, meditative rhythm. This wasn't work. This was church. Out here, with the sky beginning to blush from indigo to a soft, promising lavender, I wasn't Captain Coleridge.

I was just Austin.

When nothing bit, I reeled my line in and cast again. And again. It wasn't about the catch. It was the nervous flicker of baitfish in the shallows, the gentle tug of the current on the line. A conversation with the ocean that settled my mind and scoured away the week's tensions.

When the sun was fully clear of the horizon, throwing a glittering path of gold across the water, I reeled in for the last time. An easy, private smile touched my lips. The hook was bare, but my head was clear. A fair trade.

I walked back toward my house, the peace of the morning a comfortable weight on my shoulders. It was only as I was rinsing salt and sand from my gear at the outdoor spigot that I saw it. As if materialized out of pure nerve, a plate was propped on my porch swing, covered with a familiar faded floral napkin, a folded note beside it.

Frowning, I stowed my gear and wiped my hands as I strolled toward the patio. Hints of cinnamon carried on the breeze.

Holloway.

Iris.

Whatever.

A mix of resignation and, dammit, a flicker of reluctant anticipation settled in my gut. What culinary weapon had she deployed this time? Another batch of those surprisingly tasty cookies? Or had she branched out? Experimented? That thought was vaguely alarming, given her track record with other forms of experimentation.

I picked up the note with a sigh that felt older than my thirty-four years. Her handwriting was a loopy, enthusiastic script, the kind that probably dotted its i's with little circles or hearts.

AUSTIN,

I WAS EXPERIMENTING in the kitchen again and ended up making waaaay too much of this coffee cake. Enough to feed a very hungry army. You'd be doing me a huge favor if you could help me eat some of it, so it doesn't go to waste. Hope you like cinnamon!

IRIS

P.S. No sprinklers were harmed in the making of this cake.

"MADE TOO MUCH. RIGHT."

I arched a brow at her use of my first name, unable to decide whether that was progress or presumption, then narrowed my eyes at the plate. As if I didn't know a strategic pastry deployment when I saw one. The woman was relentless. But the excuse, the sheer, transparently well-intentioned ridiculousness of it, was so... Iris. And the postscript coaxed a rough sound from my throat that might have been a laugh. If I were a different kind of man.

I took the plate inside, the scent of cinnamon and baked apples already teasing my nostrils. When I lifted the napkin, the coffee cake looked surprisingly professional, a generous slab with a crumbly, golden-brown topping. I poured some coffee and cut myself a slice.

As if on cue, the first discordant sounds of battle erupted from next door. The guttural roar of a generator followed swiftly by the whining screech of a power saw.

My jaw tightened. "Damn it, woman."

The coffee cake, however, was undeniably edible. Okay, pretty good. Well-spiced, with chunks of apple and topped with a buttery, cinnamon-laced crumble. Blocking out the noise, I chewed slowly, savoring the taste despite myself. It was a damn pity she couldn't manage a construction crew or basic plumbing with the same competence.

After finishing, I returned outside, ostensibly to inspect the new growth on my still-recovering hibiscus hedge. I glanced at my watch, confirming I didn't need to be on the boat for another hour. But my attention, as it often did these days, was drawn inexorably toward the racket next door.

The foreman, Mick Riley, was a talker. His booming,

overly confident voice carried to my porch as he directed—or rather, gestured loosely toward—the work being done by his two-man crew. They looked like they'd rather be anywhere else, their movements slow and imprecise. Riley himself had a habit of propping one dusty boot on whatever was handy to survey the scene like a king overseeing a particularly tedious royal duty.

I studied him for a few minutes, my professional hackles on alert. They were prepping a section of the massive back wall for new siding. Riley gestured toward a roll of moisture barrier.

"Make sure that wrap is tight," he called out. "Don't want any waves in that new siding when it goes up."

The words were right. But then, Riley pulled out his phone, facing away from the wall as he launched into a loud conversation about someone's terrible golf game. I narrowed my eyes. The instructions were sound, but the problem lay in the execution. Old places like Heron House didn't forgive shortcuts. They hoarded them, magnified them, then presented you with a horribly expensive bill later.

She has no idea what she's dealing with, I thought, a familiar sense of distaste and something uncomfortably like concern stirring in my gut. *Riley might talk a good game, but if he decides not to follow through…*

"Not my circus, not my monkeys," I told myself as I turned back toward my property. It was none of my business. If Iris Holloway wanted to employ a human question mark to further butcher her inherited money pit, that was her prerogative.

Then I turned around and stared at Heron House. It stood there, an overambitious, romantic notion that a broken thing could be made whole again with just enough stubbornness and hope.

Just like Mom.

The thought landed with an uncomfortable thud.

I remembered the look on my mother's face in the years after Dad left. She'd been in over her head, too. And all of us stepped up because that was the right thing to do. You didn't let someone drown just because they were too proud to ask for a life raft.

Iris had that same look sometimes. That mix of bright-eyed ambition and the quiet panic of someone who knows they're one bad step from disaster. She was clueless, but she didn't deserve to have that grand old house fall down around her ears because of a hack like Mick Riley.

With a heavy sigh, I headed over to thank her for the coffee cake. It was a legitimate excuse.

Mostly.

I found Iris outside, conferring with Riley near the section of wall they were working on. She glanced up as I approached, her eyes widening. Riley, when he saw me, straightened, his expression shifting from bored indifference to a practiced, professional smile.

"Iris," I said, my voice neutral. "The, uh, coffee cake was pretty good."

Her face lit up with unguarded pleasure. "Oh! You liked it? I'm so glad! I was worried the apples might be a bit tart."

"It was fine." I nodded toward Riley, my gaze hardening. "Riley. Didn't expect to see you working on a project of this scale."

Riley's smile faltered for a fraction of a second. "Austin. Been a while. Good to see you, man. Yeah, Heron House is a big job, but Miz Holloway here knows quality when she sees it." He clapped a hand on a nearby ladder.

Before I could offer my unvarnished opinion on that statement, Iris jumped in. "Oh, he's been great so far,

Austin! Mick and his crew have been here bright and early every single day, and they're making such good progress. Really, it's been a relief after some of the stories you hear."

My internal alarm bells, already jangling softly, now clanged with the urgency of a four-alarm fire.

Bright and early doesn't mean doing it right, Iris.

Just then, as if summoned by the god of good timing, Riley's phone blared a jaunty ringtone. He fumbled it out of his pocket, glanced at the screen, and held up a hand with an apologetic grimace that didn't hide the relief in his eyes. "Gotta take this, folks. Talk to you later."

He winked, then strode off, already deep in another conversation. Which left Iris and me standing in a pocket of unexpected, and for me, deeply uncomfortable, silence. I studied her for a moment. The late morning sun caught the gold in her blonde hair, a line deepening between her brows. She looked hopeful, determined, and completely out of her depth. For some damn reason, the thought of Riley taking advantage of that earnest optimism set my teeth on edge.

"Iris," I began, the use of her first name still feeling a little foreign on my tongue. "About Riley."

She turned to me, eyes wide. "What about him? Is there something I should know?"

I hesitated. It wasn't my place. Not my problem. But for some reason, I couldn't stay quiet.

"He's got a history," I said carefully, choosing my words. "Sometimes he does good work. Sometimes, not so much."

Her brow furrowed. "Oh. He's been very dependable so far. And he told his crew exactly how to put up that moisture barrier this morning. I heard him."

"Telling them is one thing. Making sure they do it and do it right, that's another." My gaze drifted over the ancient manse, appreciating the potential but not negating the very real problems. "My brother-in-law, Chase, is an architect. He's told me these old houses are full of surprises, and I know a thing or two about that too. Rotted wood where you least expect it, plumbing that makes no sense, foundations that have settled in ways that defy gravity. You don't want your contractor to be another one of those surprises."

Iris chewed on her lower lip, her gaze drifting toward Riley, who was now laughing into his phone. When she looked back at me, there was a new unease in her eyes.

"Well, shit," she muttered, then clapped a hand over her mouth, her cheeks flushing a delightful shade of pink. "Sugar! Professionalism, Iris. I meant... Oh, son of a biscuit!" She looked utterly exasperated with herself.

I stared at her, my mouth open. The absurdity of her self-correction in the face of a potential structural disaster was so profoundly Iris that a strange sound escaped me. It might have been a laugh. I quickly suppressed it, turning it into a cough.

"Yeah," I said, my voice carefully neutral, though the image of her invoking biscuits in a moment of stress was going to stick with me. "Well."

She saw my reaction. "I'm, uh, trying to decrease my swearing." Her voice dropped a little, as if sharing a profound secret. "For the B&B, you know. When I become an official hostess, I'll need to use less salty language." She offered an almost apologetic smile.

I just blinked at her. The woman was trying to stop swearing while renovating a certifiable money pit with a dubious contractor. I mentally added *talks like a deranged kindergarten teacher when annoyed* to my ever-expanding list of baffling things about Iris Holloway.

"Anyway," she continued, clearly wanting to steer the

conversation away from Riley and her bizarre linguistic choices. "Mick says they'll be moving the majority of the work inside soon. Starting on the en-suite bathrooms for the guest rooms. So hopefully that will mean less noise for you." She offered me another of those hopeful, slightly anxious smiles.

En-suites. In that old wreck.

Ambitious didn't even begin to cover it.

"Right. Bathrooms." The image of tangled, ancient plumbing lines and rotted floor joists flashed through my mind. "Well. Just… keep an eye on things."

"I will," she said, her voice firm. "Thank you, Austin. For the heads-up."

The sincerity in her tone, the way she stared at me then, not with fear but with a kind of reluctant gratitude, did something strange to the usual knot in my gut. It didn't exactly loosen it, but it shifted. Made it feel less like anger and more like… Hell, I didn't know what. And I wasn't about to stop swearing.

I just nodded, a curt dip of my chin. "Thanks for the coffee cake. Gotta get to work."

Then I turned and walked back toward my property. A final glance revealed her standing there, her expression thoughtful and a little worried as the distant laughter of Mick Riley echoed across the yard.

Chapter Eight

AUSTIN

THAT EVENING, after a productive charter, the familiar scent of salt-tinged woodsmoke drew me toward the beach. A bonfire was already crackling in the family's usual spot near the home we'd grown up in, spitting sparks into the dusky sky. The residence was a distance down the beach from the resort, affording the family some privacy.

Harper and Chase were now fully settled into the house in the distance, but a quick scan showed no sign of them around the fire. Several driftwood logs were pulled up close to the flames. I hadn't planned on joining our semi-regular family gathering, but the thought of sitting alone in my house, stewing over my chaotic neighbor, was even less appealing.

Our eldest brother, Ben, was perched on one of the logs with a glossy brochure from Monroe County Community College. He'd been an EMT with the Dove Key Fire Department for a solid four months now, and by all accounts, including his captain's, he was doing a damn good job. Ben had almost blushed when he recounted to me how Rick had recently pulled him aside, told him he had a knack for it, and said he should seriously consider going for his paramedic certification. It had always been Ben's dream, the one he was too afraid to reach for. The brochure was a clear indicator he was mulling it over.

Braden was poking at the fire with a long piece of driftwood, a bucket of ice next to him. He glanced up as I approached. "And Austin makes it complete! Look at us, the last of the wild Coleridges." He let out a dramatic sigh. "The domesticated ones are no doubt at home knitting matching sweaters."

I grunted, a smile touching my lips. "Maybe they've just got better things to keep them warm than a fire and our ugly faces."

"Touché," Braden conceded, grinning. His blue eyes held equal amounts of humor and shrewdness. He grabbed the growler from the bucket and poured some into a pint glass. "This is my new IPA on tap. Hopical Storm. Figured you'd appreciate the name."

He handed me the glass, and I nodded my thanks. We Coleridges varied in our hair and eye color. Eli and Braden had the lightest hair, I had the darkest. Ben was in between, similar to Harper's shade. Only Brenna got the tinge of red.

I nudged Ben with my knee. "Contemplating a higher education, old man?"

Ben snapped his head up, alarm flashing in his green eyes before he folded the paramedic-program brochure neatly and tucked it into his pocket. "Something like that. Rick's been on my case about it." He took a sip of his Hopical Storm. "Still thinking. I just got done with EMT school. Not sure I want even more."

I knew better than to push. "Plenty of time to decide."

He barked a laugh. "Not really. The new semester starts next week. I need to fish or cut bait, to use a metaphor you'd appreciate."

"See, you're already sounding all educated. Using big words like metaphor." I lifted the glass to my lips. The beer was perfect—hoppy, crisp, with a citrusy bite that cut through the lingering taste of salt and diesel from the day. Braden excelled at his chosen profession. I gave him a nod. "Not bad."

"Just not bad?" Braden feigned offense. "That, my brother, is liquid gold. So, Captain Grumbles, how's life next to the ongoing symphony of destruction? Still getting those daily serenades via power tool and off-key pop song?"

I already regretted complaining to him about the noise. "It's a work in progress. Hers, mostly. At least I'm getting breakfast out of it." My mouth rarely betrayed me, but as soon as the sentence left my lips, I knew I was toast.

Braden, who'd been about to toss another piece of wood on the fire, froze mid-motion. He slowly lowered the log, his eyes zeroing in on me like a barracuda spotting a wounded snapper.

"Hold. The. Phone." Braden enunciated each word with deliberate, almost gleeful, precision. His usual easygoing grin widened into something positively predatory. "Rewind that last part. Did I just hear you correctly? Did the words *getting breakfast out of it* actually escape the hermetically sealed vault that is your mouth, Austin?"

I took another long, slow swallow of beer, suddenly wishing a rogue wave would swallow me whole. I ignored Ben's head swiveling toward me. "It's nothing. The woman can't seem to stop baking. Says she experiments and ends up with enough to feed half the town. Suppose it's better than her experimenting with plumbing again. Or God forbid, power tools." I attempted a dismissive shrug. It probably looked more like a full-body twitch.

Braden's eyebrows shot up. He dropped the log and leaned forward, propping his elbows on his knees, his expression a mixture of disbelief and sheer, unholy delight. "Experiments? With baking? And she's sharing these experiments with you? The guy who looks like he'd rather gargle with salt and sand than engage in polite neighborly chit-chat?" He gasped, his eyes widening. "Wait a minute. *Getting breakfast out of it…* Austin, are you sleeping with the noisy neighbor? Is that what this is? A little post-snuggle pastry offering?"

Ben roared with laughter as I choked on my beer, a spray of it nearly erupting from my lips to sizzle in the fire. "What the—Braden! Are you stupid?" My voice came out as a strangled rasp. The idea was so ludicrous, so utterly beyond the realm of possibility, it was almost offensive.

Sleeping with Holloway?

With Iris?

The woman was a walking, talking agent of chaos.

And yet, even as my mind reeled at his suggestion, a fleeting, unwelcome image flashed behind my eyes: Iris in my kitchen, the way the late-afternoon sun had caught the gold in her hair. The soft curve of her neck as she'd looked down at the basket. Her lips, full and pink, when she'd offered that hesitant, apologetic smile. The way her cleavage was revealed by the top few open buttons on her shirt…

I shoved the images away, hard, a fresh wave of heat flooding my face that had nothing to do with the fire. "Don't be an asshole," I bit out, glaring at my still-grinning brother. "She leaves the food on my patio. That's it. It's a… a neighborly gesture. To apologize for the damn noise, I assume."

Braden was practically vibrating with suppressed laughter. "Right, right. Neighborly. Of course. My mistake." He wiped an imaginary tear from his eye. "So, these purely platonic, entirely neighborly, post-noise-complaint breakfast items… are they any good? Or are we talking about those dry, crumbly things that old Mrs. Crowley used to bring to the school bake sales, the ones that could double as doorstops?"

I took another long sip of my beer, staring resolutely into the dancing flames, trying to regain my composure and project an air of complete indifference. "They're edible."

Braden threw his head back and laughed, a loud bark of amusement that echoed over the waves. "Edible! That's practically a five-star review coming from you, brother!" Then his smile faded and he grew more serious. "Just be careful, man. It's never a good idea to get all twisted up over a woman, especially an ambitious one. I know plenty about that."

He'd just left me a Mack-truck-sized opening, but I decided not to twist the knife too hard. "Yeah, well, you're the family expert, aren't you?"

"Be nice, brothers," Ben admonished softly.

Braden just rolled his eyes and turned back to me. "So what's the game plan? Are you going to keep accepting these baked goods until she's lulled you into a sugar coma so she can renovate in peace? Or is there, dare I suggest, a strategic counter-offensive involving… I don't know… offering to fix her leaky faucet? Or maybe just an effusive grunt of acknowledgment?"

Ben cleared his throat, a smile returning to his lips. Traitor. "Sounds like you've got it rough, Austin. Forced to eat free, homemade baked goods. The horror."

"I should have kept my damn mouth shut." I folded my

arms and scowled as both my brothers burst into guffaws again. Damn them. "Look. There's no game plan. She leaves food. I eat it. End of story."

Sometimes my family was more exhausting than a Category Three hurricane. The conversation shifted, thankfully, to one of Ben's calls where he ended up taking someone to the hospital in Marathon. It was good to see him so driven, so focused on building a future for himself. He'd come a long way from the rudderless, angry young man he'd been after Dad left. We all had, I supposed, in our own ways.

Eventually, we doused the fire and called it a night, three bachelors going our different ways. Back in my house, I tried to settle into my evening routine. But with the crew packed up and the relentless noise from next door stopped, the silence that descended was unexpected. A hole where the sound of saws, hammers, and off-key singing had been.

The stillness was heavier than it used to be. Deeper.

I found myself at my kitchen window, staring at Heron House, and caught a glimpse of Iris's silhouette moving behind a first-floor window.

What trouble is she getting herself into now? The thought was automatic, my default setting when it came to her.

But beneath the ingrained annoyance was something else. A low-grade hum of… what? Concern? Curiosity? I waited, almost unconsciously, for the sound of something crashing, for a yelp of frustration. For some sign of the life constantly thrumming just beyond my hibiscus hedge.

Nothing. Just the hum of my refrigerator.

In that moment, a blunt, unwelcome realization hit me. The silence was worse than the noise. Because the noise meant her vibrant, chaotic, undeniable presence. The silence just meant I was alone.

The thought was so unsettling, so alien to the man I thought I was, that I immediately dismissed it. But as I got ready for bed, the feeling lingered, a quiet, insistent thrum that sounded a hell of a lot like the beginning of a problem. A problem that had blonde hair, long legs, and a knack for baking coffee cake.

Chapter Nine

IRIS

THE THIRD-FLOOR BEDROOM, destined to be the Magnolia Suite if my grand plans ever came to fruition, currently resembled the aftermath of a plaster-eating Tasmanian devil convention. Thick, gritty dust coated every surface and hung in the hot, still air like a shroud. Piles of shattered lath and crumbling plaster formed a miniature mountain range in the center of the room. Chalk lines, white against the dark, aged floorboards, optimistically delineated where a luxurious en-suite bathroom would one day exist.

"Okay," I said to the echoing emptiness, my voice small against the vastness of the room and the task ahead. I clapped my hands, sending up another puff of dust. "This is progress. Definitely progress. Demolition is always the messy part. It has to get worse before it gets gloriously, beautifully better. Right?"

The silent, dust-mote-filled room offered no argument, which I took as a resounding yes.

I tried to visualize the finished room. Delicate floral wallpaper would complement the view of the ancient magnolia tree outside the future French doors. A ridiculously comfortable king-sized bed piled high with pillows. I could almost see the happy, relaxed guests sipping mimosas on their private balcony.

"All part of the process," I chanted, a mantra against the rising tide of overwhelm clawing its way up my gut. "Aunt Constance said it demanded resilience. And I am nothing if not resilient-ish."

It had been a week since Austin's grudging, almost-compliment about my coffee cake. And his warning about Mick. A week where I'd continued my pastry offensive with mixed results.

After the initial chocolate chip cookie and coffee cake success, I'd ambitiously attempted a batch of lemon-lavender scones, picturing them as elegant accompaniments to afternoon tea at my glorious future Heron House B&B. Unfortunately, my enthusiasm for lavender had apparently outweighed my sense of proportion. Austin had returned the plate the next day with only half a scone missing and a look on his face that suggested I'd tried to poison him with lemon furniture polish. I'd quickly sought a second opinion.

"Iris, honey," Liv Markham had said with gentle diplomacy when I'd brought her a sample at Sweet Dreams Bakery, her brow furrowed as she took a tentative nibble. "These are, um, intensely flavorful. A bit like eating an expensive scented candle." She'd then kindly shown me how to properly infuse cream for a subtler floral note, bless her practical, baker's heart.

I followed up the Great Lavender Debacle with a batch of foolproof, decadently rich double-chocolate-chip brownies to restore my somewhat battered baking reputation. Austin hadn't returned the plate for that one yet, which I was choosing to interpret as a good sign. Or possibly that he'd just thrown the whole thing, plate and all, into the sea.

One could never be entirely sure with Captain Grumpy.

But his warning about my contractor had stayed with me, a persistent stone in my shoe. I'd been watching Mick more closely, trying to reconcile Austin's grim assessment with the man who always sounded so confident, so reassuringly in control.

Which was why my stomach twisted when I heard hammering start up outside the Magnolia Suite's boarded-up window. Not inside, where they were supposed to be framing the new bathroom walls.

"What in the... sugar-coated saints are they doing out there now?" I muttered, already heading for the stairs. Not even my almost-automatic swear substitution could overcome the cloud forming over me.

Mick and I had this conversation yesterday. *Focus on the guest rooms, get them framed and ready for the plumber and electrician.* That was the plan. Yet they worked outside yesterday. I'd let it slide, sure they'd be back in this demolition derby first thing today. This constant, inexplicable jumping between tasks was inefficient, disorganized, and it was making my already frayed nerves sing a very off-key tune.

I found Mick Riley propped one dusty boot on a stack of lumber and surveying his two-man crew as they wrestled with a long, unwieldy piece of new siding on the west-facing wall. The sun, already high and hot for mid-morning, beat down on them.

"Good morning, Mick." I kept my voice even, professional. *You're the client, Iris. You have a right to know what's going on.* "I thought we agreed the priority was framing the upstairs bathrooms this week. Getting those interior walls up?"

Mick turned, his expression one of mild, put-upon surprise, as if I'd just asked him to explain the theory of relativity in Swahili. "Yeah, uh, supplies for that got delayed, Miz Holloway."

I frowned. "What about the stack of two-by-fours sitting in the room?"

"Ran out of nails. Hard to put up walls without nails." Before I could respond to that ridiculous statement, he gestured vaguely toward the sky with a sawdust-covered hand. "Figured we'd get a jump on this siding while the weather's holding. Can't let a sunny day go to waste, right?"

"But the siding on this section wasn't scheduled until much later," I pressed, a knot of frustration tightening in my chest. "And you didn't mention any delays when we talked about the bathroom layout. The upstairs bedrooms still look like a tornado went through them. I was hoping to see actual walls this week."

Riley let out an exaggerated sigh, the kind usually reserved for dealing with particularly dense children. "Look, I know how to manage a project. Sometimes you gotta be flexible, roll with the punches. Materials get held up. It happens."

His tone made my blood boil. He was treating me like an idiot, a clueless woman who wouldn't understand the first thing about construction.

Austin's quiet competence, his direct, no-nonsense assessment of Riley's history, was a beacon of sanity compared to this man's blustering excuses. For some inexplicable reason, I trusted Austin's grudging, almost-mumbled warnings more than I trusted Mick Riley's loud, confident pronouncements.

Just as I was about to argue further—perhaps demanding to know why, for mercy's sake, he couldn't trot down to one of the many stores that sold nails—one of Riley's crew members let out a yelp. The end of the long siding board he was holding slipped, gouging a fresh scratch in the piece below it. Riley swore, a sharp expletive that made me wince.

"All right, boys," he barked, his brief display of professional patience evaporating like morning mist. "That's it for today. It's a furnace out here. Too goddamn hot to be wrestling this stuff. We'll come in special tomorrow."

It was barely eleven o'clock.

"Wait, what?" I stared at him, aghast. "You can't just leave! That piece isn't even properly secured! It's just hanging there! What if it rains? Or the wind picks up?"

Riley just scowled, already turning toward his beat-up truck. His crew immediately started to pack up their tools. "If you hadn't interrupted, it would already be up. Don't worry. It'll be fine. Nothing a few extra nails tomorrow won't fix. Or Monday at the latest."

"You're just quitting for the day at eleven a.m.?"

He offered a wave over his shoulder as the three of them walked away. "Heatstroke's no joke. Gotta look out for my guys. We'll fix it when it's cooler."

And then they were gone, old trucks rattling down the drive and leaving me standing in the blazing sun, staring in disbelief at the half-finished, unsecured length of siding flapping gently in the breeze. A cold knot of dread formed in the pit of my stomach.

For a full minute, I just stood there, paralyzed by a mixture of fury and helplessness. "That… that son of a biscuit! Leaving it like this. Unprofessional. Dangerous!"

What if that heavy board came crashing down? It

could hit someone. It could damage the house further. It couldn't wait until tomorrow, let alone Monday.

As I stared at the waving board, determination filled me, making my spine stand straighter.

Fine.

If he couldn't be troubled to do his job, if he was going to treat me and this project with such disrespect, then I'd figure it out myself. How hard could it be to tack up one measly piece of wood? Secure it properly until tomorrow? I refused to believe he wouldn't return, even if it was Saturday.

The thought, born of pure, adrenaline-fueled indignation, seemed almost reasonable in that moment.

I marched into the dilapidated carriage house that served as a makeshift tool shed, rummaging through a collection of rusty implements left behind by previous, equally unsuccessful renovators. I emerged with a hammer too heavy for my hand, a handful of nails that looked suspiciously bent, and an ancient, rickety wooden extension ladder.

Setting the ladder against the side of the house was a challenge in itself. It scraped against the old paintwork, its feet sinking unevenly into the soft, sandy soil. With a grunt, I eventually had it positioned. The siding board, when I reached it from the upper rungs, was even heavier and more unwieldy than it looked from the ground. It was long, at least twelve feet, and made of some kind of composite material with all the flexibility of a granite tombstone.

And the darn thing was heavy.

My first attempt to lift it into place nearly sent me, the ladder, and the siding crashing to the ground in a tangle of flailing limbs and G-rated expletives.

"Oh, for the love of pelicans!" I gasped, clinging to the ladder as the board swayed dangerously. My heart hammered against my ribs, a frantic bird trapped in a cage.

Okay. New plan. Maybe if I just tried to secure the loose end first?

Sweat trickled down my face, stinging my eyes. The sun beat down relentlessly, turning the air into a shimmering, suffocating blanket. I fumbled with a nail, trying to hold it steady against the wood while simultaneously wielding the ridiculously oversized hammer. The first swing missed the nail entirely, grazing the side of my hand with a sickening rush that sent a yelp of pain tearing from my throat.

Tears of pure frustration and agony welled, blurring my vision.

"Shit!" I hissed, shaking my throbbing hand.

This was harder than it looked. Austin, with his reserved competence and easy way with tools when he'd repaired the hedge, would have had this sorted in five minutes flat, without breaking a sweat or resorting to invoking baffled seabirds.

My determined B&B-hostess professionalism began to crumble like the ancient plaster in the Magnolia Suite. I tried again, my movements clumsy and jerky. The nail bent in half under a poorly aimed blow. The siding, instead of becoming more secure, seemed to sag even further, pulling away from the house with a groan of protesting wood. I grabbed it quickly to keep it from falling.

A wave of dizziness, born of heat, exertion, and panic, washed over me. I clung to the ladder, my knuckles white, my breath coming in ragged, shallow gasps.

I can't do this.

The thought, cold and sharp as an icicle, pierced the fog of my frustration.

"I really can't do this. What was I thinking? Taking on this house? This town? All by myself?"

Self-doubt, that cold and familiar companion I'd tried so hard to leave behind in Abingdon, reared its ugly head, whispering its insidious, poisonous truths. Aunt Constance believed in me, but maybe she was wrong. Maybe she saw a spark that wasn't really there.

This was just like the studio in Virginia. The brilliant idea, the initial burst of energy, then the first major, impossible hurdle where I quit. The moment it stopped being fun and started being hard, I always found a reason to walk away.

Maybe I'm just not cut out for this.

Maybe I was just a disaster, like Austin no doubt thought. A walking, talking, hibiscus-drowning, siding-dropping catastrophe.

I made one last, desperate, sobbing attempt to shove the siding back into place. My hands were shaking too badly. The heavy board slipped from my grasp with a sickening scrape of wood against wood, swinging wildly for a moment before one end crashed against the side of the house with a splintering thud, hanging even more precariously than before.

The hammer clattered from my nerveless fingers, bouncing off a rung of the ladder before landing with a dull thunk in the overgrown grass below. A choked sob escaped me. Then another. The cheerful house of cards I called optimism came tumbling down as I gripped the unsteady ladder with both wildly trembling hands.

It was too much.

The only sound was the gentle, mocking creak of the loose siding in the afternoon breeze and my ragged, increasingly panicky breaths.

Chapter Ten

AUSTIN

MY DAY OFF. The three words tried to sing a quiet, contented tune in my head, a promise of uninterrupted puttering or the satisfying precision of tackle maintenance. Over the past few weeks, I'd even learned to accept some of the racket from next door. Or maybe I'd just gotten used to it.

I'd earmarked this morning for much-needed work on my favorite seven-foot casting rod. The tip guide had taken a beating on my last charter when a feisty permit did its best to impersonate a runaway submarine.

I was on my back patio, enjoying the shade while the delicate components of the rod tip were spread out on a clean canvas cloth. The old guide was off, the blank cleaned, and I was just starting the process of whipping on the new one with fine, dark-blue thread. It was a delicate operation that required a steady hand, the kind of task that usually settled my mind and allowed me to exist purely in the moment. The sharp scent of rod epoxy mingled with the salty air and the distant, sweet perfume of a blooming frangipani.

But concentration was proving hard to capture.

The sounds from Heron House, the usual roar of hammers and power tools earlier, had shifted. Now, it was a series of more sporadic, distinctly amateurish noises. The scrape of something being dragged. A frustrated grunt, sharp and distinctly feminine. Then, the thud of something heavy, followed by a faint, exasperated mutter that even the breeze couldn't quite carry.

Focus, Coleridge. Just the thread. Keep the tension even.

I tried to tune out the fact that she was right over there, to lose myself in the repetitive wrapping of the thread. I didn't think about how I'd catch her staring at that old mansion sometimes, a determined look in her eye even as she wrung her hands. I sure as hell didn't think about how good her legs looked in shorts, or how her arms were toned yet feminine.

And I absolutely didn't spare a single thought to her round, full lips.

Riley's crew was probably working inside. Or maybe Iris was experimenting again. With a sledgehammer this time, by the sound of it.

But another sound, a sharp crack of splintering wood followed by a choked cry, made my head snap up, the fine thread slipping from my fingers. My carefully constructed bubble of solitary peace popped with an almost audible hiss. I shot to my feet and rushed to the hedge.

And there she was.

Iris. Alone. Perched precariously near the top of an ancient, rickety-looking wooden extension ladder that looked like it had been left to rot by Noah after the ark landed. She was wrestling with a long, heavy piece of new siding, her frame straining against its unwieldy length, her blonde hair plastered to her sweaty forehead with a mixture of fierce determination and what looked like pure panic.

What in the ever-loving hell is she doing?

I scanned the Heron House yard, my gaze sweeping from the overgrown jungle to the peeling paint of the massive Victorian. No sign of Riley's beat-up work truck. No sign of his crew. Just Iris, a solitary, out-of-her-depth figure battling a twelve-foot plank of composite wood that clearly had the upper hand.

"Are you kidding me? Those assholes."

They left her. That son of a bitch Riley had actually walked off the job—on a Friday, no less, classic move—and left her to deal with this mess by herself. This wasn't just her being clueless anymore, or her usual brand of enthusiastic, disastrous incompetence. This was her being abandoned with a genuinely dangerous problem.

She let out another frustrated yelp as the siding slipped, the top edge swinging wildly away from the wall for a terrifying moment, nearly taking her with it. She scrambled for purchase, her body contorting at an unsafe angle.

That was it.

I dropped the rod components onto the lawn. She was going to get herself seriously hurt if someone didn't step in. And it looked like that someone was going to have to be me.

I rushed down the faint path next to the hedge, the usual irritation I felt when approaching Heron House now replaced by a grim urgency. I found her on the ladder, red-faced and sweating, streaks of dirt and maybe tears smudging her cheeks. Her knuckles were white where she gripped the siding, her body trembling with exertion and, I suspected, a huge dose of fear. She looked like she'd been through a war with a lumberyard. And lost.

"Iris," I said, my voice cutting through the oppressive afternoon heat and her muttered string of what sounded like increasingly desperate, G-rated curses.

Startled, she jumped and whipped her head around. The ladder gave an alarming wobble. For a heart-stopping second, I thought she was going to come tumbling down. My muscles tensed, ready to catch her.

"What do you want?" she snapped, her voice tight and defensive. She swiped at her forehead with her upper arm, leaving another streak of grime across her already smudged cheek. Her blue eyes, when they met mine, were blazing with defiance and unshed tears.

"Looks like that thing's about to come down on you," I said, keeping my tone as level as I could, though my insides were anything but. My gaze flicked from her unstable perch to the precariously hung siding, then back to her. "You need to get off that ladder before you break your neck."

"I've got it!" she insisted, her chin jutting out with that stubborn tilt I was starting to recognize, the one that usually preceded some new form of disaster. "It's fine! Perfectly fine! I don't need any help, thank you!"

She punctuated this bold, entirely unconvincing declaration by giving the siding another futile tug, which only made it sag more alarmingly.

"Iris, come down," I said, my voice firmer, taking a step closer to the base of the ladder. "That whole section is unstable. It's not properly braced. You keep yanking on it, you're going to bring the whole damn thing down, and yourself with it."

"I know what I'm doing!" she shot back, though the tremor in her voice betrayed her bravado. Her eyes darted from the siding to me and back again, like a cornered animal. "It just… slipped a little. I almost had it."

Slipped a little? It's hanging on by a prayer and your increasingly desperate grip.

There was a fine trembling in her arms.

"Come down," I repeated, that unwelcome knot of concern tightening in my chest, making it hard to breathe. I wasn't asking anymore. "Now. Before you get seriously hurt."

She glared down at me, her blue eyes clouded with a potent mixture of defiance, frustration, and despair. For a long, tense moment, she just clung there, a small, stubborn figure silhouetted against the vast, decaying backdrop of Heron House. I could practically feel the internal battle raging within her: fierce pride warring with the dawning realization that she was utterly out of her depth.

Then, with a defeated moan that seemed to carry the weight of the entire dilapidated mansion, her shoulders slumped. The fight visibly drained out of her. She let go of the siding. It swung free with a groan of stressed wood and a sickening scrape against the clapboard below, hanging at an even more drunken angle.

Slowly, her movements stiff and jerky, she backed down the rickety rungs. Her knees buckled slightly on the last step, and I instinctively reached out, my hand closing around her upper arm to steady her. Her skin was hot, damp with sweat, and she was trembling like a leaf.

When her feet touched solid ground, she just stood there, swaying slightly, her gaze fixed on the disastrous piece of siding as if it had personally betrayed her.

Then her carefully constructed composure shattered.

It started with a single, choked sob, a sound so raw and full of despair it hit me like a blow to the chest. Then another, and another, until she was standing in the middle of her overgrown yard, tears streaming down her dirt-streaked face, her shoulders shaking.

"I—I can't…" she gasped out between sobs, her voice hoarse and broken. "I just… I can't do this!"

I was rooted to the spot, completely unprepared. I wasn't good at this. Not with tears. Or feelings. Especially female feelings being unleashed like a Category Five hurricane directly at me. My first instinct, honed by years of practice, was to retreat. To find my quiet sanctuary and bolt the damn door. I'd just wanted to stop her from breaking her neck, not trigger a full-blown emotional meltdown I was in no way equipped to handle.

"This whole goddamn place is cursed!" she screamed, her voice cracking, all pretense of G-rated language abandoned. "And that bastard Riley just left me! With this… this shitpile! And everyone thinks I'm just some stupid, clueless girl who doesn't know what she's doing!" Her voice rose, laced with a desperate, ragged anger, her fists clenched at her sides. "But I'm not. I can do this. I will do this. I swear to God, I will finish this goddamn stubborn bastard of a house if it kills me!"

She stood still, hands scrunched into fists at her sides, dust and tears and righteous indignation emanating from every pore.

I just listened. There must have been some short circuit in my usual self-preservation instincts because I didn't walk away. My internal alarm bells were screaming at me to run. But I stayed and watched this irritating, disruptive, surprisingly good baker of a neighbor fall to pieces in front of me.

And, against everything I stood for, I moved. I closed the space between us. My hand, large and calloused from years of hauling lines and wrestling with boat engines, landed awkwardly on her trembling shoulder. It was small, bird-boned beneath my fingers, and shockingly fragile.

Before my brain could process the shift from verbal

onslaught to physical collapse, her frame was leaning heavily against my chest, her face buried in the rough cotton of my shirt. Her shoulders hitched with a final, shuddering sob.

Acting on an instinct that bypassed every wall I owned, my arms came up. They hovered uncertainly. Then, as another ragged tremor ran through her, they settled around her, pulling her loosely against me. It was an awkward embrace, foreign territory. I found myself patting her back in a clumsy, repetitive motion.

"All right, now." My voice was gruff, the words ridiculously inadequate in the face of her raw anguish. I could feel the dampness of her tears soaking into my shirt, the heat of her body, the fine trembling that still wracked her. "All right, Iris. Just breathe. It's okay."

She didn't pull away. If anything, she seemed to melt further into my arms, her hands gripping my shirtfront as if I were the only solid thing in a world that had just spun into space. The scent of her—dust, sunshine, and that faint, lingering sweetness of baked goods—filled my senses in an unexpectedly potent combination.

For a long moment, we just stood there, me holding this bewildering, sobbing woman, her ragged breathing slowly beginning to even out. The anger, the sharp edges of her earlier fury, dissipated, leaving behind a profound, bone-deep weariness. I could feel it in the sag of her shoulders, the heavy way her head rested against me.

Against everything screaming at me to maintain distance, I pressed my cheek against the top of her head, against the surprisingly soft silk of her blonde hair. It was an unconscious gesture of comfort, maybe. Or just presence. I wasn't good at words, not the kind she needed right now. But I could offer this. This private, unyielding solidity. A temporary harbor. So I just let her be.

Safe, for a moment, in the circle of my arms.

The tremors gradually subsided. Her breathing became deeper, the tension easing. Then, slowly, she stirred. She didn't pull away entirely but tilted her head back to look up at me.

Her face was a mess. Tear tracks carved paths through the grime on her cheeks. Her eyes were red-rimmed and swollen, her lips trembling slightly. But beneath the devastation, there was something else in those cornflower-blue eyes now. A raw vulnerability, a flicker of trust. And a spark of the determination I was beginning to recognize.

And then, before I could process it, she moved. One slight, surprisingly steady hand snaked up, her cool fingers sliding into the hair at the nape of my neck. Her gaze held mine, intense, unwavering. Then she pulled my head down. Her lips, soft and salty from her tears, crashed into mine.

My brain just… stopped.

Ceased all function.

Complete system shock.

All thought, all resistance, all carefully constructed defenses I'd spent over a decade perfecting vanished in an instant. Obliterated. There was only the feel of her, the unexpected, desperate heat of her mouth, the taste of her. Salt and dust and sunshine and something uniquely, undeniably Iris.

For a bare second, I was frozen, every muscle locked. Then something inside me, something primal and long-dormant, roared to life.

I kissed her back.

Hard.

My hands, acting with a will of their own, slid from her shoulders to her waist, pulling her closer, crushing the air from my lungs, eliminating the last vestiges of space between us. The kiss deepened, shifted to something shared, something hungry, that spoke of pent-up tension and a loneliness I hadn't realized I carried until this very moment. It was messy, a collision of frustration and surprise and an undeniable spark that had been simmering beneath the surface of our awkward, pastry-fueled interactions.

There was only the surprising softness of her lips under the initial force, the way she tasted, the feel of her body, slight and trembling but fiercely present, molding against mine as if she belonged there. The thought was a jolt, as shocking as the kiss itself.

Raw, unthinking instinct took over. I parted my lips in both a silent question and a demand. She answered, a soft sigh escaping her as she welcomed my tongue. The kiss transformed into a hot, wet, searching exploration, a raw claiming. No finesse, no practiced seduction, just a desperate, mutual need.

I slanted my mouth over hers, finding a better angle, a groan tearing from my throat. She met me stroke for stroke, her initial desperation fanned into answering heat. Both of her small hands were now tangled in my hair, her fingers tightening, pulling me impossibly closer.

I pressed myself against her, backing her up a step until her spine met the rough clapboard of the house. Fierce arousal, a white-hot flame I hadn't experienced in longer than I cared to admit, flared to life, coiling tight and low in my gut, hardening me against her. There was no thought, no room for the usual litany of warnings that usually governed my interactions.

Only the surprising, explosive rightness of her mouth on mine.

I couldn't stop. Didn't want to.

All the irritation, the annoyance, the walls I'd

constructed since the accident, brick by painful brick—they were just gone. Incinerated in this unexpected, bewildering, overwhelming clash of mouths.

Just as suddenly as it began, as the fire threatened to rage out of control, it ended.

We broke apart, or perhaps stumbled back from each other, breathless, chests heaving. I stared down at her, my hands still loosely on her waist. A fine tremor ran through her, or maybe it was me who was shaking. Her eyes were wide, dazed, her lips swollen and damp from my kiss, a vulnerable pink against the tear-streaked grime on her face. The remnants of her earlier despair were still there, but now mingled with a look of shell-shocked surprise that surely mirrored my own.

This was a mistake. A colossal, Category Five, no-good-can-come-of-this, what-in-the-hell-am-I-doing mistake.

Because for one breathless moment, holding her, tasting her, I had felt something other than the dull ache of the past. That feeling sent a bolt of pure, cold terror through me. It was a taste of something I could lose. A sensation like a target painted on my back, just waiting for the universe to take its shot. Again.

The sounds of Dove Key rushed back in—the distant drone of a boat engine out on the Gulf, the insistent cry of a gull circling overhead, the gentle, indifferent rustle of palm fronds in the breeze. The heat of the sun was oppressive again, pressing down on us.

What. The. Hell. Just. Happened?

I couldn't form a coherent thought, let alone a sentence. I just stared at her, this bewildering, infuriating, undeniably passionate woman. She stared back, the air between us charged with the frightening, electrifying weight of what we'd just done.

Chapter Eleven

IRIS

THE TILTED WORLD slowly and grudgingly righted itself. Or maybe that was just me, swaying on unsteady feet. The air, thick and molten only moments ago with the intensity of… *whoa*… was now frail and sharp in my lungs. I could hear my ragged breathing beside the frantic thrum of my pulse in my ears.

And Austin.

He stood less than an arm's length away, his chest rising and falling like a bellows. A loud bellows. His usually unreadable gray eyes were fixed on mine with an expression of shock, and his lips were a darker shade than usual. A muscle twitched in his jaw, a tiny, betraying sign of the storm I suspected was raging behind his stunned facade.

Oh. My. Stars.

What had I just done?

I, Iris Holloway, the woman currently engaged in a one-woman pursuit of B&B proprietorship, had just launched a full-scale, lips-first assault on my grumpy, intensely private sea-captain neighbor. After unleashing a rather un-G-rated tirade. Also after he'd saved me from almost certain bodily harm involving a large piece of siding and a terribly rickety ladder.

My cheeks, already flushed from exertion and tears, burned with a fresh, even hotter wave of mortification. My lips tingled, a phantom sensation of the surprising softness beneath the initial desperate force. At the unexpected taste of him—salt, sunshine, and something uniquely, unforgettably Austin.

And the most shocking part? The part that made my stomach perform a series of complicated, dizzying acrobatic maneuvers that had nothing to do with nearly falling off a ladder? A tiny, rebellious part of me, the part that had apparently been hibernating under layers of good intentions and silly expletives, wasn't sorry.

Not one single, solitary bit.

Austin, however, looked like he was one twitching synapse away from either bolting for the nearest horizon or spontaneously combusting into a pile of bewildered ash. The alarming flush that had risen from his collar to his hairline was receding, leaving him pale beneath his tan, his usual stoic mask shattered.

He looked… floored.

Like a complex navigation chart had just been rewritten in ancient Aramaic right before his eyes and then set on fire. For a man usually so in control, so self-contained, it was almost endearing. And also rather unsettling.

The thick silence stretched, vibrating with unspoken questions and the crackling static of a line just crossed. One of us needed to say something. Break the spell. Or the horrified paralysis.

And if history was any indication, it wouldn't be Austin.

With the almost hysterical need to inject some semblance of normalcy, however absurd, into the moment, I dredged up what I hoped was a light joke.

"Well!" I chirped, my voice sounding unnaturally bright and wobbly even to my ears, like a badly tuned ukulele. "That was, erm, unexpected." I gestured vaguely toward the wagging siding, then back to the space between us. "I, uh, feel much more… settled now. Crisis averted?" I even managed a nervous laugh that possibly sounded more like a strangled chicken.

Austin didn't respond. He didn't even look at me. Instead, his gaze, still wide and slightly wild, zeroed in on the disastrously hanging siding as if it were the only thing in the universe that made any sense.

With a rough sound that might have been him clearing his throat, or possibly just him trying to remember how to breathe, he muttered, "That siding needs to be secured. Now."

With a few brutally efficient movements, he grabbed the hammer I'd dropped, found a couple of straight nails amidst my scattered, pathetic supplies, and vaulted up the rickety ladder. With a series of precise blows that echoed like gunshots in the sudden stillness, he securely tacked the loose siding into place.

Though probably not a long-term fix, it was no longer an immediate, head-lopping hazard at least. He worked with a focused, almost desperate energy. His movements were stiff, his jaw locked, every line of his body screaming his urgent need to escape the invisible, crackling weirdness that now enveloped us.

When he was done, he climbed down and stood back, still not looking at me. His chest continued to rise and fall in short, jerky motions. "That'll hold it for now. I need… need to check on my rod. Fishing rod! The epoxy."

He turned even more crimson, whether from the rod reference, or his flimsy excuse, I wasn't sure. Then he all but scurried back to his yard, disappearing inside the house without another word or a backward glance.

Leaving me standing there, bewildered, heart still pounding a frantic rhythm against my ribs. I raised my fingers to rub my lower lip where the memory of his kiss, and the surprising, not-at-all-unpleasant roughness of his scruff, tingled with a life of its own.

THE NEXT MORNING, Saturday, dawned bright and deceptively cheerful. I was up before the sun, a bundle of nervous, restless energy. Every creak of Heron House's ancient bones, every rustle of palm fronds in the pre-dawn breeze, sounded like an accusation. I ran my tongue over my lower lip while my coffee brewed. The memory of Austin's mouth on mine, surprisingly, searchingly soft, then hard and demanding, was a vivid, full-color replay in my mind.

I kept looking out the grimy kitchen window, my gaze fixed on Austin's neat, quiet conch house.

Expecting… what?

For him to emerge, rake in hand, and deliver a stern lecture on inappropriate neighborly conduct? For him to perhaps wave, a small acknowledgment of the previous day's events? Or maybe I was searching for a sign that the earth-shattering, world-tilting kiss hadn't been a figment of my over-stressed, sun-addled imagination.

But it wasn't just the kiss that replayed in my mind. It was the moments just before it. The wobbly ladder. The unwieldy weight of the siding in my aching arms. The panic as I realized I had bitten off a mountain's worth more than I could chew. I had been alone, failing, and on the verge of either giving up or getting seriously hurt.

Then Austin was there.

He hadn't hesitated. He hadn't stood on his perfect lawn and yelled at me to be more careful. He had walked right into my disaster, taken control of the situation, and gotten me safely to the ground. He hadn't mocked my incompetence or lectured me—much. He had simply seen a problem and fixed it.

He had shown up.

And maybe that was why I had kissed him. It had been a desperate, overwhelming surge of gratitude and relief. In a moment of genuine crisis, when the man I'd hired had abandoned me, Austin Coleridge had been the one to climb into the wreckage and pull me out.

That knowledge was, in its own way, far more unsettling than the memory of the kiss itself. It was one thing to be attracted to a handsome, grumpy neighbor. It was another thing entirely to suspect that beneath the scowls and the silence lay a man who might be something more. Something that felt like a safe harbor in the middle of my storm.

But as I stared at his neat house, it remained stubbornly silent, as if hunkering down against further incursions from the lady next door.

And more pressingly, there was no sign of Mick Riley or his crew, despite him saying they'd be back today. He hadn't really meant to leave that siding half-hanging all weekend, had he?

"Of course not. That would be completely unprofessional."

The hours ticked by with agonizing slowness. Eight

o'clock. Nine. Ten. Still no familiar rumble of Riley's beat-up truck, no clatter of tools, no booming, off-key singing from his uninspired workforce. My initial annoyance began to curdle into a stomach-twisting unease.

I tried calling his cell. Straight to voicemail, a cheerful, generic recording that now sounded infuriatingly smug. I left a message, trying to keep my voice calm, professional. "Mick, it's Iris Holloway. Just wondering about your ETA today? You said you'd be here this morning."

Another hour crawled by. No call back. No truck. No crew.

"Oh Mylanta!" I exclaimed to the empty, dust-filled expanse of the Starfish Suite, where I'd gone to try and distract myself by measuring for curtain rods, a task that now felt ludicrously optimistic. "Where is he? He can't just leave that siding job half-done after practically running away yesterday."

Austin's muted, almost reluctant warnings about Mick's history and his tendency to take the path of least resistance echoed in my head. He was right. My contractor was a first-class, gold-plated weasel with the work ethic of a narcoleptic sloth.

Full of restless energy and a mounting sense of anxiety that was like a flock of angry terns dive-bombing my insides, I did what I always did when the world went sideways.

I baked.

Today, it was scones. A new recipe Liv Markham had shared at the book club, one she'd sworn was foolproof and guaranteed to produce light, flaky, buttery perfection. Cranberry-orange. Sure enough, the rhythmic, familiar process of cutting cold butter into flour, the gentle folding of the dough, and the bright scent of orange zest and tart cranberries helped to calm the frantic flapping in my chest.

The scones baked, filling the cavernous kitchen with a warm, comforting aroma that did battle with the lingering scent of ancient dust and despair. This allowed my mind, inevitably, to replay yesterday.

He's probably locked himself in his house, barricaded the doors, and is currently fashioning a garlic wreath to ward me off, I thought with a grimace. *Or maybe he's just decided I'm too much trouble. A walking, talking liability he wants nothing further to do with.*

The thought sent a sharp pang through me. That kiss had been a hurricane, tearing down all his defenses. But nothing was preventing him from waking up and starting to mortar the bricks back into place.

The scones, thankfully, emerged from the oven looking like something straight out of a glossy baking magazine—light, perfectly golden, an absolute triumph. Maybe Captain Grumpy would appreciate a scone? Or was that pushing my luck too far into the realm of desperate, slightly unhinged neighbor?

"Oh, for crying out loud, who cares? I'm already a certified disaster in his eyes. What's one more pastry offering?"

I arranged half a dozen of the best-looking scones on a plate, covered them with a fresh napkin, and, with a surge of what felt more like reckless abandon than genuine courage, marched them over to Austin's front porch. His truck was gone, so I scribbled a brief, carefully neutral note.

More kitchen experiments! These cranberry-orange scones actually turned out pretty well. Thought you might like to try one. Or six.

.   .   .

Iris.

I PROPPED it against the plate. No P.S. this time. I didn't want to press my luck with sprinkler-related humor.

I spent the rest of the long Saturday trying to lose myself in *Key West Affair*, but the romantic travails of the heroine seemed pale and unconvincing compared to the reality of the awkward and confusing drama unfolding right next door. Every creak of Heron House, every distant drone from a passing boat, made me jump, my gaze darting toward Austin's house.

I crawled into my bed that night, still out of sorts. Austin's truck was back, and the scones were gone from his porch. I'd checked, peering through the spunky hibiscus hedge like a highly caffeinated spy, but there had been no word, no sign, from him.

The silence was a deafening contrast to the explosive heat of the kiss we'd shared. And I sure hadn't imagined how he had reacted. The way his tongue had skated over mine. But with nothing to fill the silence but my thoughts and very vivid memories, a sinking feeling settled in my gut.

Sunday morning brought more of the same. Echoing stillness from Austin's house. And, more alarmingly, continued silence from Mick Riley. No truck. No crew. No returned phone calls.

The knot of dread in my stomach tightened into a cold, hard fist of fury.

"That's it," I declared to the jaunty mug I was currently filling with what was rapidly becoming my stress-fueled beverage of choice—very strong, very black coffee. "He's fired. Officially. Irrevocably. Fired."

I dialed Mick's number again, my thumb jabbing at the

screen with righteous indignation. Of course he didn't pick up.

"Mick Riley." My voice was clear, firm, and vibrating with barely suppressed rage. "This is Iris Holloway. Again. Since you have apparently decided to abandon the job and left my property in a dangerous and unsecured state, please consider this official notification that your services are no longer required. You are fired. For breach of contract and gross negligence. I expect a full refund of my deposit." I ended the call with a satisfying click, my hand trembling only slightly.

There. Done. Good riddance to bad, lazy, unreliable rubbish.

I didn't expect to hear back, let alone get my deposit returned, but I felt better for having said it. A wave of both triumphant relief and terrifying responsibility washed over me.

"Now what?"

I was alone with a half-sided house, a mountain of interior demolition that looked like a plaster-coated war zone, and no contractor. How in heckfire—*see, professionalism!*—was I going to find a replacement? Someone who wouldn't try to rip me off or treat me like an idiot? I clearly had terrible judgment when it came to contractors. Austin had been right about Riley from the start.

Austin…

My mind snagged on the memory of his words from a few days ago: *"My brother-in-law, Chase, is an architect…"*

A tiny, desperate seed of an idea began to sprout. Could I? Dare I?

I paced my chaotic kitchen, the pros and cons warring in my head. Asking Austin Coleridge for another favor, especially a favor involving his family, after I'd already assaulted his prize-winning shrubbery and then, even more horrifyingly, assaulted him with my lips… it was mortifying beyond belief. Especially since he'd been incommunicado since. He probably thought I was dangerous. Or worse, that I was chasing him?

Oh, sugar, this is awful.

My cheeks burned at the thought.

But I needed help. Real, professional, trustworthy help. And the thought of blindly picking another contractor from some anonymous online review site felt like playing Russian roulette with Aunt Constance's legacy and my rapidly dwindling sanity.

I spent a good hour, possibly two, hemming and hawing, brewing another pot of coffee I didn't need, and staring out the window at Austin's silent, shuttered house as if it held the answers to all my problems. At last, late that afternoon, the familiar sight of his dark-blue pickup truck pulling into his driveway greeted me.

It was now or never.

Taking a deep, fortifying breath that did little to calm the nerves dancing inside me, I grabbed two ice-cold Queen Conch IPAs I'd picked up at Island Market earlier that week. They were even brewed on the island, and I pegged Austin as a beer man. Clutching the cold, sweating bottles like talismans, I marched across the overgrown patch of grass that separated our properties.

Here we go again, I thought as a wave of dizziness washed over me. *Please, please, don't let him think I'm here to re-enact Friday's, uh, incident.*

He opened the door on my second knock. His shirt was three-quarters unbuttoned, like I'd interrupted him changing. I caught a tantalizing glimpse of dark hair and firm muscle. His expression, when he saw me standing with two beers clutched in my hands, morphed from wariness to something that looked suspiciously like a deer caught in the high beams of an oncoming semi-truck.

"Austin! Hi!" I tried for a bright, breezy, entirely-not-still-mortified-about-kissing-you tone as I held up the beers. "Sorry to bother you again. Peace offering? Or perhaps a bravery enhancer for the one about to ask a massive favor?"

He stared at the beers, then at me, his gray eyes unreadable.

"First," I rushed on, before he could slam the door in my face or call the authorities, "thank you so much for your help on Friday. With the siding. I was… a bit over-whelmed, as you might have gathered." I offered a weak, hopefully endearing, smile. "But I'm feeling much better now. Totally fine. I'm sorry if I overstepped the bounds of neighborly propriety. I assure you it won't happen again."

He still didn't say anything, just continued to look at me as if I'd sprouted a second head that was currently singing opera.

"The reason I'm here… well, Mick Riley hasn't shown up for two days. Since Friday, actually." I took another deep breath. "So I fired him. Officially. And now I'm kind of stuck. In a rather large, siding-deficient, contractor-less pickle. And I remember you mentioned your brother-in-law? Is an architect?" My voice was starting to squeak in response to his wall of silence. "I was just wondering… if he ever, possibly, does consultations? For, you know, disas-trous old houses and new owners with spectacularly terrible contractor luck? Just to put me in touch with the proper person for the job, you understand."

Austin blinked. Once. Twice. He looked from the beers in my hand to my face, then back to the beers. A long, agonizing silence stretched between us, punctuated only by the frantic thumping of my pulse. I was fairly certain I was going to pass out from sheer nervous tension.

Then he let out a slow breath, and the twitching muscle in his jaw relaxed. "All right. I'll… I'll talk to Chase. See if he's got any time. Can't promise anything, Iris."

The sound of my first name on his lips, so unexpected, so normal, sent another jolt through me, this one warmer, less terrifying.

"Oh, thank you, Austin!" Relief, so potent it almost buckled my knees, flooded through me as I shoved the beers into his hand. "That's… thank you! I really, really appreciate it." I started to back away, eager to escape before he changed his mind or I did something else monumentally embarrassing.

"Iris."

His voice, sharper this time, stopped me in my tracks. He still stood in his doorway, the beers still in his hand, looking conflicted. Like the words he was about to say were physically stuck, fighting their way out.

"Yes, Austin?" My voice came out polite and inquisitive. Not at all like I was scared to death I was about to get yelled at.

"You're welcome, by the way," he said finally, the words low, almost a growl. "For Friday. With the siding. I'm, I'm glad I was there when you… when you needed help." He gave a curt, almost imperceptible nod, then looked away, as if the effort of that admission had cost him dearly. "I'll let you know what Chase says."

And then his door closed with a soft, definitive click, leaving me standing on his porch, clutching nothing but the faint, lingering hope that maybe things were about to get a little less disastrous.

Austin was a man of complicated emotions; that much was clear. He was a man who obviously disliked showing them, hoarding his words like a dragon hoarded gold. But just as obviously, beneath that grouchy, barnacle-encrusted exterior, he had a sense of honor. He cared about people, even if he tried his damnedest to pretend he didn't.

And he's a darn good kisser too, my mind treacherously, inappropriately supplied as I walked back toward Heron House, a tiny, confused smile playing on my lips. The thought brought a fresh wave of heat to my cheeks. But this time, it was mixed with something else. Something suspiciously like optimism.

A fragile, Queen-Conch-IPA-fueled optimism.

Chapter Twelve

AUSTIN

THE SATISFACTION OF A JOB DONE, a promise kept, a full cooler, and happy clients—that was the feeling a successful charter was supposed to bring. But as I secured the last of *Line Dancer's* mooring lines to the dock at Sunset Siesta on Monday afternoon, the usual sense of peace was gone, replaced by a low, humming buzz. The couple from Orlando had left thrilled with the kingfish they'd landed, but our easy camaraderie was already like a memory from another lifetime.

Reality had seeped back in.

Stepping back aboard, I should have started cleaning the boat. I should have been rinsing the reels, hosing down the deck. Instead, I stood at the helm, staring out at the familiar, bustling resort but seeing nothing. My mind was a damn washing machine stuck on the spin cycle as it replayed the images of Iris's tear-streaked face, the desperate clutch of her hands on my shirt, the shocking heat of her lips on mine. How good it had felt. How I hadn't wanted that kiss to end.

Then I spent the next two days avoiding even looking in the direction of Heron House, as if it might spontaneously erupt in another geyser of feminine emotion. Two days where the memory of her pressed against me, soft and trembling, had ambushed me at the most inopportune moments. In my dreams, it had been a relentless replay of the softness of her hair beneath my cheek, the taste of her mouth, the raw vulnerability in her wide blue eyes. And my dreams had carried that encounter right into the bedroom, which only made the situation worse.

I could not stop thinking about the woman.

Then the beers. Her on my doorstep. And her high-pitched, squeaky voice, asking me for help with the Riley situation. Son of a bitch. Because she'd fired her no-good, idiot contractor.

And somehow, that had become *my* problem.

I still wasn't entirely sure how that had happened. One minute I was trying to prevent her from impaling herself on a piece of siding, the next I was practically her unwilling liaison to the architectural community of Monroe County. The two Queen Conch IPAs she'd brought over yesterday as a peace offering—or a bribe—still sat untouched in my fridge. A cold, sweating reminder of my general state of bewilderment and an increasing, unwelcome sense of obligation.

With a sigh that felt like it originated somewhere around my kneecaps, I removed the key from the starter. I wasn't a man to put off unpleasant tasks.

"And this won't get easier. Get on with it, Coleridge."

The lobby of Sunset Siesta was a work in progress. Half the ample space was sectioned off with heavy plastic sheeting, the air thick with the scent of sawdust, fresh paint, and plaster dust. A temporary check-in desk, manned by the unflappable Dana, had been set up near the main entrance. I sensed Harper's touch in the attempt to make it more welcoming and beachy with the local fish sculptures and seashells attached to the front.

I spotted Chase almost immediately conferring with a couple of workmen, his dark hair looking neat despite the surrounding entropy. A set of rolled-up blueprints was tucked under one arm, and his expression was intent as he pointed to something on a newly framed wall.

The man had a new partnership, a new wife, a new business, and *twins* on the way. This was a terrible time to ask for a favor, especially one involving the walking, talking, noise-generating complication that was my new neighbor. I almost turned around, almost convinced myself this could wait.

No. Get it done. You told her you would, so rip off the damn Band-Aid.

I waited until his workmen had dispersed before approaching. "Chase. Got a minute?"

He turned, a faint smile touching his lips when he saw me, though his hazel eyes still held that focused, assessing look he got when he was deep in a project. "Austin. What's up? Don't tell me *Line Dancer* sprouted a leak."

"Boat's fine," I said, feeling like an idiot already. I tried for casual, for the tone of a man merely passing on a piece of trivial neighborhood news. It probably came out sounding like I was about to confess to a felony. "It's, uh, my neighbor. The one renovating Heron House?"

Chase's eyebrows lifted a fraction. He knew about Heron House. Everyone in Dove Key knew about Heron House, the grand, decaying white elephant.

"The one you've been complaining about making a

racket at sunrise for weeks?" he asked, a hint of amusement in his voice. "Or is it months now?"

"That's the one. Her contractor just walked off the job. Friday, I think. Left things a mess. She's… in a bind." I shifted my weight, avoiding his perceptive gaze. "She found out you were an architect. Asked if you ever did, you know, quick consultations. Just to look at things." I waved a vague hand, trying to minimize the whole thing.

Chase was silent for a moment. He unrolled his blueprints slightly, then rolled them back up. "Heron House. That's a beast of a project. Ambitious. Contractor walked off, huh? Can't say I'm entirely surprised, some of the characters calling themselves builders down here…" He shook his head. "What exactly did he leave her with?"

I gave him the short, heavily edited version—the siding issue, the general chaos, her clear lack of experience. I definitely didn't mention the part where said neighbor had practically melted against me, or that her lips tasted like saltwater and pure, unexpected sweetness.

Chase listened patiently, his expression thoughtful. When I finished, he tapped a finger against his rolled-up blueprints. "Makes sense she'd be looking for some solid advice if her contractor bailed. How'd she know to ask for me specifically?"

Heat prickled at the back of my neck, and I scrubbed my hand over it, suddenly finding a loose floorboard fascinating. "I might have… um… mentioned you were an architect. In passing. The other day. She, uh, she asked me yesterday if I could put her in touch."

Chase's lips curved into a faint smile, the kind that said he was seeing about three layers deeper than the surface I was presenting. But he didn't press, thank God, just gave a slight nod. "Right. In passing. Got it."

That amused look lingered, making me feel like a

teenager caught sneaking in after curfew. He knew something was up, or at least that I wasn't giving him the full story.

Which, of course, I wasn't.

"She'd be happy with a quick look-see, I think."

"I'm slammed, Austin. You know that," Chase replied, waving at the half-gutted lobby. He ran a hand through his hair. "But, damn. Leaving her high and dry on a place like Heron House… that's rough." He turned his eyes back to me, a flicker of curiosity, or maybe just sympathy, in his hazel eyes. "All right. I could swing by and take a quick look. Maybe point her in the right direction, make sure nothing's about to fall on her head or cost her triple what it should. But I absolutely cannot take on another major renovation right now. I just signed two new clients last month."

Relief washed over me, followed, just as quickly, by the dawning dread of having to relay this information to Iris. Another conversation. Another opportunity for horrible awkwardness. Another attempt to keep myself from reenacting that kiss, the tempting warmth of our bodies against each other.

"Understood." My voice came out a little too quickly. Almost eager, dammit. "That'd be great. Just needs some professional eyes on it. Maybe you know someone reliable who isn't a complete hack, someone who won't try to fleece her."

"Possibly." Chase glanced at his watch. "Tell you what. I can stop by early tomorrow morning, say, seven-thirty?"

"Seven-thirty," I repeated, my mind already racing. I had no idea if seven-thirty on a Tuesday worked for Iris. For all I knew, she planned to sleep until noon and then commune with squirrels. But she wasn't exactly in a position to be picky. "Yeah, that should be fine."

"Good." Chase clapped me on the shoulder. "Now, if you'll excuse me, I have a date with some misaligned duct-work that's threatening to derail my entire HVAC plan." He offered a brief smile and unrolled his blueprints.

I said thanks to his retreating back and headed for the exit, the unpleasant task of informing Iris of her early morning architectural consultation looming before me like an ominous thunderhead.

I spent the rest of my workday rearranging tomorrow's charter to the afternoon when the client had a last-minute schedule change, then making sure *Line Dancer* was ship-shape. But as the afternoon sun began its slow descent toward the Gulf, I pulled my truck into the driveway and parked under the carport. Then, with feet that could have been fifty pounds heavier than they had half an hour ago, I veered onto the overgrown path that led to Heron House.

The place looked even more dilapidated in the afternoon light, its peeling paint and sagging porches showing years of neglect. The only sign of life was a faint, melodious humming coming from an open window on the ground floor. I knocked on the massive, ominous-looking dark front door, the sound echoing unnervingly in the sudden stillness.

After a long moment, it shrieked open with a tortured groan to reveal Iris. Her eyes flew open when she recognized me. Her hair was pulled back in that messy bun, a smudge of what looked like blue paint on her cheek, and a pair of oversized safety glasses perched on top of her head. She was wearing cutoff denim shorts that showcased an impressive length of tanned leg, and a paint-splattered T-shirt that had clearly seen better days yet still managed to look sexy.

And my eyes, those goddamn traitors, dropped immediately to her mouth. With Herculean strength, I kept them from falling to her breasts.

The memory of Friday afternoon flooded back with an unwelcome, visceral intensity. Heat rushed up my neck, into my face. I quickly looked away, fixing my gaze on a particularly alarming crack in the ancient door.

Jesus. Don't look at her mouth. Don't think about it. Don't remember it.

I was failing spectacularly on all three counts, but I finally met her clear blue eyes.

For her part, she looked equally flustered, her cheeks flushing a delicate shade of pink. "Austin! I… I wasn't expecting you." Her voice was a little breathless as she shouldered open the door further with another ear-rending shriek.

The sound was so jarring I flinched. My mouth opened, and the first thing that came out was, "You going to call an exorcist for that door?"

She laughed, the sound a welcome relief in the charged air. She patted the door. "Oh, I think it's part of the historic charm. I've named him Shrieky. He's the house's built-in security system. Scares away any traveling salesmen who might call."

The absurd image of salesmen fleeing in terror made me crack a smile despite my tense mood. "Right. You named the door."

"I suppose I'll need to replace it, though. Shrieky isn't exactly welcoming, is he?"

I just stood there, unable to think of a response to that.

"Chase," I blurted out, desperate to get this over with, to escape before my brain short-circuited even more. Or I did something even worse, like grabbing both her shoulders and kissing her senseless. "My brother-in-law. The architect. He can come by early tomorrow morning. For that consultation you wanted." The words came out too fast, too gruff, but I was helpless to change anything.

Her eyes widened before lighting up with a hopeful brightness that was hard to look at directly. Yet I couldn't look away, either.

"Oh, Austin, thank you! That's wonderful news! Really. I don't know how to thank you enough."

Her smile was sweet, unguarded, and it did something strange to the knot in my gut. Loosened it, maybe. Or just rearranged it into a different but equally uncomfortable configuration.

"Yeah, well," I mumbled, already backing away. "He's doing me a favor, fitting you in." I needed to deflect, to minimize my involvement, to put some distance back between us.

"He said early," I added. My tone implied it better be acceptable. "Before his regular workday. Around seven-thirty. That work for you?"

"Yes! Absolutely!" she assured me, her hands clasped together in front of her. "Whenever is good for him. I'll be here. I'll have coffee on! And maybe scones or something?" She offered the last part with a hesitant, hopeful little smile.

More damn baked goods. The thought was automatic, but this time, it lacked its usual venom. It was almost… resigned. But not anticipatory. Nope, not that.

"Right. Whatever you want." I turned to leave. My job here was well and truly done.

I made it to the edge of her porch, halfway to freedom, when her voice stopped me.

"Austin?"

I paused, my back still to her, bracing myself.

"Thank you," she repeated, her voice softer this time, less effusive, more sincere. "Really. For this. And for… for

Friday. With the siding. I needed help, and you were there."

I stood there for a long moment, the sun beating down on my neck, the scent of her—dust, paint, and that faint, lingering sweetness—teasing my senses. My heart felt like a lumbering bison in my chest.

I should just nod.

Walk away. End it.

But the words, rough and foreign, found their way out. "You're, uh, welcome." I cleared my throat, still not turning around. "I'm glad I was there. When you… you know. Needed it."

The silence stretched, thick with unspoken things. Then, a soft, "Good night, Austin."

"Night, Iris." The name slipped out, easy, natural, before I could stop it.

I didn't wait for a response. I walked away fast, not looking back, the echo of her quiet goodnight following me like a persistent ghost.

Back in my kitchen, I found one of the Queen Conch IPAs she'd left. The bottle was icy cold, condensation beading on the glass. I opened it, the hiss a welcome sound, and took a long, deep swallow.

The beer was good. Conch Republic always brewed a good beer, though I'd never admit that in front of Braden. Hoppy, with a clean, citrusy finish. I had to admit she had good taste in beer for a woman who probably thought a depth finder was a philosophical concept.

I fired up the grill on my back patio, the familiar ritual of preparing dinner a welcome distraction. The snapper I'd caught earlier sizzled on the hot grates, the smoky aroma filling the evening air. But even the simple, satisfying task of grilling fish couldn't quite dislodge the image of Iris, her face smudged with paint, her eyes full of that unnerving mixture of vulnerability and stubborn hope. Or the memory of her lips. Her body.

The next morning, I was up before dawn. Chase was due at seven-thirty. And for some reason I couldn't quite articulate, I'd decided I needed to be there. Purely for practical reasons, of course. To make sure nothing got lost in translation. To ensure Chase understood the full extent of the Heron House disaster and how its ongoing renovation might continue to impact my property, my peace. It was just neighborly vigilance. That's what I told myself as I sent Chase a quick text telling him to meet me at my place.

Chase showed up at my door at seven-twenty, looking remarkably awake and professional for a man with a dozen irons in the fire. "Ready to face the architectural abyss?" There was a knowing glint in his eye I chose to ignore. "Or maybe you don't think I can handle this tour on my own?"

I scowled. "I need to see how bad it really is. That's all."

We walked over to Heron House together. Iris was already on her porch, a travel mug of coffee in one hand as she wiped a palm on her dress. And, of course, after she was done, she picked up a plate covered with a napkin. I introduced the two.

"Good morning!" she said with a smile like a Sunday morning. "I made banana bread. Figured architects and helpful neighbors run on coffee and, uh, baked goods?" She offered the plate with a hopeful, slightly anxious gesture.

My stomach rumbled, betraying me. The banana bread smelled incredible, warm and sweet and laced with cinnamon.

Dammit, woman.

Chase, to his credit, accepted a piece with a gracious smile. "Smells fantastic, Ms. Holloway. Thanks."

I just grunted, trying to project an aura of detached professionalism.

"Oh, call me Iris. Please. For the love of pelicans, the house is old and stuffy, not me!"

Chase managed to look only slightly bewildered at the Iris-ism, but I had to bite back a smile. The three of us spent the next hour inspecting the property. Chase was all business, his sharp eyes missing nothing, from the precariously attached siding to the worrying sag in one section of the porch roof to the ambitious chalk lines Iris had drawn for her en-suite bathrooms. He asked Iris intelligent questions about her plans, her budget, her timeline. She answered as best she could, her initial nervousness giving way to earnest enthusiasm as she described her vision for Heron House.

I mostly lurked in the background, observing and trying to ignore the way Iris's hair caught the morning light, turning it to spun gold. Or the determined set of her jaw as she talked about her B&B. Or the fact that her notions made a lot of sense. Some were bordering on practical.

Her ideas of splitting up some of the second and third-floor rooms to ensure the bedrooms had private baths were logical and ambitious. People didn't want to share. Though when we got up there, the rooms were a wreck and more grand vision than reality.

Back outside and near the half-demolished wall, Chase turned to her. "Well, Mick Riley walking off the job, while incredibly unprofessional and inconvenient for you, might actually be a blessing in disguise. From what I've seen just on this initial walk-through, his methods weren't up to code for a historic renovation of this magnitude." He gestured toward the problematic siding. "This alone would have caused you major headaches down the line."

Iris's face fell slightly at his words, the confirmation of her fears, but then that stubborn chin came up again.

"As I told Austin," Chase continued, "I'm unfortunately not in a position to take on a project of this size right now. My firm is swamped, and Harper and I are..." —he grinned—"expecting a rather significant personal project to kick off soon. Twins."

"Oh! Congratulations." Iris offered another sunny smile.

"But now that I've seen the scope, I can make some calls. There are a few reputable local contractors I trust, guys who specialize in old houses. No promises, but I'll see who might have an opening or be willing to at least consult properly and give you an honest assessment."

Tears, actual tears, welled in Iris's eyes. She blinked them back furiously, but not before I saw them. And it gave me an unexpected, unwelcome pang right in the vicinity of my chest.

She's in way over her head, I thought, the realization hitting me with fresh force. *But damn if she isn't trying with everything she's got.*

"Oh, Chase, thank you," she said. "That would mean the world to me."

After Chase left, promising to be in touch as soon as he had any news, an awkward silence descended between Iris and me. She stood there, looking small and vulnerable amidst the grandeur of her decaying mansion, clutching the now-empty banana bread plate.

Yeah, it had been delicious.

"Well, listen," I said, needing to break the tension, needing to establish some kind of practical boundary. "I can't be running back and forth here every time Chase has an update or you have another emergency. It's inefficient."

She glanced up, eyes wide.

"I need to put you in my contacts." I pulled out my phone and tried to make it sound like a command, not a request. "If he gets hold of me first with news, or if… if something else comes up, I'll text you."

It was a purely practical measure. So I wouldn't have to keep trekking over to this disaster zone. That was all.

"Oh! Of course. Good idea." She fumbled for her phone, her fingers slightly clumsy as she navigated the screen. We exchanged numbers, the brief brush of our fingers as I took her phone to input my information like a zap of static electricity. As soon as the transaction was complete, I experienced the overwhelming, desperate urge to escape.

"Right," I said as I backed away. "Gotta go."

I turned and fled back to the sanctuary of my porch, the scent of her banana bread still clinging to me, her phone number a dangerous addition to my mind. A light sweat broke out under my shirt, despite the relative coolness of the morning.

This was why.

This was exactly why I avoided people. Women. Complications. Closeness.

I'd had a short relationship with a tourist a year or so ago. Easy, no strings. She'd left when her vacation ended. That was my speed. I never got close to women, not really. Because closeness brought… this. This acute discomfort. This unsettling awareness. These emotions.

Emotions were dangerous.

Unpredictable.

Guerrilla fighters in the carefully ordered territory of my life.

I'd spent thirteen hard years systematically suppressing mine, burying them deep beneath layers of routine and solitude and the vast, indifferent expanse of the sea. The last thing I needed was for Iris Holloway, with her disastrous DIY skills, her wide, beautiful blue eyes, her surprisingly good banana bread, and her even more surprisingly addictive kiss, to start dredging up all that old pain. And all those feelings I'd fought so hard to lock away.

But as I stood on my porch, the echo of her hopeful *thank you* still in my ears, I had a sinking feeling it might already be too late.

Chapter Thirteen

IRIS

MY HOUSE HAD a bad case of the rattles.

More specifically, the temporarily nailed siding on the west wall of Heron House played a clattering drum solo that sounded like a skeleton trying to learn the cha-cha every time the wind blew in off the ocean. It had been like that for six long days—since Austin's quick fix, which, while keeping the siding from falling, couldn't stop the clatter. And I was becoming worried that every gust of wind was making it less secure.

And five days had passed since Chase Ashworth's reassuring, if slightly terrifying, consultation. Chase had been a godsend. He'd put me in touch with two reputable local contractors. I'd scrambled to get bids, my stomach a knot of anxiety as I showed them around the glorious, crumbling money pit that was my inheritance. I'd gotten a wonderful vibe from one of them, and a quick call to Chase reinforced that Gus Davis was who he consulted when he presented with a thorny issue he needed help with. Chase also mentioned that Gus specialized in historic renovations. Yesterday, I'd signed a contract with him. And, miracle of miracles, he didn't treat me like I was a clueless child playing house.

The only catch? He couldn't start for another week. So, the siding continued to knock. A constant, visible reminder of my precarious situation.

I was out in the yard, ostensibly weeding a patch of ridiculously resilient ivy that seemed to thrive on neglect, but mostly I was just worrying. Worrying about the siding. Worrying about the budget. Worrying about the persistent flutter in my chest every time I thought about Austin and the kiss that had absolutely, positively, never happened. Except it totally had. And he hadn't mentioned it since. Not a word. Not a flicker. It was like trying to pretend a rogue wave hadn't just swamped your very small rowboat.

A shadow fell over me.

I looked up, shielding my eyes against the bright late-morning sun, my heart giving an immediate lurch.

Austin.

He stood there, a vision in faded denim and a plain gray T-shirt that did nothing to hide the impressive breadth of his shoulders. He had a sturdy-looking aluminum extension ladder propped against one of those shoulders and a serious-looking tool belt slung low on his hips. He looked too handsome, too competent, and entirely too much like he'd just stepped out of one of my more embarrassing daydreams.

"Morning, Iris," he said, his voice its usual low rumble, though perhaps a fraction less… grumpy than usual? Or maybe that was just wishful thinking on my part.

"Austin! Good morning." My voice came out a little breathless. *Play it cool, Iris. He's just a neighbor. A handsome, very good-kissing neighbor who you may or may not have accosted last week. Nothing to see here.* "What brings you over?"

He gestured with his chin toward the thumping siding. "That thing's not going to hold through another decent squall like that. Figured since I've got a free morning and you're waiting on your new contractor, we could get it properly secured. Don't need it crashing down and taking out my hibiscus."

The corner of his mouth twitched. Almost a smile. Almost.

I stared at him, dumbfounded. He was offering to help? Voluntarily? With actual tools and ladders that didn't look like they'd collapse if a strong-willed seagull landed on them? After I'd practically mauled him with my face?

"You want to help me?" I managed, my brain struggling to process this unexpected development. "With the siding?"

"Got another ladder in the truck," he said, as if that explained everything. "And a nail gun. Be faster. Unless you'd rather wrestle with it solo again. Your call."

There was no judgment in his tone, just a statement of fact, but my cheeks burned anyway at the memory of my previous, disastrous attempt.

It was like that kiss existed in some alternate universe, a bizarre, heat-fueled blip on the radar of our otherwise prickly neighborly relations. Part of me, the sensible, self-preservation part, was immensely relieved. Another, smaller part felt a ridiculous pang of disappointment.

"No! I mean, yes! Help would be, er, amazing," I stammered, pushing aside the confusing tangle of my emotions. The practical relief of knowing that siding would be properly secured was overwhelming. "Thank you, Austin. Really."

Okay, Iris. Professional. Neighborly. Pretend Friday didn't happen. Pretend your lips aren't still tingling with the memory of his. Pretend he's just a capable, somewhat grumpy, distractingly handsome, and surprisingly helpful Good Samaritan with a sexy tool belt.

"We can nail up the rest of it in no time. Can't leave the moisture barrier exposed like that."

Working with Austin was… intense. He was all focused competence, his movements economical and precise. He set up the two ladders with an efficiency that made my earlier efforts look like a slapstick comedy routine. He showed me, with patience I wouldn't have thought him capable of, how to hold my end of the long siding boards steady while he expertly wielded the nail gun, its loud, percussive reports echoing in the humid air.

There was a lot of close proximity. More than once, his arm brushed against mine as we maneuvered a particularly unwieldy board, sending a jolt of awareness zinging through me that had nothing to do with static electricity. The scent of him surrounded me. It was a potent brew of sunshine, clean male sweat, and something musky and enticingly male. I tried to focus on not dropping my end of the siding, on not staring at the way the muscles in his forearms flexed as he handled the nail gun with such easy, masculine grace.

It was not easy.

To break the charged silence, and to distract myself from the entirely inappropriate direction of my thoughts, I started asking questions.

"You seem to know a lot about old houses," I began, trying for a light, conversational tone. "And power tools. Is that a prerequisite for being a fishing captain in the Keys?"

He didn't look at me, his attention fixed on aligning the next board. For a moment, I thought he might just grunt and ignore me. But he didn't.

"Grew up at Sunset Siesta." His voice was still gruff,

but less guarded than usual as he spoke of something familiar. "It's the family resort. An old place, so something always needing fixing, something else falling apart. You pick things up. Or you learn to swim fast when the dock collapses under you."

The corner of my mouth twitched. A hint of humor? From Austin Coleridge? Wonders would never cease. "Brenna mentioned your family has owned it for a long time?"

He nodded, sighting down the edge of the board. "Over a hundred years. Coleridges have been in Dove Key longer than there's been a decent road connecting it to the mainland." There was a low-key pride in his voice, an understated connection to this place that resonated deep within me, someone whose roots felt as shallow and scattered as sea grass in a storm.

"It's in our blood, I guess," he continued, the rhythmic *thwack-thwack-thwack* of the nail gun punctuating his words. There was a touch of weary affection in his tone now. "The resort. The water. This damn island. At one point, we owned most of Dove Key, but it was sold off over the years. Now the resort is all we have left, except for what we own individually. We all learned to work hard. Had to, really, especially after Dad…" He trailed off, his jaw tightening as a shadow flickered in those stormy gray eyes.

The unspoken hung in the air between us. I didn't press. I had never heard him utter so many words in one go.

He nodded with his head back toward his property. "I bought my house seven years ago. It was a bit better off than Heron House, but I spent a lot of sweat equity restoring it. Pretty much done now."

"That's impressive," I said. "To have that kind of history, that deep connection to a place, to a family legacy.

I'm an only child, and my mom and I… well, we moved around. I don't think I've ever lived in one place for more than five years."

He turned his head then, his gaze meeting mine, direct and intent. "And this place was what brought you down here?"

"Yes, Aunt Constance." A smile touched my lips as I thought of her letter. "No one was more shocked than I was when she left it to me. And enough money to try and bring it back to life, may she rest in peace." I paused, then, driven by a sudden curiosity, asked, "Did you know my Aunt Constance at all?"

Austin picked up the last piece of siding we needed to secure, running a calloused thumb along its edge. "Not well. She kept to herself mostly. A private woman. But this house…" He looked up at the section we'd just repaired, a flash of something in his eyes. Respect, maybe, for the old structure itself. "I helped her out with a few things over the years. A loose shutter after a storm, patching a section of that old porch roof once. Nothing major. She always wanted to pay me, but I wouldn't take her money."

A wave of warmth spread through me. So, he had known her, in his reserved, practical way. Then, a teasing thought popped into my head, too tempting to resist. "You know, first the sprinkler, now the siding… Maybe Heron House has cast some kind of spell over you, Captain. Dooming you to a life of fixing its—and its owner's— never-ending disasters."

I'd expected a scowl, or at least one of his signature dismissive grunts. Instead, to my utter astonishment, the corner of his mouth lifted. Then the other. And before I knew it, Austin Coleridge was actually, certifiably, smiling.

It wasn't a wide, beaming grin. It was quieter, a subtle crinkling around his eyes and a softening around his mouth. But it was undeniably a smile. And it transformed his face, chasing away the shadows. His smile revealed a warmth and an unexpected, almost boyish charm that made my stomach perform a series of enthusiastic cartwheels.

"More like a damn curse," he said, but the words held no heat, and the smile, that rare smile, still lingered. "This whole stretch of coastline is probably built on an ancient Calusa burial ground, doomed to perpetual renovation and quirky new neighbors."

I laughed, a happy sound that echoed off the wall. "Well, I'll try to keep the disasters to a minimum. No promises on the renovations, though."

The smile faded slowly from his lips, replaced by that more familiar, thoughtful intensity, but the air between us was different. Lighter. As if that shared moment of humor had cleared away some of the lingering awkwardness, some of the unspoken tension.

He picked up his hammer again, all business once more. "Last board. Let's get it done."

We finished securing it, the satisfying thud of the last nail echoing in the sudden hush. For a moment, we just stood side-by-side on our respective ladders, a comfortable silence settling between us that was broken only by the rustle of the magnolia leaves.

"Well," I said, trying for a light tone, "I think it's safe to say I won't be quitting my B&B dream to become a professional sider anytime soon. You, on the other hand, seem to be a natural."

A faint twitch lifted the corner of his mouth. "Someone's gotta know how to keep these old places from falling into the sea. I'm starting to think I should add Disaster Mitigation Specialist to my charter business. The pay's not great, but the catering almost makes up for it."

My breath caught. Was that an actual joke? It was like spotting a rare, exotic, and possibly mythical bird. A somewhat grouchy, handsome bird, but a bird, nonetheless.

With the last piece of problematic siding finally attached, looking impressively neat and professional under Austin's capable hands, a wave of relief washed over me so profound it almost made me dizzy.

"I don't know how to thank you, Austin. You didn't have to do this. Especially after… well, after everything."

He just grunted, already gathering his tools, his usual stoic mask firmly back in place, though perhaps the lines around his eyes were a little softer.

"I was about to make some sandwiches," I said impulsively, the words out before I could second-guess them. My stomach did a nervous jumping thing. "You must be starving. And as you said, feeding you is part of my job description. Can I offer you lunch? As a proper thank you this time. No ulterior cookie motives involved, I promise."

He hesitated, his gaze flicking from me to his house, then back to me. I could practically see the internal war raging—his ingrained desire for solitude battling with whatever had possessed him to help me in the first place. I held my breath, fully expecting him to make some gruff excuse and retreat.

Then he gave a short, almost reluctant nod. "Sandwiches, huh? I could go for that, as long as it's not tuna. Can't stand canned tuna fish."

He said yes? My brain reeled. *Son of a biscuit, he actually said yes!*

"No tuna, I promise," I said, a wide, slightly giddy smile spreading across my face. "Turkey and Swiss? Or I think I have some leftover roast chicken."

"Turkey's fine," he said, and followed me, with what looked like extreme reluctance, into the unruly, paint-splattered, but suddenly much brighter kitchen of Heron House.

It was surprisingly easy to talk to him while I made sandwiches and he leaned against a counter, nursing one of the Queen Conch IPAs I'd insisted he take. When he wasn't actively scowling at me over a drowned plant or a rogue power tool, he was actually a decent listener.

He asked me, in his usual terse way, where I was from. I found myself telling him about Abingdon, about my sociology degree that had mostly just taught me how to observe people being baffling, about the string of eclectic jobs that had never quite felt right, about that milestone thirtieth birthday that had hit me like a brick to the head.

"And then," I said, spreading mustard on thick slices of rye bread, "the letter about Heron House arrived. I took it as a sign. A chance to finally build something real, something that's mine. Something that proves I'm not just drifting."

I looked up at him, expecting to see skepticism or polite indifference in those eyes. Instead, his face showed approval.

"It's a hell of a thing to take on solo." His voice was neutral, but his gaze was direct, focused.

We sat at the table and ate. "I know. Sometimes it feels totally overwhelming. Like I'm trying to bail out the ocean with a teaspoon. But then..." I gestured around the kitchen, at the piles of sketches on the table, at the new paint swatches taped to a section of relatively intact wall. "Then I remember why I'm doing it. For Aunt Constance. For myself. To create something beautiful, something welcoming. A place where people can feel happy."

The silence stretched for a moment before I asked, "So when did Captain Coleridge learn to conquer the seven seas? Or at least the local ocean?"

An almost wistful expression softened his features as he stared out the warped kitchen window toward the distant glint of the Gulf. "Can't remember not knowing how to fish. Dad had me out on a boat before I could walk properly. Spent more time with him out on the water than any of the rest of my siblings. He taught me everything. How to read the tides, the currents, the birds. Where the snook hid in the mangroves, where the tarpon rolled at dawn."

When he spoke of his father, his voice held a wistful warmth, a depth of longing that surprised me. It was a glimpse of the boy he must have been, before the world, or something in it, had taught him to build such formidable walls. It was a precious, fleeting thing.

Then, just as quickly, the warmth vanished, his face clouding over, the shutters slamming down over his eyes. "He took off. Long time ago, when I was barely a teenager. Left Mom, left us, left the resort high and dry. Just gone. He never came back."

The shift was abrupt, jarring. The earlier easy camaraderie, the shared task, the tentative connection we'd been building all seemed to evaporate in the face of this new, stark revelation.

And there it was again.

That deep, hidden wound I sensed in him, the one that spoke to his guarded nature. My heart ached for him, for the boy who had loved being on the boat with his father, only to have that world shattered.

I didn't know what to say. Platitudes sounded cheap, intrusive. So I just nodded, my sandwich suddenly tasteless in my mouth.

After a moment of thick, uncomfortable silence, I ventured carefully, "Well, whatever happened back then… it seems like Sunset Siesta is thriving now. And with you as captain, I'm sure *Line Dancer* is one of the most popular charters in the Keys." I offered what I hoped was an encouraging, non-prying smile.

He studied me, a long, considering moment, his gray eyes searching mine. Then, another small smile touched his lips. Two in one hour!

"Things are looking up," he admitted, his voice a low rumble that sent a tickle across my shoulders. "For the resort. For Dove Key."

For a breathless second, warmth rose between us, a fragile, unspoken understanding that passed between us. Then it was gone, his expression shuttering once more, but the memory of that brief, unguarded moment lingered.

He helped me. He talked to me. He even smiled at me. Twice.

Maybe there was hope for peaceful coexistence between Heron House and its grumpy, sexy-tool-belt-wearing—heck, there was no point in denying it—capably hot next-door neighbor.

Or maybe even something more.

The thought sent a fresh, confusing, exhilarating roll of heat through my core. Because no matter how much I tried to pretend that kiss hadn't happened, it most definitely had. And I hadn't imagined his wild, passionate response, either. He'd been like a man who'd crawled across a desert and found himself at an oasis at last. And now he was doing his best not to partake of the forbidden fruit.

Or something like that.

My metaphors might be a bit jumbled, but the fact remained. There was a question hanging in the air between Austin Coleridge and me, one that had nothing to do with siding or sprinklers. And as I stared at his full, sensual mouth, I realized I wanted him to ask it.

Chapter Fourteen

AUSTIN

HER LAUGH. That was the problem.

It cut through the lull of my afternoon, a bright, musical sound carried on the breeze from her porch as she talked with someone on the phone. It landed straight in my gut like a lead weight. I stopped my sweeping motion, the orbital sander humming uselessly in my hand, my knuckles white where I gripped it. The porch railing I was working on didn't need sanding. I'd refinished the whole damn thing a year ago. The wood was as smooth as sea-worn glass. But I needed to do something, needed to burn off the restless, angry energy that had been rushing through my veins for days.

Iris Holloway had taken up residence in my brain, an uninvited renter who refused to pay rent, ignored all eviction notices, and apparently redecorated the place with images of her own damn self.

It had been several days since I'd helped her with that siding job, days since we'd shared those turkey sandwiches in her ancient, yet somehow homey kitchen. And the way she'd looked at me like I was some kind of puzzle she was determined to solve. Days since she'd looked up at me with those wide, earnest blue eyes, a smudge of something—flour? drywall dust? who the hell knew with her?—on her cheek.

And the kiss.

Son of a bitch.

That was always where my thoughts snagged, replaying in my head with the relentless persistence of a bad pop song you couldn't get unstuck, like those Sutton Vale tunes Brenna loved. Iris's initial surprise, followed by that answering heat from me that had ignited from nowhere. The pull of her surprisingly strong hands gripping my hair and bringing me closer.

Giving up, I dropped the sander on the floor and went back inside where I couldn't hear her. I moved to the kitchen sink and poured myself a glass of water, drinking it in a single shot. Yet my gaze found the window and the shadowy mansion barely visible through the vegetation.

The new contractor hadn't started yet, a delay that left Iris puttering around next door, mostly on her own, tackling whatever ill-advised projects she could conjure up to fill the time. And because I was apparently a masochist, or just losing my goddamn mind, I'd found myself helping with more of these minor catastrophes in the interim. Small things, really.

Or so I told myself.

Each brief, neighborly interaction was a fresh form of torment. Her laugh, when she'd nearly collided with a paint can, was a bright, unexpected sound that lodged in my memory, replaying at odd, inconvenient moments. The way she'd bite her lower lip when she was concentrating on some complicated instruction I was giving her about, say, the proper way to use a pry bar without taking off a finger or demolishing an entire load-bearing wall. The curve of her neck when she bent over the sketches for Heron House that were always spread across her kitchen table. How her blonde hair caught the beams of sunlight.

I was losing it.

My iron control was fraying at the edges, unraveling thread by stubborn thread.

My routine was shot to hell. I was now timing my trips to my truck, my pointless inspections of my damn hibiscus hedge, to moments when I might catch a glimpse of her and exchange a few words.

Me! Exchanging words!

One afternoon, a package for I. Holloway had been misdelivered to my porch. Probably more books on how to turn a crumbling mansion into a charming B&B with nothing but pluck and a glue gun. Or perhaps it was a bulk order of G-rated swear word substitutes.

More importantly, that box was a legitimate reason to go over. My heart hammered against my ribs with a force that was entirely disproportionate to the simple task of returning a misdelivered parcel.

She answered the awful front door looking surprised, a little flustered, her blonde hair escaping a sunny yellow bandana in soft tendrils that clung to her damp forehead. She'd been painting something, judging by the streaks of pale blue on her arm that somehow managed to look artistic. The faint, sweet, chemical smell of latex paint clung to her.

"Oh! Austin. Hi." Her expression quickly gave way to a pleased, unguarded smile that somehow managed to rearrange the air in the room. I felt her gaze on me, not a quick, nervous glance, but a deliberate, appreciative sweep. It traveled from my face down and skated across my shoulders. Then her eyes moved back up, pausing for a notice-able moment on my mouth before she seemed to realize what she was doing. She glanced away then, a faint blush staining her cheeks, but the message had been sent. And received. It had landed squarely in my core, a knot of heat that hardly ever went away these days.

"Package for you," I grunted, thrusting it at her, desperate to make the interaction as brief as possible, yet wanting to prolong it. All at the same time. "Came to my place by mistake."

Our fingers touched as she took it. Just a fleeting contact, skin against skin. But it was like grabbing a live wire. A jolt, hot and sharp and entirely unwelcome, shot up my arm, straight to my chest, then lower. I instantly got hard, a raw, insistent physical ache coiling low and tight in my gut, an ache that was both infuriatingly distracting and undeniably, agonizingly real.

Her eyes widened, filled with a sultry heat that almost made me step toward her. The air between us grew thick and humid, making it hard to breathe.

I snatched my hand back like I'd been burned, mumbled something incoherent about needing to check my crab traps, even though it was the middle of the damn afternoon. I retreated fast, the sensation of her skin still searing my fingertips long after I was back in the supposed safety of my house.

What the hell is wrong with me?

The question had become a relentless refrain. It had been a long, long time since any woman had provoked that kind of immediate, visceral reaction in me. Years. And certainly not one who represented everything I usually went out of my way to avoid. Chaos, complication, and the very real threat of emotional entanglement.

I tried to work it off. Took *Line Dancer* out for a run later that day, even though I didn't have a charter, pushing the throttles until the twin diesels roared and the hull slammed against the building chop, the salt spray cool and sharp on my face. But even the vast, indifferent expanse of the sea offered no escape. Iris's delicate face was superimposed over the endless blue horizon.

Sleep was no better. When I did manage to drift off, my dreams were a relentless, Technicolor replay of all that had happened and more that hadn't. They left me waking in a tangle of sweat-soaked sheets, my body aching with a frustration that was almost unbearable, the phantom scent of her still clinging to my pillows.

Now it was late afternoon a couple of days later. I was on the verge of heading out to the sander again when Braden showed up in my kitchen. He carried a growler of his latest experiment in one hand, two glasses in the other.

"Heard you were communing with your inner hermit again," he said, bypassing any greeting and heading straight for my table to pour the beer. "Figured you might need some actual human interaction. Or at least my charming company and some quality craft brew."

"What do you want, Braden?" I grumbled, not bothering to turn from the window where I'd been staring, unseeing, at the rustling palm fronds.

He finished pouring and handed a pint glass to me. "Just checking on my favorite brother. You've been even more of a ray of sunshine than usual lately. Which is saying something. Anything you want to talk about? Like, say, the mysterious woman next door who seems to have you tied up in more knots than a tangled fishing line?"

I took a long pull of the beer. It was good, hoppy and bitter, but it did nothing to soothe the jagged edges of my mood. "There's nothing to talk about. I'm just in a mood."

"Sure." Braden leaned against the counter, taking a sip

of his beer, his eyes—those damn perceptive Coleridge eyes—studying me. "So the fact that you look like you haven't slept in a week and are currently exuding enough negative energy to power a Caribbean island has nothing to do with the new neighbor who, I've heard, is both very attractive and has a rather sweet disposition?"

"How would you know? You've never seen her," I snapped, then immediately regretted it.

Braden's grin was slow, wolfish. "A little bird. Or rather a big one. Named Hunter. Who heard it from Brenna. And others who have met her. This is Dove Key, Austin. New people stay unknown about as long as a block of ice on a July sidewalk. I can see why that particular combination of good-looking and very nice would cause this reaction in you. So spill."

"There isn't anything to spill," I bit out, the memory of her tear-streaked face flashing through my mind, an unwelcome pang of what I was pretty sure was protectiveness. "She's my obnoxious neighbor. And the whole thing is none of your goddamn business."

"Ooh, defensive." Braden's grin widened. "Getting a little proprietary about the neighbor, are we, big brother? Is this more than just a boundary dispute?"

"Shut up, Braden." My voice was low and dangerous. I didn't know why I was so on edge, so ready to lash out. It wasn't just Braden.

It was her.

It was everything.

Braden's smile faltered. He put his beer down, his expression shifting from teasing to something more serious, more concerned. It was rare to see him drop the easygoing facade, and it caught me off guard. "Hey. Okay. Seriously, man, what's going on? You're... you're wound tighter than I've seen you in a long time. You look like you're terrified to let yourself have something good because you're already convinced it's going to end. Trust me, I know the look. I wrote the damn book on it, remember?"

"Too bad we're not talking about you, huh, asshole?" I snapped.

Braden held out a hand, then added, his voice softer, "I'm just saying, I have a feeling you're thinking about the past. Which always makes me a little worried…"

He didn't finish the sentence. He didn't need to. We both knew what he meant.

The air in the kitchen thickened, heavy with unspoken things, with old ghosts. The casual, sunlit space filled with the shadows of the past, shadows I'd spent years trying to outrun. Or bury, whichever was easier at the moment.

I turned away from the window, my fists clenching and unclenching at my sides. "I'm fine. Just… a lot on my mind. Boat stuff." It was a weak excuse, and we both knew it.

Braden didn't call me on it. He just nodded slowly, his gaze still searching, still worried. He picked up his beer again, but the earlier lightness was gone from his expression. "Uh-huh. Boat stuff. Well, if the boat stuff gets too heavy, you know where I am. Or Eli. Or even Ben, when he's not trying to save the entire population of Monroe County one call at a time." He gave me a brief, conciliatory smile. "We're still your brothers, Austin. Even when you're being a world-class asshole."

The unexpected gentleness in his tone, the quiet understanding, was worse than the teasing. It chipped away at my anger, leaving behind a raw, aching vulnerability I didn't know what to do with.

"I know." My voice was barely a croak. I cleared my throat. "Sorry for snapping. Just tired."

"You're forgiven. Get some rest, man," Braden said,

draining his beer. He clapped me on the shoulder, a brief, solid pressure. "And maybe lay off the neighbor's cookies for a while. Sounds like they're giving you indigestion."

He tried for another grin, but it didn't quite reach his eyes this time. Then he was gone, leaving me alone again with the silence and the relentless, consuming thoughts of Iris Holloway.

Braden's visit and concern had somehow made it worse. I paced my house like a caged animal, the four walls now feeling like a prison. I couldn't read. Couldn't focus on the TV. Couldn't even stomach the thought of food. Every sound from next door amplified the edgy, humming energy that was making my skin itch, making my blood heat.

Because I was acutely aware of her.

I stopped pacing in the middle of my living room. A sudden, almost deafening stillness descended in my head. The internal argument, the constant battle to suppress and deny, simply ceased.

And a single, stark realization hit me with the force of a snapped anchor line in a storm.

I couldn't fight this anymore.

I didn't want to fight this anymore.

The energy it was taking to resist, to maintain this constant, exhausting state of vigilance against my thoughts, my body, was more depleting than just giving in.

"Enough."

The word was a murmur in the hushed room, but it sounded like surrender. To what, I wasn't entirely sure. To her? To this… this consuming, relentless craving that had taken root in my body and refused to be dislodged? I didn't care anymore. The control I'd maintained over my life, over my emotions, for thirteen long, hard years had finally, irrevocably, shattered.

I needed this to stop. I needed her.

The thought was terrifying. Liberating.

And utterly reckless.

A grim sort of acceptance settled over me, cold and hard as a submerged reef. Let it happen. I yanked open my front door, the familiar scrape of wood on wood a jarring sound in the sudden, intense focus of my new resolve. I didn't grab a tool. Didn't concoct an excuse. Didn't even pause to consider the monumental risk of what I was about to do.

I just started walking.

My stride was heavy, purposeful, each step a deliberate act of will. It carried me across my neatly edged lawn, through the narrow gap in the hibiscus hedge that separated our properties, onto the overgrown, chaotic territory of Heron House.

Toward Iris.

The unforgiving late-afternoon sun beat down on my face, but I barely registered it. The crunch of shells and dry, untamed grass under my boots was a rhythmic counterpoint to the frantic hammering of my heart against my ribs.

Heron House loomed larger with every step. But it wasn't the mansion I was focused on. Iris's shadow crossed behind a third-floor window. One of the demolished bedrooms.

No more thinking. No more fighting it. I was going inside and straight upstairs. No knocking on the front door this time.

And whatever happened, happened.

I was beyond caring about the consequences. I needed the consuming, relentless fire in my mind and body to either be quenched or to burn me straight to the damn ground.

Chapter Fifteen

IRIS

THE CHUNK of plaster hit the pile in the center of the third-floor bedroom after I tossed it, sending up a puff of golden dust in the late-afternoon light. It was a pointless task, tossing debris from one spot to another, but it kept my hands busy. My mind, however, was a different story.

The last few days had been an exercise in exquisite torment. A low-grade, pulsing tension followed me from room to room. A constant awareness of Austin, just a stone's throw away in his fortress of solitude. His brief yet frequent visits had only made me want him more. Each brush of his skin against mine, every shared, increasingly loaded look wound the spring between us tighter and tighter.

The way his eyes would catch on my mouth when he thought I wasn't looking, how his entire body would tighten when I got too close. The two of us were a storm building just offshore, the air growing staticky and electric before the first drop of rain.

A heavy thump from the doorway made me jump, my heart leaping into my throat.

I whipped around.

Austin stood framed in the empty doorframe, looking... undone. His hair was a mess, as if he'd been dragging his hands through it. His face was tight, his jaw locked, and his gray eyes burned with a raw, intense emotion I'd never seen before.

Not anger. Not annoyance.

Something else. Something elemental.

"Austin?" My voice came out as a shaky murmur. "What are you doing up here?"

"I saw your shadow in the window. The kitchen door was unlocked."

He took a step into the room, then another, closing the distance between us until he was only a few feet away. The sheer heat radiating from him was a physical force, changing the atmosphere of the dusty room. My body responded instantly with a deep, primal clench low in my belly, a current of pure awareness that made the fine hairs on my arms stand on end.

He wasn't here to talk about contractors. He wasn't here to check on loose siding.

He was here for me.

"I can't stop thinking about you." His words were low and strained, as if they'd been torn from him against his will. "I try to work, I try to sleep. It doesn't matter. You're just... everywhere. All I can think about is more."

The storm had made landfall. This wasn't the grumpy, guarded neighbor. This was a man whose cement walls were completely demolished. All my carefully rehearsed witticisms, my G-rated swear substitutes, evaporated into the dusty air.

There was only this.

Him. Here. Now.

The torture was clear in his expression, the battle he was losing with himself. What had happened to this man to make him fight so hard against something he clearly wanted so much?

"What about me being your peace-wrecking neighbor?" My voice, when I found it, was strong. I needed to be sure, to understand this sudden reversal. "The prize-winning hibiscus destroyer?" I used his own accusations against him, needing to hear him deny them. Needing to know that he saw me, not just the mess I'd made.

His expression tightened, a flicker of self-reproach crossing his features. He took a half-step closer, his gaze so searing it was like a physical touch. "You are. You're all of those goddamn things. You've turned my life upside down." He paused, his eyes dropping to my mouth for a fraction of a second. "And none of that matters. Because you're so much more."

That was the confirmation. The unvarnished, utterly Austin-like admission. It was an acknowledgment that, despite all the reasons he shouldn't, emotion was overriding everything else.

He crossed the remaining distance between us in two urgent strides, his hands framing my face. His trembling thumbs traced my cheekbones.

"If you don't want this, you need to say so." His voice came out in a low, choking growl. "Now. Because I'm at my breaking point here, Iris. I'm dying."

There was no more awkward dancing around. He was laying it all on the line, giving me the final choice. The power in that moment, the sheer force of his need mirroring my unspoken want, was euphoric.

I managed a single, jerky nod. "You're not wrong. I

want this. You've been living in my head for weeks, Austin. I can't… I can't get you out either."

He surged forward and slammed his lips to mine.

It was deep, hungry. A kiss that said *yes*, that said *don't you dare even think about stopping.*

He groaned into my mouth, a sound of surrender and victory all at once, and the charged atmosphere between us ignited. His hands plunged into my hair and yanked me closer, deeper, as if he could consume me entirely. I could taste his desperation, his weeks of pent-up need as I plunged my tongue into his mouth, and it made me wild.

We were a tangle of frantic hands and desperate mouths in the stifling room, tearing at the barriers of clothing between us. Urgent. Primal. A button popped off my shirt as he tore it open, skittering away into the plaster dust, forgotten. I yanked his shirt over his head with clumsy, desperate fingers, needing to feel his skin against mine like I needed air.

"Christ, Iris," he rasped against my throat, his voice breaking. "I've wanted you so bad."

His confession sent liquid fire straight to my core. I fumbled with his belt, and he groaned when my knuckles brushed against the hard ridge of his arousal straining against his jeans. I slid them down until they dropped to the floor. He was steel wrapped in denim, and knowing I did that to him made me dizzy with power.

"God, you turn me on," I breathed.

He answered by gripping the waistband of my shorts and yanking them down my legs in one swift, possessive motion. I kicked them away, along with my underwear, suddenly desperate to be bare for him.

Our clothes were strewn over the dusty floor in a heap of denim and cotton. I inhaled the dusty air as my eyes drank him in. His body was lean, corded with the hard, functional muscle of a man who worked with his hands and body. A light dusting of dark hair covered his chest, trailing down his abdomen. He was beautiful. Raw and real and overwhelmingly male.

The way he stared at me made my knees wobble. Like he was starving, and I was his salvation.

He backed me up against the wide windowsill of the demolished room, his hands sliding up my sides, leaving trails of fire in their wake. He lifted me onto the sill, the dusty wood cool under my heated skin. For a moment, he just looked at me, his eyes so dark they were almost black, his chest rising and falling with harsh breaths.

"Jesus, you're beautiful," he choked out. "I've imagined this… God, I've imagined this."

Then his mouth was on me again, exploring, claiming. His lips traced a burning path down my throat, and I could feel his desperation in every kiss, every nip of his teeth. When he reached the sensitive spot where my neck met my shoulder, he bit down gently, and I cried out, my back arching.

"More," I gasped, my hands fisting in his hair. "Austin, please."

His mouth moved lower, his tongue flicking out to taste my skin. When he reached my breasts, he paused, his breath hot against my skin, and looked up at me with eyes so intense they burned.

"I need you," he said simply, and then his mouth closed over one peak.

The sensation was a jolt of pure pleasure that shot straight to my center. A sharp, ragged gasp escaped me. His scruff was a delicious abrasion against the sensitive skin, and his mouth was hot, wet, and demanding. He licked and sucked, one hand coming up to cup my other breast, his calloused thumb stroking, teasing the peak into a tight, hard bud.

My head fell back against the cool, grimy windowpane, and my mind dissolved into pure sensation. But I wasn't content to simply receive. An answering need surged through me, a desperate hunger that demanded I touch him, claim him back. I slid my hand down his sweat-slicked torso, over the hard ridges of his abdomen, feeling the muscles jump under my touch.

"Shit," he hissed, his hips bucking forward involuntarily. "My G—"

His words cut off on a strangled groan as I wrapped my hand around his thick, hot length. He was heavy and hard, throbbing in my palm. I stroked him once, twice, learning the feel of him, and he shuddered against me.

"You're killing me," he gasped, his forehead dropping to rest against mine. "I won't last if you keep doing that."

"Then don't," I said, my voice bold despite the tremor in it. "I want you to lose control. I want to see you fall apart in front of me."

Something wild flashed in his eyes, and suddenly his hand was sliding across my stomach, leaving a trail of fire in its wake. His calloused fingers, so competent and sure, dipped lower, threading between my legs. I gasped and opened them wider, my back arching against the windowpane as he found me slick.

"Jesus," he muttered. "You are ready for this, aren't you?"

I could only nod, beyond words, as his thumb found the sensitive bundle of nerves at my center and began to move in slow, deliberate circles. The coil of pleasure inside me, already tight from his mouth on my breast, wound impossibly tighter.

"Austin," I breathed, my hips moving against his hand. "Please."

His motions were relentless, his thumb never stopping its maddening circles. I cried out, my body clenching, and he cursed under his breath.

"You feel so good," he said, his voice strained. "I need to be inside you. Now."

The raw desperation in his voice made me clench harder. He was coming apart at the seams, and I loved it. I loved that I could reduce this controlled, careful man to base need and pleading.

I watched, dazed and gasping, as he fumbled for his wallet with shaking hands, retrieving a condom and rolling it on with clumsy, desperate efficiency. The sight of him preparing himself for me, his jaw clenched with concentration and need, was almost my undoing.

Then he positioned himself between my legs, his hands gripping my hips, and I could feel the blunt head of him pressing against my entrance. He entered me in one deep, decisive thrust that drove the air from my lungs in a sharp cry. My back pressed against the windowpane. The sensation of being filled by him was everything. He was perfectly big, stretching me in the most delicious way, and for a moment we both just breathed, adjusting to the perfection of it.

"God," he growled, his face a mask of intense concentration. "You're so tight. So right."

He began to move, and the rhythm he set was frantic, almost desperate. This was not the man who methodically repaired fishing rods and hung siding. This was someone else entirely. Someone raw, untamed, driven by weeks of suppressed need.

I wrapped my legs around his lean waist, pulling him deeper, meeting him thrust for powerful thrust. The friction was exquisite, building a fire inside me that threatened to consume us both. I raked my nails down the hard muscles of his back, feeling the skin ripple, earning a sharp hiss from him.

"Yes," I cried out, as my back slammed against the window again and again. "God, yes. Harder, Austin. I need more."

He slammed into me again, deeper this time, harder, and I screamed his name. The sound seemed to drive him wild, and suddenly he was moving with a wild fury, his hips snapping against mine.

"Is this what you want?" he rasped, his voice almost unrecognizable.

"Yes!" I cried, my nails digging into his shoulders. "Don't stop."

The coil inside me wound tighter and tighter, past the point of bearing. I was so close, balanced on the knife's edge of release. Austin must have sensed it because suddenly his hand was between us, his thumb finding that sensitive bundle of nerves and pressing hard.

The wild glare in his eyes, combined with the relentless pressure of his thumb, shattered me. A cry was ripped from my throat, my body convulsing around him as wave after wave of pleasure crashed over me. Through the haze of my climax, I felt him stiffen, his release tearing through him with a force that made him shake.

"Iris," he groaned, my name a prayer on his lips as he climaxed inside me.

We stayed like that for a long time, entwined at the window, breathing hard. Our bodies were slick with sweat and coated in a fine, gritty layer of plaster dust. The reality of what we had just done, and where we had just done it, began to slowly seep back in. As did the uncomfortable press of the window against my spine.

Then worry washed over me, chilling my overheated skin. Was he going to bolt? Put his walls back up and pretend this was just a momentary, regrettable lapse in judgment? I braced myself for the inevitable withdrawal.

But he didn't pull away.

Instead, he leaned down and kissed me again. This time, it was different. His brush of lips was soft, slow, almost questioning, completely opposite to the furious passion of moments before. He ran his mouth gently across my jaw, his scruff a pleasant, tingling abrasion, then down to the sensitive skin of my neck, to the hollow of my collarbone. Every movement was tender. A reassurance.

This tenderness, this simple act of staying, was almost more shocking and more intimate than the frantic passion that had preceded it. Hope, fragile and beautiful, bloomed in my chest. Bolstered by his unexpected gentleness, I found my voice.

"Stay tonight," I whispered in his ear. "With me."

He pulled back enough to look at me, his eyes dark, still unreadable. But the frantic, panicked energy was gone, replaced by something deeper and more thoughtful. After a long moment that stretched into an eternity, he gave a single, steady nod.

After we gathered our clothes, I reached for his hand and led him from the dusty, chaotic demolition of the Magnolia Suite, down the hall to my bedroom—a temporary island of relative order amidst the glorious mess of Heron House. We fell together onto my bed, and its clean sheets were a soft, welcoming haven.

He pulled me against him, his lips finding mine again in the semi-darkness of my bedroom. His kiss was softer now, a question asked without words. I answered by melting into him, my body boneless and sated. We didn't speak. There were no words for what had just happened in that dusty, deconstructed room. No easy labels for the raw, messy, undeniable thing that had exploded between us.

All I knew was that the silence that had so often felt vast and lonely was now different. And as I drifted off to sleep, curled against the warm, solid reality of Austin Coleridge, Heron House didn't feel quite so daunting anymore.

Chapter Sixteen

AUSTIN

I'D BEEN awake for at least five minutes, listening to the unfamiliar creaks of this old house. Listening to the soft, even rhythm of Iris breathing beside me. The light in the room was a soft, hazy gray filtering through an unfamiliar window, not the sharp stripes of sunlight that usually cut across my bedroom floor.

I was in her bed. In Heron House.

The fact registered with a dull, heavy certainty, not the sharp panic I would have expected. I turned my head on the pillow. She was a mess of blonde hair and bare shoulders, smelling of sleep and cinnamon. The woman who had bulldozed her way into my life was now curled up in the middle of it.

Iris let out a soft, contented sigh in her sleep. One small hand, which had been resting on the mattress between us, flopped over to land right on the center of my bare chest.

And I froze.

I lay there, rigid, the warmth of her hand a five-pointed brand against my skin, and I waited. Waited for the usual panic to set in, the claustrophobic sensation of walls closing in, the desperate need to escape back to my solitary space where everything was under my control.

But it didn't come.

Instead, there was calm. Not just in the room, but inside my head. The relentless energy and frustration that had been my unwelcome companions for weeks—the very things that had driven me across the yard and up her stairs yesterday like a man possessed—were gone. It was like a massive pressure valve, one I hadn't even realized was tightened to the absolute breaking point, had been released in the raw, frantic honesty of last night.

The world hadn't ended. The sky wasn't falling. It was just morning.

And I didn't want to leave.

The realization was as shocking, as disorienting, as our first kiss had been. It was a foreign concept, an alien emotion, and it threw me.

Iris's eyes fluttered open, the blue hazy and dark with sleep. They landed on me, and for a long moment, there was sleepy recognition and the slow processing of the reality of me, here, in her bed. Then awareness dawned, and a faint, self-conscious blush crept over her face, coloring her cheeks a delicate shade of rose. She looked young, vulnerable, and so devastatingly beautiful in the soft morning light that it made my chest ache.

I cleared my throat, the sound jarring.

Say something, you idiot. Anything other than 'I need to go check my crab traps.' Don't be the asshole you usually are.

"Morning," I managed.

Her lips curved into a tentative, shy smile. "Hi." Her voice was soft and husky. "You... you stayed."

It was both a statement of surprised fact and a question filled with a fragile, tentative hope that I felt all the way down to my bones.

"Seemed like the thing to do," I mumbled, the heat rising in my face.

She propped herself up on an elbow, the sheet slipping down to reveal the graceful swell of her breast. "Did it now? I wasn't sure what the protocol was for... you know. Post-conflagration snuggling."

The words, so ridiculously formal and yet so accurate for what had happened between us, had me fighting a smile. "Don't think there is one."

"We should write one." Her voice was still soft, but with a new, teasing lightness. "Chapter one—the gentleman does not flee the scene of the... conflagration at first light."

In a move that went against every rule in the Austin Coleridge playbook, I got up, not to flee, but to act. I found my discarded jeans on the floor where we'd dumped the whole pile last night and pulled them on.

"Chapter two," I said with my back to her. "The gentleman makes coffee."

I didn't wait for her response. I just walked out of the bedroom, my heart beating in a strange, unfamiliar rhythm.

I didn't do coffee.

I didn't do mornings after.

Yet here I was.

I entered her kitchen and navigated around a stack of blueprints that looked a hell of a lot more professional than Mick's chicken scratch I'd glimpsed when she made me lunch. She had a fancy new coffee machine, a beacon of modern convenience inside a mausoleum. I found fresh coffee in the fridge and managed to get a pot brewing without setting anything on fire.

She emerged a few minutes later, wrapped in a faded blue chenille robe that looked ancient and invitingly soft, her hair piled into an even messier, more precarious bun on top of her head. And despite that, she was radiant. Almost ethereal.

She leaned against the doorframe with a gorgeous upturn to her lips. "You know your way around a coffee maker. I'm impressed. I was half-expecting you to try and brew it with seawater and a blowtorch."

"Very funny," I grumbled as I grabbed two cups from a mug tree. One had a cartoon manatee wearing a top hat on it. Of course it did. I automatically handed it to her. "I've been making damn good coffee for years. I even provide it on charters."

"Uh-oh. Now I've got coffee expectations." Her fingers stroked mine as she took the steaming mug, sending that now-familiar, not-at-all-unpleasant jolt up my arm. She winked over the rim as she sampled it. "Okay. You've got the job."

I just snorted.

She moved around me with a careful, charged aware-ness, pulling a covered plate from the counter. "I was experimenting yesterday afternoon. Mango shortbread. It should still be fresh. Want one?"

"Uh, sure. Thanks."

The simple domesticity of it all—her in that soft robe, me pouring coffee, the sweet scent of mango as she warmed the squares in the microwave—was both deeply foreign and surprisingly pleasant.

She set the shortbread on the cluttered kitchen table between us. It tasted incredible. Light, flaky, with a tropical sweetness from the mango that was unexpected and damn near perfect with the strong, black coffee. I took several bites before I realized she was watching me, waiting for a verdict. I swallowed.

"It's delicious." I met her gaze, and the memory of the night before flashed through my mind. The taste of her, the feel of her silken skin. "Kind of like you."

Her eyes widened slightly, and a slow smile bloomed on her face, a warmth that chased away the last of the morning-after awkwardness. She didn't look away. Didn't make a joke. She just held my gaze. For a long moment, the air was filled with nothing but the low hum of the refrigerator and the unspoken truth of what was happening between us. The weirdness was gone, replaced by something milder and more solid.

She sighed after taking a bite. "I have to admit this is better than my usual breakfast of Nutter Butters and long, soul-searching conversations with dust bunnies."

"You eat cookies for breakfast?"

She turned, a mischievous glint in her eyes. "Sometimes, on days that end in y. Don't judge my coping mechanisms, Captain. They are varied and highly effective."

It felt like a regular morning. Like something normal people did. And that thought was absurd. I was an imposter, a trespasser in a life that wasn't, and could never be, mine. Yet it didn't feel entirely wrong, either.

"So I've wanted to ask you about something for a while." She took a sip of coffee, clearly trying not to smile. "And I think we've been suitably introduced now. You mentioned your hibiscus was award-winning when you were yelling at me during the Great Sprinkler Incident."

Heat flamed over my face. Of all the conversations we could have had over our first shared breakfast, she had to pick the most embarrassing moment of our entire acquaintance. "I didn't yell during Sprinklergate."

"You yelled a little." Her grin was growing now as she

clearly enjoyed my discomfort. "With your eyes. Highly intimidating eye-yelling. So what's the story about that hedge? What award?"

I stared into my coffee mug like it might offer me an escape route. The hibiscus story was exactly the kind of ridiculous, overly invested behavior that revealed too much about who I really was. It showed the part of me that got obsessive about things, that couldn't do anything halfway, even when it was supposed to be casual.

"It was a stupid bet," I said. "With Braden."

"One of your brothers, right?"

"The youngest of us. I'm close to him."

"Tell me about the bet."

Her words were soft but insistent. When I glanced up, she was leaning forward slightly, chin propped on her hand with curiosity written across her features. Not mocking, not preparing to laugh at me—just interested.

I took a long sip of coffee, buying time. But something about the way she stared at me, patient and encouraging, made me want to tell her. Made me want to share this piece of my history.

"Braden said I was too uptight to grow anything that wasn't practical. No flowers, no pretty plants, nothing that didn't serve a clear purpose. Just trees and landscaping."

"Sounds like something a little brother would say."

"He wasn't wrong, exactly. My landscaping was all function and no form. Gumbo limbo trees, some grass, nothing flashy." My ears were starting to burn, but I pressed on. "So I bought a bunch of hibiscus plants. Bright red, the most impractical, purely decorative thing I could find. Planted them to make a hedge right down the edge of my backyard just to prove him wrong."

"And?"

"And I got invested." The admission was huge, exposing. "I started researching proper care techniques, optimal soil conditions, fertilizer schedules. I bought a pH testing kit and started tracking rainfall patterns. I likely spent more on those plants than most people spend on their entire garden."

Iris was trying not to smile now, but I could see the delight dancing in her eyes. "Of course you did."

"When they finally bloomed, it was…" I paused, remembering the moment I'd walked out to find that first massive flower unfurling in the morning sun. "Spectacular. Bigger and more vibrant than anything I'd ever seen. The blooms were easily six inches across, this incredible deep crimson with yellow centers. Perfect symmetry, perfect color saturation. It was like something out of a magazine."

"Prize worthy. So you entered some sort of competition?"

"Oh, no. That was another dare from Braden. He said I'd never have the guts to actually show the thing off."

Braden had gaped at my hedge before turning to me with that irrepressible, shit-eating grin firmly in place. The one that always made me suspect he knew something I didn't, usually something I wouldn't like. He shared an excessive sense of humor with our older brother Eli, but Braden's was milder. Eli's version occasionally came equipped with sharp teeth.

He made a wild flourish with one arm. "Come on, Austin. Share your floral genius with the world. Blow those little old ladies from the Garden Club out of the water with your brooding botanical brilliance."

Of course I scoffed, a sound of pure disdain. Me, at the county fair, fussing over flowers like some retired dentist with too much time on his hands? Ridiculous. The idea was offensive to my image of rugged, seafaring solitude. But, also like Eli, Braden could be relentlessly, charmingly persuasive when he set his mind to it.

I refilled Iris's manatee mug. "So I cut the best bloom, drove it down to the county fairgrounds, and filled out the paperwork to enter it."

"And you won!"

"Grand Champion, Division of Horticulture." I couldn't quite keep the satisfaction out of my voice or the smile off my face. "Beat out Mrs. Lowry's roses, which had won three years running. The judge said it was the finest hibiscus specimen he'd seen outside of a professional greenhouse."

Iris burst into laughter. Not the polite, social kind, but genuine, delighted laughter that filled the kitchen with warmth and light. The sound should have annoyed me, should have made me feel exposed and foolish. Instead, the last residual tension in my shoulders dissipated. Her laughter wasn't mocking or condescending. It was pure joy, the kind of reaction that made the story funnier and more endearing instead of embarrassing.

"Austin Coleridge, champion hibiscus grower," she said when she could speak again. "I absolutely love it. I love that you got so invested in proving your brother wrong that you became a hibiscus expert. I love that you won first place with your spite flower."

"It wasn't a spite flower," I protested, but my smile grew.

"It absolutely was a spite flower, and it was glorious. You grew something beautiful just to prove you could, and then you won a prize for it. That's not ridiculous, Austin. That's..." She paused, studying my face with an expression I couldn't quite read. "That's very you, actually."

Before I could figure out how to respond to that—to her ability to see something admirable in behavior I'd always considered slightly obsessive—her emotion shifted, became more serious, though not heavy. The laughter was still in her eyes, but it was joined by something more thoughtful.

I couldn't respond because I was too busy dealing with a baffling new reality—her teasing didn't make me feel suffocated or uncomfortable. It made me feel at ease.

She looked down at her coffee cup and traced the rim with her finger. "So what does this mean, Austin? Us? Last night?"

The question should have sent me running for the door. But it didn't. Staring at her, with her robe, messy hair, and earnest blue eyes, all I could feel was a surprising, unsettling need to answer her with the same honesty.

"I'm not sure. I don't do coffee mornings…" I gestured vaguely between us. "Labels. Complications."

"Me neither, usually," she admitted, a brief, self-deprecating smile touching her lips. "My life is complicated enough right now."

"But," I continued, the word hanging in the air, "I just know… I like this." It was a huge admission. The biggest one I'd made to anyone, including myself, in a long time. "Maybe we just see what happens? No labels. No pressure. Just you and me."

She studied me for a long moment, then another sweet smile returned to her lips. One that reached all the way to her eyes and did something warm and dangerous to my chest.

"I like this too, Austin," she said. "I'd like to see what happens."

But time was marching on, and I had a group to prep for, a boat to see to. I pushed my chair back and stood, the sound scraping loudly in the quiet kitchen. "I need to get ready for work. Got a charter this morning."

"Of course. I've got a full day too." She stood up with me but didn't move away. Just stood there on the other side of the cluttered table, her gaze soft and a little uncertain.

I closed the space between us. Before I could overthink it, before my usual defenses could slam back into place, I cupped her jaw, my thumb stroking the soft skin just below her ear. Her eyes widened slightly, her lips parting on a soft, surprised breath. I meant to lean in for a simple goodbye kiss—a soft, brief confirmation of the words we'd just shared.

But the moment my mouth touched hers, that plan went to hell.

She tasted of coffee and sweet mango. Her lips were soft, yielding, welcoming. What started as a gentle press deepened instantly to a magnetic pull I was powerless to resist. The memory of last night's desperate heat flared, a coiling warmth in my gut. She pressed against me, and her hands came up to rest on my chest, right over my thumping heart. It wasn't a frantic, messy collision like yesterday. This was something else.

Slower. Deeper. More dangerous, maybe.

I lingered for a moment longer, then forced myself to pull back. Her eyes were dark, color high on her cheeks.

My hand was still on her face. I brushed the back of my fingers down her cheek, the skin unbelievably soft. "Will I see you later?"

She gave a small nod. "You will."

As I stepped onto her porch, a brand-new, clean Ford F-250 with crisp lettering for *On the Level Remodeling & Restoration* pulled into the Heron House driveway. A man got out, maybe in his mid-fifties, with a calm, confident air about him that was the polar opposite of Mick Riley's lazy swagger. He was tall and broad-shouldered, and the ebony skin of his weathered face was framed by a neatly trimmed, salt-and-pepper goatee. This had to be Gus, the guy Chase had recommended and Iris had chosen. I'd heard of him but never met the man.

Iris joined me on the porch and squeezed my bicep. "He's right on time. Come on. You should meet him since you're the one who made it happen."

"I'd like that."

We crossed the walkaround porch and descended the steps to meet the man.

"Gus! Good morning!" Iris called out, her voice bright.

Gus smiled as he walked up the path, a clipboard tucked under his arm. "Morning, Iris. Ready to make some real progress?" His voice was a deep, steady baritone that inspired confidence. He nodded toward me.

"Gus, this is my neighbor, Austin. He was the one who put me in touch with his brother-in-law, Chase," Iris explained.

I extended my hand. "Austin Coleridge."

Gus's grip was firm, dry, no-nonsense. "Gus Davis. Pleasure to meet you. Chase told me you know your way around these old houses yourself."

"I know enough to stay away from them, usually," I replied, and Iris laughed.

Gus's smile widened. "I know the feeling. Well, no time to waste." He turned to Iris, all business. "As I told you last week, my exterior crew is on the way to get this siding situation permanently resolved and make sure you're watertight. We'll have this whole west wall finished by the end of the day tomorrow. My interior guys will continue the third-floor demo for those en-suites. I've got a third team finishing up a job across the bay, and they'll join us here in about a week. We'll hit this place from all sides. Should have you ready for plumbing and electrical in no time."

He laid out the plan with such calm, logical efficiency

that I found myself nodding in approval. I watched Iris's face as he spoke. The anxious frown line that had seemed a permanent fixture between her brows was gone, replaced by an expression of pure happiness.

"That's amazing," she said. "I can't tell you what a relief that is to hear."

Seeing her like this, so happy and hopeful, did that unsettling thing to my chest again. Warmth spread through me, a feeling of satisfaction on her behalf that was profoundly, dangerously unfamiliar. With Gus and his competent crew taking charge, my presence was no longer required.

"Well," I cleared my throat and addressed them both. "Sounds like you've got it handled. I have to get to work."

The contractor gave me another firm nod. "Good to meet you, Austin."

"You, too. We'll get to know each other, I expect." Couldn't hurt to let the guy know I'd be around.

Iris turned to me, her blue eyes shining. "Thank you again, Austin."

"You're welcome. Uh, see you later." I gave her a nod, unable to articulate the mess of conflicting emotions churning inside me, and retreated.

As I headed back to my place to shower, my world felt like it had spun sideways. I'd spent the night with the chaotic woman next door. I'd made her coffee in her kitchen. I'd talked, I'd laughed. And now, her biggest problem was on its way to being solved.

Things were changing, whether I wanted them to or not. When I pulled my shirt off in the bathroom, I caught a whiff of Iris's scent. The unfamiliar lightness in my chest battled with a deep, familiar sense of dread. And hell if I wasn't entirely sure which one was going to win.

Chapter Seventeen

IRIS

"YOU'RE certain that going with cypress on the porch ceiling is the right call, even with the humidity?" I squinted up at the bare joists of the wide, wraparound veranda. My gaze dropped to the sample board, which was undeniably lovely. I could already imagine the tight grain with its natural honey-to-reddish-brown tones stretching along the length of the ceiling.

Gus glanced up from the support beam he was inspecting. "Hundred percent." His deep voice resonated with an authority that soothed my nerves. "We seal it right, front and back, it'll outlast both of us. It's what this house wants, Iris. You try to put cheap composite up there, an old girl like this, she'll just reject it. Spit it right back out in the first decent tropical storm."

A smile burst across my face. It had only been a week since Gus and his crew descended upon Heron House, and already the entire property felt different. The air, once thick with the lonely scent of dust and decay, now smelled of freshly cut lumber, sawdust, and the determined energy of progress. A crew of four men swarmed the exterior, their nail guns creating a steady, reassuring rhythm. Inside, another crew was deep in the demolition of the third floor, their work careful and planned.

Gus was a direct answer to a prayer I hadn't even realized I'd been screaming internally. He was calm, professional, and he actually listened to my ideas before gently explaining why some were brilliant and others would lead to structural collapse. I sensibly nixed those.

But now I was left with a restive energy. Gus had a detailed schedule, a binder thick with permits, and a crew that knew exactly what they were doing. My role had shifted from crisis manager to, well, the lady who occasionally brought out cold lemonade and cookies while trying not to get in the way.

Which left my mind with entirely too much free time to drift next door.

My phone buzzed in my pocket. I pulled it out, a hopeful flutter in my chest. It was a text from Brenna.

Brenna: Tour of Dove Key still on? I'm in desperate need of a non-book-related conversation. Meet me at Driftwood Beach in a half hour?

I typed back quickly.

Iris: Absolutely! See you there!

A thrill ran through me. I'd been looking forward to this all morning. With Gus and his army of capable workers handling Heron House, I finally had an outlet for that new restlessness—an exploration of my new town. To see it through the eyes of someone who knew its secrets.

"Gus, I'm heading out for a bit," I called over the rhythmic hammering. "My friend is giving me a tour of the area."

He looked up. "Good for you. This old house is in

good hands. We'll keep making progress while you're gone."

"I have no doubt. I'm so grateful to have you here."

Maybe spending a few hours with Austin's sweet, friendly sister would help me get a better handle on the complicated man himself. Or at the very least, it would be a conversation that didn't involve me wondering if he was thinking about jumping me half as much as I thought that about him.

The past week had been a revelation. We had fallen into a strange, unspoken rhythm. He'd leave for a charter early, and I'd wake up to find a large, steaming thermos of his strong, black coffee left for me. A silent offering that was more intimate than a dozen roses. In the evenings, he'd find a flimsy excuse to come over, to "check on Gus's progress" or to return an empty plate from whatever test bake I'd left for him.

And we'd actually talk. Austin was still reserved, but his walls were lower, the silences between us more comfortable. He acted less like heavy dental work was preferable to conversation. We'd even worked together on his hibiscus hedge one afternoon, a surprisingly easy and companionable task that ended with a long, hand-in-hand stroll along the north-shore beach as the sun melted into the horizon. And later…

Oh my stars.

We had spent nearly every night together since… well, since the conflagration, as I had taken to calling it. It had been a blur of tangled sheets and a raw, consuming passion that left me breathless and sore in the best possible way. When he touched me, when he looked at me in the quiet moments after, his gray eyes soft and unguarded, I felt seen. In a way I wasn't sure I ever had before.

I walked to Driftwood Beach on the eastern edge of

the Key, then down a long, zigzagging wooden staircase. Brenna was already there, her long, auburn hair a bright spot of color against the dark wood and pale sand. Her smile was pure warmth.

"There you are!" she called, waving me over. We headed toward the south end of the beach, where a structure grew larger as we neared. "This is our local celebrity: The Driftwood Dragon."

The dragon was even more impressive up close—a whimsical, silent sentinel pieced together from the sea's offerings. Its twisted driftwood body curved gracefully along the shoreline, weathered smooth by salt and time, creating something both ancient and timeless.

"It's beautiful," I said, brushing my hand along one of the dragon's smooth curves. "How long has it been here?"

"The first one was built ages ago." Brenna patted the arching neck of the sculpture. "But this version? Only a year or so. Every big storm takes some or all of it, and the community just rebuilds it. It's never exactly the same dragon twice."

There was something soothing about that—the idea of something being destroyed and rebuilt over and over but somehow maintaining its essential spirit. Like resilience made manifest in salt-smoothed wood.

We strolled back up the beach in comfortable silence, watching the waves roll in.

"So," Brenna said, "how are things going with the house? And with life in general?"

"The house is going amazingly well, thanks to Gus. Your brother-in-law has impeccable taste in contractors."

"Chase is outstanding at what he does," Brenna agreed as we headed up the staircase. "How about we continue our tour on the way to lunch? We've got a great local diner, and I can point out some places on the way."

"That sounds wonderful. I'm more than ready for lunch."

The Island Breeze Bistro was a classic small-town diner, all red vinyl booths, black-and-white checkered floors, and the delicious, life-affirming scent of burgers on a flattop grill. We tucked into a booth by the window. A middle-aged, plump waitress with a friendly face and a name tag that read *Marge* came to take our order. We both ordered cheeseburgers and iced tea, a decision that required zero deliberation on my part.

After Marge delivered our food, I patted the pink box on the table. "It was very nice of Liv to give us dessert."

"Too bad she couldn't join us, but duty calls. She seemed happy we dropped by."

I had to admit that as much as I liked my new bakery-owning friend, I wanted a little privacy for this conversation. I stuffed a French fry in my mouth and took a sip of iced tea.

"I'm glad to hear things are going well at Heron House." Brenna leaned forward conspiratorially. "Which brings me to my next question. How are things on the neighborly front? Is my brother still a world-class grouch, or has he at least stopped scowling at your general existence?"

I couldn't help laughing, even as a blush crept up my neck. This required some tact. As nice as Brenna was, I had no idea how she would feel about me dating her brother. "Let's just say we've turned over a new leaf. I initiated a pastry offensive that appears to have brokered a fragile peace."

"A pastry offensive?" Brenna grinned. "Iris, I love that. So you're just pelting him with baked goods until he surrenders? That's a brilliant strategy. I'm surprised no one's tried it before." She took a sip of her water. "So he's being civil? That's progress, I suppose. I was worried he'd put up a barbed-wire fence and a *No Trespassing* sign aimed directly at your porch."

I wriggled in my seat. I couldn't keep this from her, no matter how she reacted. She was my friend, and I owed her honesty. "It's a little more than civil, Brenna."

Her teasing smile faltered slightly, replaced by genuine curiosity. "Oh? What does that mean? Did he actually help you with something without you having to bribe him with a whole pie?"

"He helped me with the siding, actually," I said, the memory still warming me. "And he's been… well, wonderful. We've been spending a lot of time together." I let the words hang in the air, watching her face.

Her lips curved further. "A lot of time? That's great. It's good for him to have a friend next door." Then her face went blank, and she tilted her head. "Wait. What kind of time are we talking about here?"

I took another deep breath, my heart galloping. "That kind. Like… he's been over almost every night for the past week."

The reaction was immediate and profound. Brenna's fork, which had been poised over her coleslaw, clattered onto her plate. Her eyes widened, losing their teasing light and filling with absolute shock.

Oh no. She hates the idea of me with him.

Before I could respond and try to pull our friendship train back onto the tracks, she held up a palm. "Wait. Every night? As in… that kind of together? As in, Austin Coleridge, the man who considers small talk a form of psychological warfare, is in a relationship with you?"

A cold dread washed over me, extinguishing the warm, happy optimism I'd walked in with. I had overstepped.

"Oh, dear. Oh Mylanta. Brenna, I'm so sorry," I

rushed out, my voice filled with sudden panic. "Maybe I shouldn't have said anything. I know it's unexpected with the rocky start we had, and he's your brother. Please don't let this be weird between us. I really value your friendship."

Brenna just stared at me, her stunned expression becoming unreadable. Then her face became calculating. I could see the wheels spinning as her eyes darted over my face. "Oh, Iris. Honey, no. It's a little weird, but I'm not upset." Her gaze was shrewd now, intensely focused. "I'm just shocked. How long has this been going on?"

I laughed, though it came out nervous. "Well, I don't know if we're putting labels on it yet. It's new. Like I said, only a week or so. And I know we didn't hit it off right away. I practically flooded his yard. He was probably ready to have me arrested."

"No," Brenna said, shaking her head slowly, her eyes still locked on mine. "No, Iris, you don't understand. It's not about you. Or the sprinkler. Austin doesn't do relationships. Not for a very long time."

Goosebumps pebbled my arms at the realization that her reaction wasn't about me being with her brother.

It was about him being with *anyone*.

The mood at our table shifted from lighthearted gossip to something heavier. I picked at the coaster under my iced tea, my cheeseburger now unappetizing.

"He hides a lot behind that grumpy persona, doesn't he?" I said, testing the waters. "I've seen another side of him. A side that's kind and really protective."

Brenna nodded, her gaze soft with affection for her complicated older brother. "He's both of those. Austin cares more deeply than almost anyone I know. And he's the most dependable person on the planet. He built walls a long time ago, Iris. He built them high and thick, for a reason."

The unspoken hung in the air between us, a ghost at our lunch table. "A reason? Brenna, what happened to him?"

She was silent for a long moment, her gaze drifting out the window to the sunny Main Street traffic, a sad look in her eyes. When she looked back at me, her expression was full of a pained apology.

"That's Austin's story to tell," she said softly, her voice firm but kind. "It's not mine to share. I'm sorry."

My cheeks flushed as if I'd just read a page from her private diary. Of course she wouldn't betray her brother's confidences. "No, I'm sorry. I shouldn't have asked. I didn't mean to pry."

"It's okay." Brenna reached across the table and patted my hand, her warmth chasing away some of the chill that had settled over me. "Listen, Iris. Austin is complicated. You've seen that already. But he's the best man I know. He deserves some happiness. He's been on his own for too long." Her gaze sharpened with sisterly affection, and her smile returned. "I'm not going to pretend I'm not surprised, but it's high time someone besides his family breached those walls. And we haven't been friends all that long, but I think I know you. I'm glad that someone is you."

Tears welled in my eyes. I dabbed my napkin at them, feeling a little silly. "Thank you for saying that. Your friendship already means a lot to me. And Austin does too. Cranky, perfectionist tendencies and all."

That made both of us laugh, ending the serious moment. She took a bite of her burger. "Come on. Eat."

As we finished our meal, my mind whirred.

After we paid the bill, Brenna gave me a smile. "I should get back to the bookstore. But don't be a stranger, okay?"

"I won't. Thanks for the tour, Brenna. And for, you know, the burger and everything."

"Anytime. Honestly, Iris, you've given me a lot to think about today. Good things." She paused, her expression thoughtful. "I'm happy for you. And for Austin, too, even if he is a stubborn grump who doesn't know what's good for him half the time. He's got a good heart under all those barnacles. He just doesn't let many people see it."

Her eyes held a silent message, a clear, sisterly plea. *Be patient with him.*

I nodded, understanding the unspoken request. "I'm starting to see that."

She waved at me through the window as she walked away. I returned it as I sat at our table, processing. I was truly happy to have made real friends, to feel the first tentative threads of community weaving around me.

But this new feeling of belonging now competed with a profound, gnawing unease. This was no longer a simple case of winning over a grumpy man with good cookies and a stubborn spirit. Austin had experienced a significant trauma that still affected his sister and probably his whole family, not just him.

"What happened to you, Austin Coleridge?" I whispered to my empty iced tea.

Chapter Eighteen

AUSTIN

WORKING on *Line Dancer* usually settled something deep inside me, a mechanical meditation that smoothed the frayed edges of my thoughts. But as I hosed down the deck with the sun setting behind me, the familiar scent of salt and diesel offered no comfort.

I retreated to the boat's tiny cabin, a space usually reserved for paperwork and refuge from sudden squalls. It was my sanctuary within a sanctuary. The neat berth contained a double bed and a tiny marine head. On the other side, a desk where I logged my trips and repaired my reels stood next to a minuscule galley. It was all me, all orderly. But the confined space offered no escape from the relentless replay of the last few weeks.

Her laugh. Her passion. The way her hip flared and dipped.

The terrifying, exhilarating plunge into something I hadn't realized I was starving for. And couldn't get enough of.

My phone buzzed on the desk, the sound unnaturally intrusive in the quiet cabin. I stared at Brenna's name on the screen, a knot tightening in my gut. Brenna didn't usually call just to chat on a Friday evening. I let it ring twice more, a small act of futile defiance, before swiping to answer. "Brenna."

"Well, hello to you too, Captain Sunshine," her voice came through the phone, but with an underlying, sing-song quality that immediately put every one of my defenses on high alert. "I was just calling to see how you were. And to mention I had the most interesting afternoon yesterday."

"And you need to tell me about it?" I dropped into the desk chair, pinching the bridge of my nose.

"I gave your neighbor a little tour of Dove Key," she continued, her tone deceptively casual, as if she were commenting on the weather. "Iris is really lovely, Austin. So full of life and enthusiasm for that old house."

Oh, hell.

I didn't realize they knew each other. How did that even happen? The island was small, but not that tiny.

"That's nice, Brenna." My response was flat, clipped, a verbal dead end designed to shut down this entire line of conversation before it even began.

But Brenna had never been one to be deterred by a dead end. She just saw it as an opportunity to find another route. "It was. We had a good time. And she mentioned you two have been spending some time together. That was... interesting news, Austin."

I could picture my little sister perfectly, sitting in her cozy, book-lined office at the shop, that knowing, perceptive, infuriatingly gentle smile on her face. She was tossing out her line, and I was the damn fish, already feeling the insistent prick of the hook.

"She's my neighbor," I said, the words stiff. "We live

next door. It happens." It was a weak defense, and we both knew it. It sounded flimsy even to my ears.

"It happens? She told me you've been over there almost every night. She seems to really care about you."

My sigh was a harsh, rasping sound, and the fight went out of me. There was no point in denying it. I leaned forward and rested my forehead on my palm, elbow propped on the desk. "All right, Brenna. Yes. We're seeing each other. It's new. It's not a big deal."

"Oh, Austin." The relief in her voice was a warm wave that traveled through the phone. "Deny it all you want, but that's wonderful news! I was surprised, obviously, but… happy for you. You know we all worry about you. It's been a long time." She hesitated, and I knew what was coming next. The one topic that was off-limits, the one door I never, ever opened. "Maybe… maybe she can help you. You've never really dealt with what happened."

Ice.

Sharp, paralyzing ice shot through my veins, freezing blood and silencing the chaotic thrum of my thoughts.

"Do not go there." My voice came out low and cold and hard. Each word was a chip of ice. "That has nothing to do with this. That has nothing to do with her. And I did deal with it. I buried it. End of story. Drop it, Brenna."

There was a long, heavy silence on the other end of the line. "Okay," she said finally, her voice subdued, full of a soft, aching regret. "I'll stop. But I'm here, all of us are here, if you change your mind, okay? Or if you want to talk to Iris about it. Please?"

I closed my eyes and leaned my forehead against the desk. "I know. I do. I'm sorry I snapped at you."

"It's okay. Really." She took a breath, and I could hear her regrouping, shifting gears. "But you can't keep her a secret. People are going to see you two together. It's a small island. When are you going to introduce her to the rest of us? As more than just the neighbor?"

The ice in my veins began to melt, replaced by a weary, heavy resignation, and I sat up straight. She was right. Of course she was right. I couldn't keep Iris in a separate, isolated box labeled *neighbor* while the rest of my life went on around her. Life and my family were already seeping in around the edges, blurring the lines I had drawn so carefully, so desperately.

I scrubbed a hand over my stubble. "Yeah, I know. And I will. Just keep it to yourself for now, okay? I need a little time to figure things out."

"Okay," she agreed, though the reluctance was clear in her voice, the unspoken promise that this conversation wasn't over. "For now. But I really like her. She's good people."

"Yeah," I said, the single word feeling like a massive concession. "She is."

"I love you, you big, stubborn hermit," she said softly.

"Yeah, love you too."

The call with Brenna left a bitter taste in my mouth, like stale coffee. I drove home in a funk. Her words, so full of gentle, loving concern, had been worse than any argument.

"You never really dealt with it."

The four walls of my house felt like they were closing in, the silence suddenly suffocating. Needing air, I went out to my yard, telling myself I needed to check the tension on the new guide wrappings on my fishing rod, a task that required focus and a steady hand. My hands were far from steady, and my real reason for being outside was standing in plain sight. My gaze, as if drawn by its own magnetic pull, went straight to Heron House.

Gus's crew was packing up for the day, the professional

hum of their work winding down into the easy camaraderie of men ready for a cold beer and a hot meal.

Iris was on the porch, a clipboard tucked under her arm, talking with Gus. Her blonde hair was pulled back, but tendrils had escaped to frame her face, which was tilted up toward him, her expression focused and intent. She wasn't smiling or laughing. She was working.

I was still annoyed that my sister and my neighbor had somehow formed an alliance, a book club conspiracy that was now apparently focused on the state of my emotional well-being. I assumed Iris had sought her out, maybe to get the inside scoop on the grumpy sea captain next door.

But I found myself drifting closer, down the property line, keeping to the shadows of my trees. I told myself I was just making sure Gus wasn't giving her the runaround, that this new contractor was as good as his clean truck and professional demeanor suggested.

It was vigilance. That was all.

I got within earshot just as Gus was pointing to a section of the second-floor exterior.

"…so we can ensure there's a proper air gap behind the siding," he was explaining, his voice a calm, steady baritone. "It'll let the whole wall breathe, which is critical in this climate. Prevents moisture buildup, rot, the whole nine yards."

"Right," Iris said, and I saw her make a note on a sheet attached to her clipboard. "And the flashing you're using for the new window installations, is it a self-adhering, or a fluid-applied one? I was reading that with these older, uneven clapboards, a fluid-applied membrane can create a more seamless seal."

I stopped dead. My feet just halted, half-hidden behind a large bush.

Fluid-applied membrane?

I must have heard her wrong.

But then Gus nodded, an expression of professional respect on his face. "Good question. We're using a high-quality butyl tape. But you're right, on a house this old, a fluid application around the sills is a smart secondary measure. I'll add it to the work order. Good catch, Iris. You've been doing your research."

"I'm trying," she said, and I could hear the quiet pride in her voice. "This house has been neglected for a long time. I want to make sure we do right by her."

I stood hidden in the shade, absolutely poleaxed. This was not the same woman who had tried to fix a sprinkler with a pair of rusty pliers and a vague memory of a YouTube video. Or who had blushed furiously over a story about catching a trout at summer camp. This was a woman discussing building envelopes and flashing techniques with a seasoned contractor.

She was a business owner.

And the respect I experienced was a companion to the relentless physical attraction that was a constant, low thrum in my blood. It made her more real. More formidable. And infinitely harder to dismiss as just a temporary complication.

The conversation between Iris and Gus wound down. He tipped his hat to her, said his goodbyes, and headed for his truck. Iris remained on the porch, her back to me, staring at the blueprints still spread across the makeshift table. Her posture was straight, confident.

The twitchy energy that had been plaguing me since Brenna's call coalesced into a single, undeniable impulse. My feet started moving before my brain gave them permission.

I found my sharpest pruning shears, the ones I used for nothing else, and walked over to my hibiscus hedge. The one she'd almost sent to a watery grave, the one we'd worked on together just a few days ago. It was recovering beautifully, new growth dotted with vibrant, defiant blooms. Carefully, with the precision of a surgeon, I snipped one flawless crimson flower. Its petals were a rich, bright velvet.

After dropping the shears, I walked through the gap in the hedge where a path was slowly but surely being worn. I went up the steps of her porch, the flower held carefully in my hand. The bloom felt both foolish and incredibly important.

It was an apology for every grumpy thought I'd ever had about her.

And a question I still didn't know how to ask.

She must have heard my footsteps on the old wood. She turned, a question on her face, and her eyes widened when she saw me standing there holding the flower. I stopped in front of her, feeling strangely, uncharacteristically shy. I didn't say anything. I just held out the flower.

She stared at the crimson bloom, then up at me, her blue eyes searching mine for a long, breathless moment. A slow, wondrous smile spread across her face, an expression of unguarded delight that made my heart do a two-step.

"Austin," she breathed, her gaze dropping back to the perfect, velvety petals as she took it from me. She lifted it to her nose, inhaling its faint, sweet scent, her eyes gently closing for a second. "It's beautiful. Thank you."

"It's a good one," I managed, my voice rough. "Figured it belonged with you."

She looked up at me again, her smile so soft it made my chest ache. I stepped forward and cupped her jaw, my thumb stroking the soft skin of her cheek. Her eyes fluttered, her lips parting on a soft breath.

Lowering my head, I touched my mouth to hers.

Her lips were soft, yielding, welcoming. The memory of our first, explosive encounter flared, but this was different. This was a slow, deliberate coming together. Slower. Deeper. More dangerous, maybe, because it felt less like a loss of control and more like a conscious surrender.

She leaned into me, the hibiscus still held carefully in one hand. This quiet, intimate moment on her porch, with the scent of sawdust and her perfume filling my senses, was more real than anything I'd allowed myself to feel in thirteen years.

I pulled back, reluctantly, my hand still cradling her face. Her eyes were dark, dazed, color high on her cheeks.

The memory of my phone call with Brenna, the one I'd been trying to shove into a dark corner of my mind, suddenly surfaced. The absurdity of the situation, of me standing here, kissing my neighbor just hours after my sister had interrogated me about her, hit me. A soft, unexpected laugh escaped me.

Iris blinked, a confused little frown appearing between her brows. "What's so funny?"

"I, uh… I talked to Brenna earlier," I admitted, feeling a fresh wave of heat creep up my neck. I dropped my hand from her face, needing the distance. "She mentioned her little tour of Dove Key yesterday."

Iris's eyes widened in dawning horror, then narrowed with a sharp glint of amusement. "Oh, did she? She casually mentioned knowing about you and me?"

"Something like that," I grumbled, my usual defenses starting to reassert themselves now that our lips weren't touching. "She has a way of extracting information in unexpected ways. I didn't even know you two had met."

"Well, you knew I joined her book club," she teased, her smile returning. "It's not a huge leap in logic to think I might have gotten to know the woman who is a huge part of it."

"I don't pay attention to all that… day-drinking club crap," I said, the familiar gruffness a welcome, if slightly ill-fitting, shield.

"It's a book club, you heathen." She laughed again, a full, honest sound that settled something deep inside me. "And the wine is purely for literary enhancement, I'll have you know."

The ease between us, the shared humor, was a new and dangerous territory. It felt good. Too good. And the look in her eyes, the way she was smiling at me as if I were the most interesting, baffling man she'd ever met, made it hard to think straight.

The smile faded from my face. "It suits you," I said, my voice suddenly rough again as I nodded toward the crimson flower she was still holding. "The color."

She looked down at the bloom, then back up at me, her expression softening. "Thank you for bringing it to me."

"You're welcome." The words sounded inadequate. "Listen, I… I have a really early charter tomorrow. A full day." It wasn't true. My calendar was no busier than usual. But it was a necessary lie, a desperate attempt to create some space, to give myself a chance to process the monumental shift that was occurring inside me. "I should turn in soon, and I don't want to wake you when I leave before dawn."

"Oh," she said, a flicker of disappointment in her eyes that she couldn't quite hide. "Of course. I understand."

"I'll… I'll call you tomorrow," I added, the promise leaving my lips before I could stop it.

Her face brightened instantly, that thousand-watt smile returning. "I'd like that."

I forced myself to turn and walk away. I didn't look

back, couldn't look back, as I left her standing on the porch and holding my flower. The scent of her and a future I didn't know what to do with followed me all the way home.

I walked through my living room, a space I had designed for peace and order. The carefully chosen nautical charts on the wall looked flat, lifeless. The fabric of my sofa, usually so inviting, offered no comfort. I moved to my back patio, where the sky was now a deep, bruised purple streaked with the last fiery remnants of the sunset. The lights of Heron House flickered next door, a warm, inviting glow against the deepening twilight. Her silhouette moved behind a window, maybe putting the hibiscus I'd given her in a bowl of water.

I replayed the moment on her porch over and over. The soft, unguarded delight on her face when I gave her the flower. The way she'd laughed at my stupid, gruff joke about her book club. The easy way she'd teased me. The way my mouth had curved into a smile without my permission.

It was real.

The thought landed not with a jolt, but with a weighted certainty. This thing with her wasn't just about the physical pull anymore, the raw, undeniable chemistry that had exploded between us in that dusty, demolished room. That was the easy part, the part a man could understand and compartmentalize. This was something more dangerous.

I liked the sound of her laugh. I liked the way her eyes lit up when she was passionate about something. I liked her stubborn determination, her ridiculous G-rated curses, her surprisingly good baking.

I liked her.

I had real, developing feelings for her.

And I could, if I was foolish enough to let my guard down for more than a few stolen moments, picture a future. Waking up with her. Sharing coffee. Listening to her talk about her plans for Heron House. Seeing her smile that blinding smile because of something I'd said, something I'd done.

And that was the most terrifying thing in the world.

Because it inevitably brought the ghosts rushing back from the deep, dark places where I kept them chained. The jagged memory of a different life—a different future—crashed back, a world snatched away in an instant.

Caitlin.

The echo of her laughter, so different from Iris's, but bright in its own way. The memory of a day on the water, the sun warm on our faces, the whole world vast and endless, like it would never run out.

Until it did.

I gripped the kitchen counter, my knuckles white, grounding me in the here and now. I wanted to leave the past where it was. Over. Forgotten. I'd told Brenna as much.

But I was beginning to realize the truth. That maybe you can't bury the past and be done with it. If I wanted a real future, a life, I might have to unlock the one door in my mind I had bolted shut. It wasn't just grief that lived behind that door. It was the frigid memory that happiness could come at a terrible price. And the thought of letting Iris all the way in was like tempting fate to come and collect its due all over again, with her as the payment. And I knew exactly what that looked like.

The chaos, the screaming, the terrifying water, the silence…

And the crushing, suffocating weight of my survival.

I didn't know if I had the strength to turn that key. And I was terrified that if I did, the guilt I'd spent all these years trying to outrun would finally end me for good.

Chapter Nineteen

IRIS

ONCE A SPLINTERED MESS of sagging boards, the porch of Heron House was now a solid, welcoming expanse. I worked on a section of railing, the rhythmic swipe of my paintbrush a soothing meditation. Primer. A clean slate.

The scent of sawdust and the nearby sea filled the air, a perfume of progress and possibility that was finally feeling more like home than a challenge. This was the part of the renovation I loved—the tangible work of bringing something beautiful back to life.

In a way, it reminded me of Austin. A small, secret smile curled my lips, my thoughts drifting back to the other night. The day following his tense retreat after giving me the flower, he'd been true to his word and called me.

His voice on the phone had been its usual low rumble. "Caught some fresh yellowtail. Enough for two. Come over for dinner at six o'clock?"

The fact that he had called, that he was initiating contact, had sent a happy flutter through my chest. He was a man who couldn't be rushed. Like the hibiscus he'd given me, he'd open up on his own schedule. At times, that was frustrating to me. But when we were together, the outside world didn't matter. Dinner at his place had been an education. Everything had a place; every surface was clean. We'd moved around each other in the space, a charged dance of awareness. He'd grilled the fish, and I'd made a salad, the air between us comfortable, full of the low hum of undeniable attraction.

And in the darkness that followed, the storm we'd unleashed only grew in intensity. But this time, it was different. There was a raw, almost desperate intensity to his lovemaking, a fierce possessiveness in the way he touched me, as if he couldn't quite believe I was real and truly there in his arms, in his bed. But it was tempered with a new tenderness. Slow, lingering kisses that spoke more than his carefully rationed words ever could. The feel of his calloused hands, so gentle as they traced the curve of my spine. He'd held me all night, a solid, warm weight against my back, his breathing a steady rhythm in the darkness.

The soft crunch of boots on the shell path made me look up. Austin walked with that familiar, easy stride, two sweating bottles of beer in one hand. He didn't say anything at first, just set one of the bottles on a sawhorse near me as we exchanged nods. He leaned against a support post with his arms crossed over his chest and watched me for a moment.

"Are you painting that or just giving it a light dusting?" he asked, that dry humor filling his deep voice. "My grandmother moves faster."

"This is called precision, Captain," I said without looking at him, a smile touching my lips. "Something a man who wrangles fish for a living likely wouldn't understand. Besides, look at you, over here and willingly participating in whimsical renovation." I dipped my brush and drew a clean, perfect line before gesturing with it toward his property line. "That spite-flower hedge of yours is looking awfully friendly these days."

He snorted. "Don't get cocky. And again, it's not a spite flower." Pushing off the post, he came over. "Give me that. You're holding it wrong."

"I am not." But I let him take my hand, his fingers wrapping around mine to adjust my grip. The simple, practical touch sent a now-familiar jolt straight to my core.

"Like this," he said, his voice close to my ear. "Lets you control the stroke better."

He grabbed his own brush, and we painted in silence for a few minutes, the only sounds the whisper of our brushes and the chirping of songbirds. The work was easier with him here, the load lighter. I had to admit his advice on holding the brush made the job easier.

"So," he said, breaking the stillness. "What are you going to call these rooms when you're done? The Room of the Rodent Attack?"

I shuddered theatrically at the war I'd raged getting a family of squirrels to vacate the premises. "Very funny. I was actually thinking of naming them after the things you can see from their windows. The third-floor suite, the one you, uh, found me in? That'll be the Magnolia Suite. And the one I was painting yesterday, at the other end of the hall? The Sea Turtle Suite. I saw one from the balcony last week." My vision for the B&B looked sharper and more real as I said it out loud to him. "I want Heron House to be a sanctuary. A place people come to feel peaceful and rejuvenated."

I risked a glance at him, half-expecting a cynical grunt. Instead, his gray eyes were thoughtful, his expression open.

"It's not just a business for you, is it?" he asked.

"No. It's more than that." The words were out before I could stop them. "It's not just my dream, you know. It was hers, too."

"Whose?"

I took his paintbrush and set it down with mine, the mood between us shifting from easy banter to something more intimate. "Come here. I want to show you something."

He followed me without question, his boots thudding softly on the newly sanded floors. I led him through the demolished but promising great room to the window seat that overlooked the magnolia tree in the backyard.

I opened the drawer and set aside the dried magnolia sprig before pulling out the letter. "I found this a while ago."

After unfolding the pages of cream-colored stationery, I handed them to him. It felt like handing over a piece of my heart. He took them carefully, his large hands gentle with the fragile paper.

I studied him as he read. His gaze slowed as he took in my aunt's words, the confession of her regrets, the hope she had placed in me. A muscle in his jaw tightened, and his throat worked as he swallowed.

He was silent for a beat after he finished, his gaze still on the page. Then he carefully folded the letter and handed it back to me. His eyes, when they met mine, were full of deep, quiet understanding. He didn't offer platitudes. He didn't say he was sorry for my family's past. He just reached out, his thumb gently brushing across my jaw.

"A warm, determined heart." His voice was quiet while he quoted the letter. He studied me, a whole world of respect and validation in his steady gray gaze. "Constance knew what she was doing, leaving it to you."

"I sure hope so."

He smiled and leaned over to kiss me, his lips soft and warm against mine. It was a kiss of acceptance. Of seeing me and not flinching. And in that sunlit room, with the presence of my aunt's hopes hanging in the air between us, something new and solid clicked into place. He wasn't just my neighbor anymore. He was part of this. Part of my home.

THE SIPS and Pages book club meeting was winding down. A few days after sharing the letter with Austin, I'd walked into Pam's bungalow with a bottle of white wine and a confident stride. The air was a familiar, happy mix of wine, Liv's incredible miniature lemon tarts, and the excited chatter of women who had found their tribe.

As we discussed our latest romance novel, a second-chance romance, I caught Brenna's eye across the circle. She gave me a wink. This was so different from my first meeting, where I'd felt like an outsider on display. Now, I was one of the girls, debating the merits of fictional men and real-world desserts.

As the meeting began to break up, the conversation splintered into smaller clusters. A chic woman with sharp, stylish dark hair approached me, her smile warm.

"You're Iris, right? The one tackling Heron House?" She extended a hand. "I'm Suzanne Hainey. I have a marketing firm in town. I couldn't help but overhear you talking about your B&B plans. It sounds amazing. If you get to the point where you're thinking about websites or branding, give me a call. I'd love to help you tell the story."

A surge of professional excitement rose within me. "I'm not quite there yet, but I absolutely will. Thank you."

"Of course," she replied with a warm smile. "And

another tip from one business owner to another. If you need help with your financial planning, Dean Mercer on Main Street is the best. He's a certified financial planner and fairly new in town. He was a huge help getting my firm on solid footing."

"Thanks for the recommendation." I made a mental note. Another piece of my new life was clicking into place, a network of support I knew I would need sooner than later.

As Suzanne turned to say her goodbyes to Pam, a soft touch lighted on my arm.

"Don't run off yet!" Liv beamed at me, her brown curls bouncing. She held an empty platter, a single, eloquent crumb the only evidence of her tarts. "I've been dying for a real peek at the progress."

I laughed, a rush of affection for this whirlwind of positive energy rolling through me. "You have to come see it! The floors are sanded in places, and I even painted some of the porch railing. I'll give you the grand tour."

"Fabulous! I'd love to!"

"How about coffee tomorrow?" I offered. "My treat this time, to thank you for the lavender-scone intervention."

Liv's eyes twinkled. "It's a date! But I'm bringing the pastries. It's the least I can do for the woman who will probably single-handedly boost my lavender supplier's quarterly profits. I can swing by about one, if that works?"

Her easy, supportive friendship felt like another piece of my new life clicking into place. I wasn't just building a house. I was building a home, a business, while surrounded by a community of strong, smart women who had my back. And the thought made me feel more capable than I had in years.

· · ·

THE NEXT AFTERNOON, the rich scent of coffee and fresh pastries battled with the aroma of sawdust and primer in my kitchen. Liv sat at my cluttered table, a pink bakery box open between us, her expression one of professional admiration.

"Iris, you are killing it," she said before taking a sip from the *World's Best Proprietress* mug I'd bought myself as a joke. "This place has incredible bones. I can totally see your vision now."

My lips rose. We'd just finished the tour, and showing off the progress to someone who understood the grit and grind of building a business from scratch was incredibly validating. "It's getting there. I love how the house is showing itself piece by piece since Gus started working."

"It's going to be gorgeous." Liv took a bite of a flaky croissant she'd brought. "Listen, just a heads-up, the health inspector is a real stickler for hand-washing sink placement. He made me move mine twice. Make sure Gus has it exactly to code, or he'll make you tear it out."

"Oh, wow. Thank you for the warning." I made a mental note to double-check with Gus. This was the kind of practical advice I needed. "See? This is why I need you in my life. You're my construction fairy godmother."

Liv laughed, a rich, throaty sound. "Us small-business gals have to stick together. Besides, I know a local woman who does custom linens for half the price of the big suppliers. She's a genius. Here's her number." She slid a business card across the table.

I picked it up, and a wave of gratitude filled me to bursting. "Liv, thank you. I don't even know what to say."

"Don't say anything. Just make sure you save me a room for a girls' weekend when you open." Her gaze drifted to the window, which looked out over my jungle of a yard and, beyond the hibiscus hedge, to Austin's neat, orderly conch house. "So how's the grumpy neighbor situation? Has he called the noise police on you yet?" I'd explained the situation in rather broad strokes when I sought her out for the lavender-lemon scone intervention.

A blush crept up my neck, and I busied myself by pouring more coffee. "Actually, things are better. After a lot of apology cookies and one very precarious ladder incident… we kind of figured things out. And now we're a couple. I still can hardly believe it."

"A couple? With the hibiscus guy?" Liv's face broke into a wide, delighted grin. "Get out! Who is he?"

"Austin Coleridge." It felt good to say it out loud to a friend who wasn't a Coleridge. A sense of relief, of normalcy, washed over me.

"Austin? Really?" Liv's face broke into a wide, delighted grin. "Well, good for you! I've met him a few times when he's come into the bakery. He doesn't say much, but you can just tell he's a solid guy. He has that quiet, dependable vibe, and he's Brenna's brother to boot. A great reputation on the island, too." She paused, her expression turning thoughtful. "Thank God the Coleridge-Markham feud is officially over."

"A feud?" My eyes widened. "Brenna mentioned something about that once. Oh my gosh, was it like the Hatfields and McCoys, but in flip-flops?"

Liv roared with laughter. "Not quite that dramatic, but close enough for Dove Key. Just old family stuff. But that chapter is closed. Brenna and Hunter's romance basically forced a truce. You don't need to worry about being involved with a Coleridge."

Her easy acceptance, her positive view of Austin, was the final piece of the puzzle. It solidified the feeling that I was on the right path, both with the house and with him.

I stared out the window at the vibrant red of the

hibiscus hedge, the one I had nearly drowned, the one he and I had worked on together. Not that long ago, I'd been an outsider, an amateur wrestling with a haunted house. Now, sitting here with a new friend and Austin's strength just a stone's throw away, I experienced something else entirely. A deep and wonderfully solid hope.

Chapter Twenty

IRIS

ISLAND MARKET on a weekday afternoon was a different beast than on the weekend. The aisles were less crowded, the energy more focused. Locals on their way home from work were picking up something for dinner. A few sunburnt tourists wandered aimlessly, looking for aloe vera and souvenir keychains.

My gaze landed on a display of dubious-quality toolkits at the end of the aisle. Screwdrivers, pliers, all neatly arranged in molded plastic cases. It sparked an idea, a welcome distraction from my Austin-centric thoughts. With Gus and his crew making such progress, I was spending less time putting out fires and more time thinking about the finer details of the B&B. I needed a better system for keeping track of it all. A proper notebook was what I needed. A dedicated place to record my observations and chart the course for Heron House's grand resurrection.

I marched toward the school and office supply aisle tucked away at the back of the store. A proprietress ensconced in a major renovation should, at the very least, have a pretty notebook to document her journey. The aisle was a surprisingly cheerful oasis of color and order in the sprawling market. I was pleased upon spotting my target, a surprisingly wide array of notebooks. I studied them, debating the merits of college-ruled versus wide-ruled, modern gray marble versus a more optimistic floral pattern.

A man stood further down the aisle. He wore the dark-blue uniform of the Dove Key Fire Department, the crisp white lettering stark against the fabric. He was tall, with a muscular, capable build, and was intently studying a display of brightly colored index cards. As he turned slightly to reach for a package, I caught a glimpse of his profile, the strong line of his jaw. He must have sensed me watching because he glanced over, his gaze meeting mine for a brief, fleeting moment. He gave a short nod of acknowledgment, which I returned before turning my attention to the notebooks. His bright green eyes immediately reminded me of Brenna. They were the same shade, though his were more guarded.

An employee with her cart bustled down the aisle, her sensible shoes squeaking on the tile. She had a sour expression with frown lines embedded around her mouth. She stopped cold when her gaze landed on the man in the uniform, and her lips thinned further.

"Ben. Finding everything you need in the school supply aisle?" Her voice dripped with an icy politeness that was somehow more offensive than outright rudeness.

The man—Ben, apparently—didn't flinch. He turned to face her, his expression flat, unimpressed. "Looking for some new index cards."

"Index cards," the woman repeated, drawing the words out as if they were a strange and exotic contraband he had no business possessing. My eyes widened. She looked him up and down, as if studying him for stolen merchandise.

Ben's gaze remained steady. "Because I'm in school, Francine," he replied, his tone still flat, but with an underlying edge of steel. "Hence, school supplies."

"Fine." Francine sniffed. She gave him another long, hard look, a look that was full of a history I couldn't begin to understand, then huffed and pushed her cart away without another word.

I stood there with a floral-print notebook clutched in my hand, a hot flare of indignation burning in my chest on his behalf. I didn't know what the story was, but I knew rudeness when I saw it.

Ben was staring after Francine, the cool reserve in his green eyes now tinged with weary frustration.

"Wow. And I thought I got the third degree around here sometimes." I offered a sympathetic smile. "Maybe being new in town is easier than being a local."

His head snapped toward me, his brows reaching halfway up his forehead. Then a laugh escaped him, a short, sharp bark that transformed his face and chased away the shadows. The coolness in his eyes warmed instantly, replaced by a friendly, appreciative light. "You might have a point there. Sometimes, no matter how hard you try to make a new start, people will only see the past." He gestured with the package of index cards in his hand. "I'm trying to make one, actually. A new start."

"Oh?" I asked, curious now as I strolled closer.

"Just started the coursework to become a paramedic." The flicker of pride in his voice was quickly dashed as he looked at the floor. He continued in a lower tone, "Trying to get a jump on the memorization. Figured flashcards couldn't hurt."

"That's amazing! Congratulations." The thought of

someone so dedicated and serious on the local rescue squad was reassuring. "That sounds like a huge amount of work."

A small, self-conscious smile returned to his lips. "It is. But hopefully worth it." He paused, then his expression shifted, his gaze direct and polite. He held out a hand. "Ben Coleridge, by the way."

My brain did a little stutter-step. Coleridge. Of course. The green eyes. The reserved intensity. Austin's brother.

I shook his hand, his grip firm and warm. "Iris Holloway. It's nice to meet you, Ben. I'm… I'm Austin's neighbor. The one trying to resurrect Heron House."

His eyes widened in recognition. "Oh, right. The B&B." He smiled again, and this time it was warmer. "Chase was telling me about it. Said you've got a hell of a project on your hands, but a great vision for it."

So the family knew about the project. That made sense. But Ben's open demeanor gave no indication that he knew anything more. That he knew his reclusive brother was spending his nights tangled up in the sheets of the new neighbor.

"It's a beast," I admitted with a laugh, "but I'm getting there. My new contractor, Gus, is fantastic."

"That's good to hear. You need a good team on a job like that."

I could see the family resemblance now, not just in his features, but in the underlying steadiness he projected, that same solid, dependable quality I'd come to recognize in Austin. But where Austin's steadiness was wrapped in layers of grumpy, keep-your-distance armor, Ben's was more approachable.

"Well," he said, lifting his package of index cards. "Gotta get these home and put them to use. Pharmacology isn't going to memorize itself, unfortunately." He gave me another one of those smiles. "It was nice meeting you, Iris. Welcome to Dove Key, officially."

"You too, Ben," I said.

Then he walked away, his stride confident and his uniformed shoulders straight. I absently grabbed a notebook with a vibrant floral cover, but my mind was no longer on stationery. I paid for my groceries in a daze, the earlier contentment now replaced by a swirling mix of new thoughts and questions.

Meeting Ben, seeing that brief, ugly flash of small-town judgment from the woman in the aisle, hearing the pride in his voice as he talked about his new path… it solidified something for me.

The Coleridges weren't just a family. They were an institution in this town. For better or for worse, they were known. Their history, their triumphs, and their failures were all part of the local lore. I knew the solitary, intense, surprisingly tender man next door, the man who built walls so high it was a miracle anyone could scale them.

I didn't know the respected fishing captain.

And most importantly, I didn't know the brother, the man who was part of this complex, tight-knit, deeply rooted family.

In that moment, a more painful realization hit me. Ben's friendly but polite demeanor gave no indication he knew anything more about me. To him, I was just the neighbor. Austin hadn't told them about us.

The thought was a hard thud in my chest. I needed to see that other side of him, to understand the place that had shaped him. It wasn't just idle curiosity. It was a necessity. If this was going to be real, we had to exist publicly as a couple. If I was going to have any hope of understanding the man, I had to understand his world.

And I was determined to find a way to get him to let me in.

THAT EVENING, a comfortable, almost domestic rhythm had settled over my kitchen, one that had become familiar over the past weeks. Austin leaned against the counter near the sink as I put the finishing touches on dinner. He'd shown up at my door half an hour ago, flimsy excuses long gone. Now we shared a quiet, unspoken understanding that this was just what we did.

The air was filled with the scent of the roast chicken I'd made, the sharp, herby aroma of the vinaigrette for the salad, and the warm, yeasty smell of the crusty bread I'd picked up at the market.

I pulled a bottle of chilled Sauvignon Blanc from the refrigerator and held it up. "Wine? Or are you sticking with beer tonight?"

"Depends." His eyes glinted with a humor I was starting to get used to. "Are we celebrating something?"

"We could be. We could celebrate the fact that my house isn't actively trying to collapse on top of me today. Or that I met another one of your siblings without any major international incidents."

He pushed off the counter and closed the space between us, taking the wine bottle from my hand. "I'll get it." He found the corkscrew in the jumble of my utility drawer with an ease that spoke to his growing familiarity with my kitchen. "And for the record, all my siblings are pains in the ass. Don't let them fool you."

I laughed as I pulled two wine glasses from the cupboard. "Too late. I'm already friends with Brenna, remember?" I watched as he uncorked the wine, his hands moving with that unexpected grace. "I admit, I'm shocked, Captain. I had you pegged as strictly a beer-and-black-coffee man. Are you sure you can handle a fancy white wine?"

He finished pouring and handed me a glass. Then, to my complete shock and delight, he winked—a real, honest-to-goodness, slow wink that made my heart do a little stutter-step.

"Have to keep you on your toes. Besides," he added, his gaze dropping to my lips for a fraction of a second, "I figure drinking wine with you earns me some brownie points. Maybe I can cash them in later."

The joke, a clear callback to my pastry offensive, landed squarely in my chest, a warm, blossoming thing. This was easy. This was fun.

We sat at my kitchen table, the sounds of the island night just beginning to stir outside the open window—the chirp of crickets, the distant hum of a boat out on the water. The chicken was juicy, the bread crisp yet soft inside, the wine cold and perfect.

"Which sibling did you run into?"

"Ben, at Island Market."

He nodded, chewing on a piece of potato.

"We had a nice chat." I took a breath, mustering my courage. This was the moment. "It made me realize… I know you, but I don't really know you. Not all of you. I know the solitary, intense man next door, the one who likes my baking and who helped me with my siding." I looked up, meeting his gaze, trying to convey the sincerity, the real need behind my words. "But I don't know the world you come from. I'd love to see Sunset Siesta, Austin. The place your family built. I want to understand that part of you."

He stilled, his fork halfway to his mouth. The easy humor of a moment ago vanished, replaced by that familiar, guarded intensity. He put his fork down slowly, his gaze dropping to his plate as he considered my words. The silence stretched, and I held my breath, my heart starting to pound again as I prepared for disappointment.

When he glanced up, his eyes searched mine, a silent, internal war raging in their depths. I could see the instinct to refuse, to shut me down, to retreat back into safety. Then, he let out a slow, heavy breath, a sound of a decision made. "Yeah. All right. I suppose I can show you around the place."

Relief, and more than a little surprise, flooded through me. A wide, uncontrollable smile broke across my face. "Really? Austin, I can't wait."

He tilted his head to study the sky outside the window. "How about tomorrow? If the weather holds, we could take *Line Dancer* out for a bit afterwards. See a proper sunset from the water."

My jaw actually dropped. This was more than I had hoped for. He wasn't just agreeing to let me into his world. He was inviting me into his most sacred space: his boat, the ocean.

"I would love that. So much."

The tension in the room shifted again, the earlier ease replaced by a new, humming, electric current. The tour, the sunset, that was all for tomorrow. My mind was no longer on the future. It was on him. Right here. Right now.

My dinner was forgotten. I pushed my chair back and stood, closing the space between us until I was standing beside his chair. He looked up at me, his eyes dark and questioning.

I didn't say anything. I just leaned down, tangling my fingers in his thick, dark hair, and skated my lips over his. It was a kiss full of the gratitude, hope, and spooling desire that was coursing through me. He responded instantly, his hand coming up to cup the back of my neck, his thumb stroking my skin as he pulled me deeper. The kiss was hot, hungry, a confirmation of everything that had been building between us.

I pulled back just enough to trail my lips along the rough, stubbled line of his jaw, inhaling the masculine scent of him—salt, sea, and pure, complicated Austin.

"You know, all this talk about tomorrow is great." I kissed the corner of his mouth, and his breath stuttered. "But I'm very concerned about the structural integrity of my bedroom. After all that demolition upstairs." My voice was pure, playful seduction. "It needs a thorough inspection."

A low growl rumbled in his chest, and I felt it vibrate all the way to my toes. He turned his head, capturing my mouth again for another deep, soul-stealing kiss. When he pulled away, his eyes were burning, all traces of the guarded, grumpy neighbor completely gone, replaced by the raw, possessive man I was coming to know in the darkness of my bedroom..

"Is that right?" His voice was a low, rough purr. "Maybe I should come check it out for you."

He stood, his tall frame dwarfing me, and took my hand, his calloused fingers lacing through mine. He led me from the kitchen, leaving our half-eaten dinner and the bottle of wine forgotten on the table. Halfway up the grand staircase, on the second-floor landing, I pushed him against the wall and slammed my lips into his. With a groan, he spun me around and grabbed my ass, lifting me and holding me against the plaster. We didn't even make it to my room. Instead, we ended up checking the structural integrity of the staircase.

Chapter Twenty-One

AUSTIN

"OH MY," Iris breathed, stepping inside. "Austin, this is simply beautiful."

We stood within one of the newly completed rooms in Room Block One. The resort had two of these cinderblock units, each containing two floors. The room was clean and modern, but we'd been careful to keep the Old Florida charm intact. The walls were a soft, sandy white, the furniture a mix of solid teak with live-edge details and crisp, soft-blue linen upholstery. Glass doors at the far end of the room opened onto a private balcony with a breathtaking, unobstructed view of the ocean.

Yesterday, agreeing to show her the resort had seemed simple. Natural. Hell, I'd even thrown in a trip on *Line Dancer* without a second thought. But now the reality felt more like a treaty I'd signed without reading the fine print. Walking Iris through the resort was putting my entire life under a microscope. This place was my history, my family, my failures, and showing it all to her was the first, terrifying clause.

The idea was almost as daunting as the next stop on our tour. I just hoped my brothers would keep their damn mouths shut for five minutes. It was a fool's hope, and I knew it. When I'd mentioned casually in a group text that I might be bringing her by, I could practically see them rubbing their hands together in anticipation.

Despite my disquiet, a flicker of pride ran through me at her reaction to the resort. "It turned out pretty well."

"Pretty well? It's incredible!" She walked over to the balcony door and peered out. "The colors, the view... it feels so peaceful. Like you could just leave the whole world behind out here."

I pointed across the resort grounds toward the building currently shrouded in scaffolding and construction netting. "That's Room Block Two over there. Looks like hell now, but it'll have the same result. We learned a few things from this block that Chase is applying over there."

"I can see why having him for a partner is such a boon." Stepping away from the door, she ran a finger over the back of the sofa, a wistful expression on her face.

"His ideas are smart, even if he does need to be reined in from time to time."

We walked back outside, the late-afternoon sun warming our faces. I led her past the renovated pool area and pointed to the subtly textured gray surface. "Chase designed the deck finish. Palm fronds are embossed right into the concrete."

She bent down, tracing one of the elegant, ghostly leaf patterns with her finger. "Beautiful. It's those little details that make a place special."

She got it. Her immediate appreciation for the craftsmanship, the thought that had gone into it, impressed me. We passed the new pool bar, a tiki-style hut with a gleaming mahogany top, where a few guests were enjoying a cocktail. Chase was there, talking to the resort assistant manager, and he gave us a quick wave.

"Driftwood Grill is over there." I gestured toward the main resort restaurant. "We're renovating it in stages so it can stay open. It's a logistical nightmare, according to Harper."

"But you're making it work," she said, her tone full of admiration. "I hope I can bring a similar feel to Heron House when it's all said and done."

I nodded toward the pier and the two boats bobbing gently in their slips, their hulls reflecting the glittering water. "That's where we're headed eventually. But first, a drink." I pointed toward the cheerful structure of Tidal Hops. "My brother Braden's place."

"A tour and a beer?" she said, a teasing smile playing on her lips. "Be still my heart, Captain. You're spoiling me."

I just grunted, but I couldn't stop the smile that raised the corner of my mouth. I wanted her to see this place the way I saw it—as more than just a business. But that feeling was unsettling, and I pushed it down to focus on the familiar path to the pub. I had enough to worry about with my brothers lying in wait.

Tidal Hops buzzed with the easy, late-afternoon energy of people who had spent their day in the sun and were now ready for a cold beer. The air smelled of hops, salt, and Braden's grilled fish tacos, and its turquoise walls and hung surfboards always made the place lively. But walking in with Iris beside me was like stepping onto a stage, the spotlight uncomfortably bright.

Braden was behind the bar, laughing at something a customer said. Eli and Ben sat at the far corner of the L-shaped bar. Eli was telling some story, his hands gesturing wildly, while Ben listened with his usual patience, a half-empty beer in front of him.

Three brothers. Three pairs of perceptive Coleridge eyes. Three different forms of interrogation.

Here we go.

Braden spotted us first and a slow grin spread across his face. It was the same look he got when he knew he had a winning hand in poker.

"Well, well, well," he said, his voice loud enough to draw the attention of Ben and Eli. "Look what the tide dragged in."

Our brothers turned on their stools. Eli's face broke into a wide, charming grin nearly identical to Braden's, though his dark-blue eyes held a sharper, more assessing light. He nodded, which caused a lock of sandy hair to fall over his forehead, and he swept it back casually. Ben just gave me his usual slow, perceptive nod. When his gaze slid to Iris, a flash of recognition swept over his face.

As we reached the bar, I gestured to the lineup. "Iris, this is the rest of the circus. My brothers—Braden, Eli, and you've met Ben."

"It's good to see you again, Ben," Iris said with a warm, easy smile.

"You too, Iris."

"So, this is the ambitious neighbor," Eli said, leaning forward. He looked slightly bewildered as he extended a hand. "The one who has my brother acting even stranger than usual. I'm Eli. It's a pleasure to meet the woman who has successfully weaponized baked goods."

Iris laughed as she shook his hand. "It's lovely to meet

you too. And the pastries are purely for diplomatic purposes, I assure you."

"What can I get you?" Braden asked Iris. "First one's on the house. A thank you for keeping this one," he jerked his head toward me, "semi-socialized."

Iris laughed. "I'll have whatever IPA he's having," she said, pointing to Ben's glass of Hopical Storm.

Eli let out a low whistle. "Likes a hoppy IPA. Good taste." He winked at her.

Then Harper appeared, moving through the crowd with the slow, deliberate grace of the heavily pregnant. She came to a stop beside us, her hand on her back. She was all belly now, a month from her due date, if she made it that long. She smiled warmly at Iris. "You must be Iris. I'm Harper. Welcome to Sunset Siesta."

"Thank you," Iris replied. "It's so good to meet you. And congratulations."

"Thanks. We're very excited." Harper's eyes flicked to me, warm and approving, but they contained a deeply curious look I felt more than saw. "Terrified, but excited."

"We saw Chase for a moment, but I didn't get a chance to thank him again," Iris continued. "His help at Heron House was invaluable. My new contractor is a godsend."

"That's my Chase. Miracles guaranteed." She stayed for another minute, chatting easily with Iris about the horrors and joys of renovating an old Keys property, before patting her belly and making her excuses. "Okay, these two are demanding I go put my feet up. It was so nice to meet you, Iris."

She gave me another one of those searching looks and then she was gone, leaving me feeling like I'd just passed the first round of a subtle, complicated interview.

"So, Iris, Austin tells us nothing," Eli said with the

subtlety of a whale shark. "What's the story with Heron House? Are you finding any pirate treasure? Any ghosts in the attic?"

"Not yet," Iris said, playing along easily as I cupped my hand around her waist. "But I did find a family of squirrels living in the chimney, which was its own kind of terrifying treasure hunt. We had to call a specialist to lure them out. It was a whole three-day saga involving marshmallows and a lot of very angry chittering noises."

The way she told the story, with self-deprecating humor and dramatic flair, had Eli roaring. "A squirrel saga! I love it! See, Austin? This is what we're missing. Stories! All you ever tell us about is barnacles and bait."

"Someone around here has to work," I grumbled good-naturedly, taking a sip of my beer. But I watched Iris, almost hypnotized, as she effortlessly charmed my brothers. She wasn't intimidated. She wasn't trying too hard. She was just herself, and they were clearly eating it up.

"Oh, for the love of pelicans," she said, shaking her head as she finished her squirrel story. "It was an absolute mess."

Eli, who had been mid-sip of his beer, choked and sputtered into a fit of coughing hysterics. "Pelicans?" he wheezed, looking at me with unabashed delight. "She invokes seabirds in moments of high drama?"

Iris shrugged. "Well, I find a little whimsy in speech adds flavor to the conversation."

Silent for a moment, Eli just stared at her. Then he turned to me. "Austin, where have you been hiding this woman? Don't you dare screw this up."

I just glared at him over the rim of my glass, but the corner of my mouth was twitching again. I patted her waist with my hand. Eli was still smiling, but as he held my gaze, his eyes were serious, evaluating. He liked to play the humor card, but few people were more perceptive. As Eli took a drink, successfully this time, Iris turned to Ben, who had been listening with a quiet, amused smile.

"So, Ben." Her tone changed, becoming more curious. "How are the paramedic studies going? Are you enjoying it?"

The shift was subtle, but I saw it. The way she gave him her full attention, remembering their conversation from the market. Ben straightened up slightly, pleased by her interest, and began to tell her about a particularly challenging pharmacology section he was working on.

As I watched them, a new and unfamiliar feeling settled in my chest. Pride. I was proud of her. Proud of the way she was navigating this gauntlet of my family with such easy grace and humor.

Braden chose that moment to lean toward me. "Hey, Austin." His earlier teasing was gone, replaced by a more serious tone. "Come check out the new glycol setup for the keg lines in the back. I want your opinion on it."

Eli, ever the opportunist, immediately chimed in. "Yeah, I've been wanting to see this too. Ben, you hold down the fort."

It was a setup. The glycol lines had been working fine for months. But I also knew there was no getting out of whatever they wanted to say. With a sigh, I pushed back from the bar and followed my brothers into the back room. A cold sense of dread settled in the pit of my stomach.

The back room of Tidal Hops was a cluttered space that smelled of yeast and cleaning solution. Stacks of kegs, some gleaming and new, some scarred and dented, lined one wall. Shelves overflowed with spare parts, coiled hoses, and boxes of pint glasses.

And right now, it was more like an interrogation chamber.

Braden pulled the door shut behind us. The cheerful noise of the brewpub instantly muffled, leaving us in a humming silence broken only by the low thrum of a cooling unit. He didn't head for the glycol lines. Instead, he leaned back against a stack of kegs. The easygoing, charming bartender was gone.

Eli moved to stand beside him, his posture relaxed. But the playful light in his eyes had been extinguished, replaced by the same focused intensity he got when he was mapping out a deep wreck dive.

"Okay," Eli's voice was low but direct, leaving no room for bullshit. "What's the real story, Austin? She seems great. Genuinely great. Are you serious about this?"

Even though I'd expected something like this, I bristled at the question, at the sudden shift from casual banter to intense scrutiny. I took a half step back to create some distance, crossing my arms over my chest.

"I like her," I said, my voice flat. "We're seeing what happens. It's not a big deal." The words were a practiced litany of deflection, words I'd been telling myself for weeks. They sounded hollow, even to me.

"Not a big deal?" Braden pushed off the kegs. "Austin, you haven't brought a woman around us, around the family, in… ever. You don't do 'seeing what happens.' You do 'keep your distance.' You do 'don't get involved.' So don't treat us like we're idiots."

"We're happy for you, man," Eli added, his voice softer but no less pointed. "Really. But don't try to bullshit us that this isn't a big deal for you."

"Jesus, if I knew I was going to get the finger screws, I would have stayed away."

"Austin, we couldn't help but notice," Eli added. "The blonde hair. The blue eyes. That sweet but stubborn way she has about her…"

Every muscle in my body went rigid. I knew where this was going. An icy dread, heavy and familiar, seeped into the room, chilling the air. I could almost smell the ozone of a coming storm.

"He's right." Braden stepped closer. He lowered his voice, making the words, when they came, hit even harder. "Iris is great, Austin. But she's so much like… like her. We have to ask, man. Are you trying to create another Caitlin here?"

The name hit me like a fist to the gut. Knocked the air from my lungs and left me cold, the walls of the small room suddenly closing in.

Caitlin.

A name I hadn't heard spoken aloud in this family for thirteen years.

Freezing, white-hot anger surged through me, a desperate, defensive fury. "What the hell did you just say?"

"Austin…" Eli raised a palm, his expression full of caution.

"Don't say her name," I warned, my voice tight, my hands clenched into fists. "This has nothing to do with her. Nothing to do with them. Do you understand me?"

The thought was ludicrous. Insulting.

I had never, not for one single second, compared the two women. Iris, with her chaotic energy, her growing competence, her ridiculous G-rated curses, and her mostly irresistible baking… she was nothing like Caitlin. She was her own unique, infuriating, wonderful person. The idea that my brothers could think I was just… what? Trying to fix the past? It was obscene.

But I saw it in their eyes. The quiet pity. The concern. The fact that they weren't convinced. And that pissed me off more than anything. I pressed my trembling hands against my hips.

"This is about me and Iris." My voice came out in a low growl. "That's it. It's not about… before. It's not about anyone else. I'm not some damn charity case you all need to manage." I took a deep, shuddering breath, trying to get my emotions under control. "We're done here. Drop it. Now."

I didn't wait for them to respond. I turned, yanked the door open, and strode back out into the noise and light of the brewpub. The ghosts of the past swirled around me. I walked back to the bar, my whole body tight with a cold, protective anger as my brothers followed. The easy, cheerful atmosphere of the brewpub sounded abrasive. I could feel Eli and Braden's gazes on my back, but I refused to turn around.

Iris glanced up as I approached, her smile warm, then questioning. The light in her eyes dimmed slightly, her smile faltering as she took in my stony expression. "Is everything okay?"

The honest answer was no. Nothing was okay.

My brothers had just ripped open a thirteen-year-old wound and poured salt all over it. The old, familiar instinct screamed at me.

Push her away before it gets too deep, before the risk becomes too great. Before you have something you can't bear to lose again.

But then I looked at her.

At the genuine concern in her eyes, the way her brow was furrowed with worry. For me. And something inside me stronger than the fear, something more stubborn than the pain, made a choice.

I would not let the specters of my past poison this. I would not let my brothers' well-meaning but misguided fears dictate my future. I forced the tension from my shoulders and deliberately unclenched my jaw. I manufactured a smile. It probably looked pathetic, but it was the best I could do.

"Yeah." My voice was a little rough. I cleared my throat and tried again, my smile feeling steadier. "Everything's fine. Braden was just showing me his new collection of artisanal bottle caps."

She knew I was lying. I could see it in the way her eyes searched mine. But she didn't push. She just gave an accepting nod.

"Ready to get out of here?" I placed my hand between her shoulder blades to ground myself in her presence, pleased my tone was gentler now. "The sun's starting to set, and the water should be like glass."

"Absolutely," she said, her smile returning.

We said our goodbyes, a chorus of "Nice to meet you, Iris!" and "See you later!" following us out the door. I could feel my brothers' eyes on us the entire time. I didn't care.

As we walked along the pier, the scent of salt and frangipani heavy in the evening air, she gently bumped her shoulder against mine. "So was everything really okay back there? You seemed, uh, tense."

I looked down at her, at the line between her brows that hadn't been there before. "Just stupid brother shit." I caught the word as it left my mouth. "Uh, stuff. Stupid brother stuff."

The unconscious correction, the automatic softening of my language for her, was both ridiculous and scarily significant.

She smiled. "I get it. Stupid sibling stuff is a universal language, even to an only child."

The wooden planks were solid beneath our feet and soon the warm air with its gentle breeze worked its magic on me. The sky was beginning its nightly spectacle, streaks of orange and pink painting the western horizon.

She pointed toward the two boats bobbing gently in their slips. "Which is which?"

I nodded toward the larger, more functional-looking vessel. "That's *Sunset Diver*. Eli's domain. It's set up for a dozen divers, gear racks, a big platform to jump off." I gestured to my boat. "And that's *Line Dancer*. Smaller, faster. More agile. Built for finding and fighting fish, not for sightseeing. But," I added, turning to smile at her, "she cleans up nice for a sunset."

We stopped next to the stern of my boat. The water lapped against the hull in its gentle, rhythmic song.

Iris shifted her gaze from the boat to me, her eyes sparkling in the golden light. "Permission to come aboard, Captain?"

I stared at her, this beautiful, resilient woman who had turned my entire world upside down. I thought of my brothers back at the bar, watching through the windows and still dissecting my every move. I thought of their words, of Caitlin, of the past.

A surge of pure, defiant possessiveness washed through me.

Let them watch.

I leaned in, cupped her face in my hands, and lowered my mouth to hers.

It was a statement. A public, deliberate claiming. I kissed her deeply, possessively, right there on the dock in the golden light of the setting sun. A clear, unmistakable message to anyone who might be looking.

She was with me.

This was real.

This was happening.

She gasped into my mouth, then melted against me,

her hands coming up to grip my arms, returning the kiss with an answering fire of her own.

When I pulled back, her lips were swollen, her breath faster. I darted a glance past her toward Tidal Hops, then dropped my gaze back to hers. "Permission very much granted. Let's go."

I took her hand and led her aboard.

Chapter Twenty-Two

IRIS

MY LIPS WERE STILL TINGLING, my entire body humming with the aftershock of Austin's kiss. It hadn't been a tentative kiss. It had been a message. A clear signal sent right across the water to his entire nosy, well-meaning family at the brewpub.

A sharp, tremulous thrill shot through me.

I reeled from the emotional whiplash of it all. The easy camaraderie at the bar, Austin's stony face when he returned from the back room, and now… this. His possessive and possibly world-altering kiss. A certainty settled deep in my bones that something significant had gone down in that back room, something that had pushed him to make this public statement. And I understood this man well enough to know that pushing him to talk about it would be fruitless.

Austin moved on his own timeline.

Stepping onto *Line Dancer* was like stepping into another world. Austin's world. It wasn't a luxury yacht,

"

designed for champagne and indulgent selfies. It was a serious, hardworking fishing machine that exuded competence. The deck was spotless, every rope coiled with a precision so quintessentially Austin it made me smile. Rods stood at attention in their holders like well-disciplined soldiers. The air smelled of salt, diesel, and the faint, clean scent of the sea itself. I had a strange sense of privilege, a feeling that he was sharing a part of himself he didn't share with many people.

He moved with an easy, practiced grace, his body perfectly in tune with the rhythm of the boat. He untied the thick mooring lines with a few efficient movements, his muscles flexing under his shirt. Jumping behind the helm, he flicked a series of switches, and the twin diesel engines rumbled to life, a low, powerful thrum that vibrated up from the deck and through the soles of my shoes.

"You can sit there." He nodded toward the cushioned bench seat beside the helm. "Or hold on. Whatever you do, don't fall overboard. The paperwork is a nightmare."

The corner of his mouth twitched, his way of cutting through the lingering intensity of the kiss. And the mysterious meeting.

My lips curled in response as I settled onto the bench seat. "Aye, aye, Captain."

He guided *Line Dancer* away from the pier and through the channel, the setting sun glinting off the water and turning it to molten gold. The tense, cornered man from the back room of Tidal Hops was gone. In his place was Captain Coleridge, a man in his element, at peace with the vast expanse of the sea.

Once we cleared the last of the channel markers, Austin pushed the throttles forward. *Line Dancer* surged ahead, the bow lifting as we sliced cleanly through the turquoise water. The wind whipped my hair back from my face, tasting of salt and freedom. Austin stood tall with one hand resting lightly on the wheel, his gaze fixed on the horizon. He wasn't staring at the glowing GPS screen or the complex-looking radar display.

"How do you know where you're going?" I had to raise my voice slightly over the roar of the engines.

He glanced at me, a flicker of surprise in his eyes, as if the answer was something he never even thought about.

"See that dark patch over there?" He pointed to a section of green-tinged water about a half-mile off our port side. "That's a grass flat. Good for bonefish. The channel runs just to the east of it. And that distant smudge on the horizon?" He gestured straight ahead. "That's Pigeon Key. I've known these waters since I was a kid. Don't need a machine to tell me where I am. The GPS is for fog and tourists."

The quiet confidence in his voice, the deep, ingrained knowledge of his home, was more impressive than any display of bravado could ever be. Relaxing, I enjoyed the shifts in color of the water and the birds circling in the sky.

After another ten minutes, he throttled back, guiding the boat into a protected cove, the water here an other-worldly, jewel-toned aqua. The silence was sudden and profound, broken only by the gentle lapping of water against the hull.

"All right." He turned to face me, his expression open and at ease in the soft, golden light. "Let's see if we can do better than a rainbow trout."

"You're going to teach me to fish?" I asked, clapping my hands. "After my less-than-impressive story?"

A smile touched his lips. "Consider it an effort to redeem your angling reputation. My first rule of fishing is don't hook yourself or, more importantly, the captain."

"Duly noted," I said with a laugh. "That seems like a solid life rule in general."

He moved with that easy competence I found so alluring, selecting a lighter spinning rod from the impressive arsenal arranged in the rocket launchers overhead.

REACHING INTO HIS BACK POCKET, he pulled out a small, worn canvas pouch. His nimble fingers untied the drawstring and selected a small, sharp hook with a short piece of line attached. He tied it to the rod with a series of swift, intricate knots.

"Ah, a man prepared." I had to smile. "Do you always carry fishing hooks around in your pocket?"

He glanced at me, a flicker of amusement eyes. "I keep this pouch on the boat. Then in my pocket when I'm on board. It's kind of a part of me."

He tucked it away carefully before baiting the hook with a piece of shrimp in a few swift, practiced movements. "Okay, come here."

I slid off the bench seat and stood in front of him at the rail. He stood behind me, his body a solid wall of heat at my back. One of his calloused hands covered mine on the cork grip, the other gently adjusted my fingers on the reel. A hint of his scent wafted toward me. I was intensely, overwhelmingly aware of every point of contact—his chest against my shoulder blades, the rough texture of his jeans against the back of my legs, his warm breath stirring the hair near my ear as he leaned in to speak.

"It's all in the wrist." His voice was a low rumble close to my ear. "You don't need to throw it a mile. Just a quick flick. Bring it back here…" He guided my arm back. "And snap it forward. Like this."

He helped me with the first cast, our bodies moving

together in a single, coordinated motion. The line sailed out, the light weight plopping neatly into the water about twenty feet from the boat. It was far more graceful than any cast I'd ever attempted on my own.

He let me try the next few casts by myself. Most were clumsy, landing with an ungraceful splash much closer to the boat. But Austin was a patient teacher, correcting my stance, reminding me to keep my wrist loose, his instructions calm and clear. There was no hint of the impatient, gruff man who had glared at me over a broken sprinkler head. Out here, he was a different person. Calm, confident, and in control.

On my fifth or sixth attempt, something tugged on the line.

"Got one," he said, his voice instantly sharp, professional. "Okay, reel it in. Steady. Keep the tip up."

My pulse hummed with excitement. I cranked the reel, the rod bending with the weight of the fish. It wasn't a huge fight, but it was a battle. With Austin's coaching, I brought it alongside the boat. He leaned over with a net and scooped it out of the water.

According to him, the fish was a grunt. Maybe six inches long, its silver scales flashed in the setting sun, a jewel from the sea.

"Well, look at that." The warm approval in his voice made my chest swell. "You're a natural."

He showed me how to hold it carefully, avoiding the spiny dorsal fin, his fingers brushing mine as he guided my hands. The fish was surprisingly solid, its life force a vibrant, wriggling thing in my palm.

"Oh, look at him," I breathed, grinning completely. "He's kind of small, though. Bigger than my trout, if I recall, but maybe we should throw him back."

"Yeah, he's still got some growing to do."

He gently took the fish from me, removed the hook, and slid it back into the clear, blue water. It gave a flick of its tail and was gone.

The moment was significant, a quiet act of respect for the ocean. I glanced up at Austin and found him smiling at me, an unguarded smile that made crinkles appear at the corners of his gray eyes. And seeing him in his element, with the golden light of the setting sun on his face, something shifted inside me. Not just a flutter of attraction anymore.

My chest filled with something that felt dangerously, wonderfully, like falling.

The sun was a fiery orange ball now, kissing the horizon and painting the underside of the few stray clouds in brilliant streaks of pink and gold. The water around us transformed into a sheet of shimmering, liquid copper. It was the most beautiful thing I had ever seen.

After thoroughly washing our hands, I leaned back against the cushioned seat. A contented sigh escaped my lips. The tension of the last few weeks—the constant worry about the house, the contractors, the budget—all melted away out here, dwarfed by the sheer, magnificent scale of sky and sea.

Austin disappeared for a moment into the cabin before emerging with a thick, navy-blue blanket. Without a word, he draped it over both our shoulders as we sat side by side on the bench. We sat in a companionable silence for a long time, just watching the sky put on its nightly spectacle.

But my mind drifted back to the scene at Tidal Hops. The easy camaraderie between the brothers, then the jagged shift in the atmosphere after Austin had been pulled into the back room. Bolstered by the easy intimacy of the sunset, by the simple, solid weight of his arm now resting over my shoulders, I ventured into more dangerous waters.

"So," I said softly, my gaze still on the horizon, "I know we mentioned this, but was everything really okay at the brewpub? With Eli and Braden?"

Austin was quiet for so long I thought he was going to ignore the question. He tensed beside me, the easy relaxation of a moment ago evaporating. I almost wanted to take the question back, to fill the silence with some trivial comment about the beauty of the sunset.

"It's nothing," he said finally. "They like to give me a hard time."

It was a dismissal, a clear don't-pry signal, but this time I didn't let it go.

"It seemed a little more than that," I said gently, still not looking at him. "You were upset."

He let out a slow, heavy breath, a sound of pure, weary resignation. "They were thrown. I don't bring women around the family. Well, ever."

My heart gave a little squeeze at the admission. "Ever?"

He paused again, his gaze fixed on the last sliver of sun disappearing below the horizon, turning the water to a deep purple.

"I haven't been seriously involved with anyone in over a decade. The last time, a long time ago…" He paused, and I could feel the struggle in him, the immense effort it took to even speak these vague words. "The relationship ended badly. Unexpectedly. It—it shook me."

A vast, cold ocean of pain lay beneath that one, simple phrase.

It shook me.

Something had fundamentally changed a part of him, a part he had spent thirteen years carefully walling off. This was the reason for his solitude, his grumpy armor, his fierce, almost pathological, need for control.

With absolute certainty, I knew this was not the time to ask for more. He had just handed me this broken piece of his past in a profound act of trust, a gift more precious than any flower. My role now was not to question or pry, but simply to hold his trust, to show him it was safe with me.

I nodded, leaning my head gently against his shoulder. "Thank you for telling me that, Austin."

He didn't reply, but the tension in his shoulder eased. He shifted slightly, his arm tightening around me, pulling me into his warmth, his scent of salt and sea and safety.

We sat as the first stars began to prick the velvety darkness, the silence between us no longer awkward or charged, but full of a fragile and deeply felt understanding. He hadn't told me everything. He hadn't even told me much. But he had opened the door a little.

And for a man like Austin Coleridge, that was everything.

Eventually, he started the engines, the low rumble a comforting sound in the deepening twilight. He guided *Line Dancer* back toward Sunset Siesta. I stood near him, the soft blanket still draped over my shoulders, the warmth of his body a solid presence next to mine.

When we reached the dock, I moved with newfound confidence, helping him secure the lines as if it were the most natural thing in the world. I wasn't just a guest on his boat anymore. I felt like a partner, a first mate, however temporary.

Once the boat was secured, he turned to me in the soft glow of the dock lights and pulled me close. "I never mix drinking and boating. But now that we're safely tied up… how about a glass of wine?"

A slow smile spread across my lips. The earlier vulnerability was gone, replaced by the thrilling, electric hum of building desire.

"Oh?" I took a step closer, my hand skating across the stubble of his cheek. "Trying to earn more brownie points?"

He covered my hand with his own, his thumb stroking my skin and sending a bolt of searing heat through me. A lazy, devastatingly sexy smile touched his lips, the one that made my brain short-circuit.

"Do I need them?" His voice was a low, husky purr.

I leaned in, my lips brushing his, a silent promise of what was to come. "Absolutely not, Captain. Lead the way."

Chapter Twenty-Three

AUSTIN

I LED Iris into the cramped, stuffy cabin, a space so private and intrinsically mine that few people other than family had ever set foot in it. None of them had been a woman I'd just spent the evening falling even harder for. The thought was a fresh shock to my system. I flicked on the low cabin lights, and the space immediately became smaller and more intimate with her presence. I started the modular air-conditioning unit, its quiet hum a welcome buffer against the outside world.

I pulled a bottle of chilled Chardonnay from the tiny onboard fridge, a bottle I'd gotten from a server at Driftwood Grill earlier.

"A man of hidden talents." Iris's voice was full of amusement. "I didn't know you were a wine connoisseur."

"I'm not," I admitted with a smile as I worked the corkscrew. "But I know who to ask."

The cork came out with a soft, satisfying pop. I poured

the pale gold liquid into two sturdy, stemless glasses I'd also liberated from the restaurant.

I handed her a glass, our fingers brushing. The only real place to sit comfortably in the tight quarters was the double bed that took up the forward part of the cabin. I sat on the edge of the navy blanket, and she settled beside me, her knee just touching mine. The space was charged, alive with unspoken energy.

"Do you sleep in here much?" Her gaze took in the space—the neatly folded charts on the desk, the single book tucked beside my bunk.

"Not often," I said, taking a sip of wine. It was crisp, cold, with a hint of oak. "Once in a while. If I need to get away from everything. I'll take the boat out to one of the outer anchorages and just… be. It's peaceful out there."

"I can imagine," she said softly. She looked at me, her blue eyes searching, serious. "Thank you for showing me this side of you, Austin. The tour, the boat, your world."

The sincerity in her voice made my chest tighten. It was hard to breathe, hard to think. I didn't have the words to tell her what it meant to have her in my space, to explain the feeling of rightness, of peace, that had settled over me while we were out on the water and watching the sunset together. I settled for the only truth I could manage, a confession as risky and momentous as any deep-water dive.

"It feels different." I stared into my wine glass, unable to meet her gaze. "Being out there. It's freeing and honest. I… I liked showing that to you. Experiencing it with you."

When I finally risked a glance at her, her expression was one of acceptance and understanding. She gave me a soft smile, a look that seemed to see right through all the walls I'd spent years building. In that look, I knew she'd heard everything I couldn't say.

The silence that followed was a tangible thing, a warm

blanket settling over us. Iris held my gaze, her eyes full of a deep awareness that made my skin prickle. Reaching out, she took my wine glass and set it, along with her own, on the desk with a soft click.

The message was unmistakable. The talking was over.

She turned back to me, then leaned in and kissed me. This was a kiss of pure, confident intent—slow, deep, a mutual exploration that spoke of a conscious choice to fall into this together.

My attention was wholly consumed by her. By the taste of her—wine and sweetness and Iris. By the soft sigh that escaped her lips and slipped into my mouth. By the feel of her hands, no longer the tentative touch of a new lover, as they moved from my shoulders to cup my face, her thumbs stroking the rough scruff on my jaw.

When she pulled back just enough to look at me, her eyes were dark and luminous in the low light of the cabin. She straddled my lap, her knees sinking into the firm mattress on either side of my hips, her body fitting against mine with a rightness that sent a fresh jolt of heat straight to my groin.

"My turn to take charge, Captain." Her voice was a husky promise that made my pulse hammer.

This confident, assertive Iris was intoxicating. I found myself nodding, my hands settling on her waist, letting her know I was hers to command.

She undressed me. Slowly. Deliberately. Her gaze never left mine as her nimble fingers worked the buttons of my shirt, pushing the fabric aside. Her touch was light and inquisitive, tracing the lines of my collarbone, the curve of my shoulder, before she pushed the shirt off.

I was mesmerized, a willing captive. This slow, deliberate act of claiming me was a new kind of intimacy, a new power she held over me. I didn't want to fight it. At all.

I was already so hard it was painful. I didn't want this to end, yet I yearned for release. She slid gracefully from my lap to kneel on the fiberglass floor in front of me. The light caught in her hair, creating a messy, beautiful halo. Her eyes, full of sultry confidence I'd never seen before, lifted to meet mine as she reached for the button of my jeans.

"Let me," she whispered, and the command in her soft voice made my shaft twitch.

Her gaze held me pinned as she slid the zipper down, her knuckles a deliberate, searing brand against my straining length. She hooked her fingers into the waistband of my jeans, then my briefs, and slowly, inch by excruciating inch, pulled them down my legs and off, tossing them aside into the shadows.

I was completely exposed to her, physically and emotionally. She sat back on her heels, her eyes drinking me in. The way she looked at me—like I was something she wanted to devour—nearly undid me.

"You're beautiful," she said simply, and then she leaned forward and took me in her mouth.

A sharp, ragged breath tore from my lungs. The sensation was immediate, overwhelming, a bolt of pure, white-hot pleasure that obliterated all thought. Her mouth was hot, wet, and impossibly soft, her tongue a masterful torment.

And her eyes… she never broke eye contact.

She watched me, her eyes dark with concentration and a fierce, feminine power, as she gave me long, slow, deliberate sweeps. Her tongue traced, tasted, teased. The sight of her lips wrapped around me, the feel of her taking me deeper, was almost more arousing than the physical act itself.

My hands, acting on their own volition, came up to gently cup her head, my fingers tangling in the soft silk of her hair. A silent communication.

Yes.

Like that.

More.

A low, guttural groan tore from my throat, a sound of absolute surrender.

"Christ, Iris," I managed to rasp. "You're killing me."

She hummed around me, the vibration sending shockwaves through my body, and I had to bite back a curse. The pressure built inside me, coiling tighter and tighter, an urgent climb. I was close. Too close.

Gritting my teeth, I tightened my fingers gently in her hair and pulled her back.

"No." My voice was a raw, strained whisper I barely recognized. "Not yet. Your turn now."

She looked up at me with slick, swollen lips, her eyes dazed with arousal. She just nodded, a slow, sensual dip of her chin, and allowed me to pull her to her feet.

I had to tilt my head to keep from hitting the low cabin ceiling, a familiar motion, but everything else was brand new. I undressed her with a reverence that felt foreign, almost holy. My hands, which had spent a lifetime wrestling with nets and lines and boat engines, were gentle as I opened the buttons on her blouse, peeling it from her shoulders to reveal the simple, pretty lace of her bra. I kissed the warm, smooth skin of her shoulder, then the hollow of her throat, tasting her, breathing her in. Her dress pooled at her feet in a whisper of soft fabric.

I knelt before her, my mouth tracing a path down her stomach, swirling my tongue around her navel and earning a sharp, hitched breath from her. I pressed her gently back onto the bed, the cool air from the A/C unit blowing over my back as I tugged her panties down her long, shapely legs. I parted her thighs, revealing the flesh at her center. The scent of her was the most intoxicating thing I had ever known.

And then I took my turn.

I tasted her with focus and dedication, my tongue finding all the places that made her gasp and arch beneath me. I loved the shape of her, the taste of her, the involuntary sounds she made when I found a particularly sensitive spot. I listened to her body—to the way she gasped, her moans growing deeper, the way her muscles tensed beneath my hands as I held her hips. I experienced her pleasure as if it were my own, a rising tide of sensation that I was both controlling and at the mercy of.

"Austin," she gasped, her fingers fisting in the bedsheets. "Oh God."

I answered by increasing the pressure, the rhythm of my tongue quickening. She was close. I could feel it in the way her body began to tremble, in the sharp, staccato rhythm of her breathing. I pushed her farther, higher, determined to give her everything.

And then she shattered.

Her back arched off the bed, a sharp, piercing cry tearing from her throat as a wave of pure, convulsive pleasure ripped through her. Her release was a victory, a powerful, stunning moment of connection that left me feeling tremendously possessive.

I moved up onto the bed beside her as the aftershocks of her orgasm still trembled through her body. Her skin was flushed, her eyes dazed and unfocused, her lips parted on soft, ragged breaths. She looked completely unraveled, utterly beautiful, and entirely mine.

She turned her head on the pillow, her gaze finding mine as she reached for me. "I need you now."

I found my wallet and retrieved a condom. As I tore open the packet, Iris took it from me. Her fingers were deft and sure as she slowly, deliberately rolled it on, her warm touch a silken torment that nearly sent me over the edge.

"Easy," she whispered, her voice thick with desire. "I want to feel every second of this."

I was throbbing so fiercely I could barely think, a raw, aching need that was a physical pain.

We fell back onto the berth together, a blending of limbs and urgent need in the cool, conditioned air of the cabin. She parted her legs, welcoming me as I positioned myself between them. I looked down at her face, at the trust and undisguised desire there, and pushed into her in one deep, slow thrust.

Her gasp was a soft, breathy sound against my ear. The feeling of being inside her, so hot, so impossibly right, obliterated every coherent thought. There was no past, no future. No Heron House, no *Line Dancer*. There was only this. Only her.

The rhythm we found was slow and deep. Deliberate.

I pushed in.

She met me, her hips rising from the mattress.

Deep. Slow. Again.

Each movement was a conversation, a nonverbal confirmation of everything that had passed between us. Then she shifted, her hands on my shoulders. With a lithe movement, she rolled me onto my back, the mattress groaning in protest, and straddled me, taking me inside her again.

The sight of her above me, in control, sent a bolt of pure lust through my system. This was what I'd been craving without knowing it. Her confidence, her power, her complete ownership of the moment.

She sat up, her back arching, her hands threading through her wild, blonde hair and lifting it off her neck. The low light of the cabin sculpted the curves of her breasts, the flat plane of her stomach, the gentle flare of her hips.

And I was lost.

The sight of her, so confident and beautiful, was the most arousing thing I had ever seen. She was a siren in the low light of my cabin, claiming me. I was powerless to resist. I had no desire to resist.

"You like this," she said, her voice husky with satisfaction as she watched my face. "You like me taking charge."

"Yes," I managed to rasp, my hands gripping her hips. "God, yes."

She began to move, a slow, sensual rhythm that was pure, exquisite torture. My hands came up to grip her hips, my thumbs pressing into the soft skin, helping to guide her, to increase the friction, the pleasure, for both of us. But she was setting the pace, controlling the depth, the angle, everything.

"Faster?" she asked, her voice breathless but commanding.

"Whatever you want," I groaned. "You're in control."

The admission seemed to ignite something in her. She leaned forward, her hands braced on my chest, and began to move with more urgency. The pace quickened, her movements becoming more demanding, her breaths coming in sharp, ragged gasps that matched my own.

I watched her face, saw the moment she found the angle that made her cry out, saw her eyes flutter closed as she chased her pleasure. She was magnificent—wild and uninhibited and mine.

The wave built between us, a shared, rising tide. The coil of pleasure inside me spooled, past the point of bearing.

"Iris," I gasped out, my control shattering. "I'm—"

"Yes," she breathed, her movements becoming frantic. "Now."

She threw her head back, a cry tearing from her throat as her climax hit. It was that—her complete and total surrender in the midst of her dominance—that sent me over the edge. A deep, ragged groan ripped from my throat as my world exploded into a wave of white-hot, blinding release.

I don't know how long we lay there afterward, her body a welcome weight on top of mine. The only sounds were our harsh, ragged breathing slowly returning to normal. Her head was tucked into the curve of my neck, her hair tickling my chin. I held her, my arms wrapped tightly around her, my hand stroking her sweat-slicked back as the whirring A/C slowly dried it.

In the breathless aftermath, with the gentle rocking of the boat a soothing rhythm beneath us, the wall inside me cracked. I sensed the shift, a tectonic movement deep in my soul. This was a terrifying, undeniable connection to another human being.

Whether I wanted it or not, whether I was ready for it or not, this woman was a part of me now. She had burrowed her way past years of defenses, past all the warning signs and tripwires I'd so carefully laid. She was here, in my arms, in my sanctuary, in my head.

Most of all, I could no longer deny that she was deeply lodged in my heart.

Chapter Twenty-Four

AUSTIN

THE MORNING SUN beamed through the porthole, warm and gentle as it painted a gold stripe across Iris's bare shoulder. The side of my body was half propped up against the cool, curved fiberglass of the hull. She nestled next to me with my arms wrapped loosely around her.

For the first time in forever, my mind was quiet.

The usual pre-dawn litany of worries and old ghosts was absent. In its place was the steady rhythm of her breathing, the warmth of her skin against mine, and the sweet scent of her hair mingling with the comforting smell of saltwater and old wood that permeated every inch of *Line Dancer*. It was a fragile peace, an unfamiliar contentment that I was almost afraid to breathe, for fear it might shatter like glass.

She stirred, her sleepy blue eyes finding mine. A slow, languid smile spread across her lips, a smile meant only for me. "Morning, Captain."

"Hello there." I tightened my arm around her and pulled her closer.

Her gaze drifted to the corner of the cabin, where a half-dozen rods stood in their custom-built rack.

"Now that I'm a seasoned angler, I have to know." Her voice was full of lazy, morning curiosity. "What's the biggest fish you ever caught?"

A smile touched my lips at the memory. "A marlin. Just over eleven feet, I'd guess. Maybe four hundred pounds. Hooked him about twenty miles south of the reef."

Her eyes went wide. "You're kidding me. Four hundred pounds?"

"I was out alone a few years back. It was a grueling battle. Took me almost four hours to get him alongside the boat. My arms felt like they were going to fall off. My back was screaming. He was magnificent."

I could still see it, the brilliant cobalt blue of his back, the flash of silver. The sheer, raw power of the animal as he leaped from the water, silhouetted against the afternoon sun.

Her mouth hinged open. "An eleven-foot marlin! Austin, that's the fish of a lifetime. You have it mounted somewhere, right? I haven't seen it at your house. Where is it?"

I shook my head, the memory still vivid. "No. A beast that noble, that fierce… It fought too hard to end up as a dusty decoration on a wall." I paused, remembering the exhausted elation of that moment. "I got him alongside and took a quick picture with my phone for proof. Then I leaned over, worked like hell to get the hook out clean, and watched him swim away."

Iris was quiet for a moment, studying my face with new awareness. "None of this is about the sport for you, is it? The catching, the trophy. It's something more."

I glanced out the porthole to the glittering water. "I like being a part of it. Part of the process. The waves, the wind, the life humming just beneath the surface. It's… honest. Pure." The words were inadequate to explain the deep, spiritual connection I felt out on the open water. I gave a rough snort, a sound of self-deprecation. "As long as the wind isn't blowing a hundred miles an hour, anyway."

I'd meant it as a dark joke, a way to deflect from the depth of the conversation. But her smile faded, replaced by thoughtful curiosity.

"Have you been caught out in a bad storm?" She said the words in a soft voice, completely unaware of the land-mine she had just stepped on.

Everything inside me went still.

The gentle rocking of the boat, the warmth of Iris's body against mine, the soft morning light—it all vanished. Replaced by a sudden, roaring darkness, a memory so potent and so deeply buried it was like a physical thing clawing its way up my throat. The air grew thick with the taste of salt, ozone, and a freezing, metallic dread. My smile vanished as I went rigid. I squeezed my eyes shut, but it didn't matter.

The images were burned onto the backs of my eyelids.

Iris placed a gentle hand on my forearm. Her touch was a warm anchor in the sudden, violent maelstrom in my head. "Austin? I'm sorry. I didn't mean to touch a wound."

Neither her soft contact nor her murmured apology stopped the memory. But both steadied me, kept me from shoving her away and retreating into the cold silence I'd lived in for so long.

I opened my eyes and met hers. The trust there, the patient waiting, was the only thing that made the words possible. At long last, my guts unclenched. Not all the way, but enough.

"Maybe that wound finally needs to be touched." My voice came out a low, rough rasp I barely recognized. "Yes. I was in one terrible storm. The one that changed my life."

At her encouraging nod, I took a deep, shuddering breath.

"I was twenty-one. Thirteen years ago. It was supposed to be a perfect day. A double date. My girlfriend, Caitlin, and I. And my best friend, Leo, with his girlfriend, Beth. Leo had just bought his first boat, a twenty-two-foot center console. He was so damn proud of it. We were all just kids. Stupid kids who thought we were invincible."

My gaze went distant, past Iris, past the walls of the cabin, to that morning.

"The sky was gorgeous when we left the dock, but the air felt wrong. Heavy. I looked at the barometer before we cast off. It was falling like a stone thrown from a cliff. A voice in the back of my head, the voice my dad had spent years training into me, was pointing out that maybe this wasn't the best idea. That the ocean was getting ready to do something ugly."

I looked down at my hands, seeing them not as they were now, but as they had been then. Young and so sure. "There was barely a cloud in the sky, and Caitlin was so excited. Leo wanted to show off his new boat. So I ignored that voice. I told myself the barometer was just hinting at a temporary little squall. That we'd be fine if we stayed in the shallows. I knew better, Iris. I was the experienced one of the four of us. Yet I went anyway."

The guilt, still knife-sharp after all these years, was a lead weight on my chest, making it hard to breathe.

"We went out to a little cove an hour away that was nice and protected. Snorkeled for a while, hung out on the beach, laughing. It was perfect. One of those days you think you'll remember forever." I gave a short, bitter, humorless laugh. "I will remember it forever. Just not the way I was supposed to."

Iris turned so she could see me better, maintaining her gentle hold on my arm.

"We saw the line on the horizon around noon. It looked like a bruised, angry wall of darkness. We decided to head back. Thought we could outrun it. We couldn't."

My voice dropped, the memory taking over. I wasn't in the cabin with Iris anymore. I was back on Leo's boat, the deck pitching beneath my feet.

"The storm hit us like a locomotive. One second, it was choppy and spitting rain. The next, the world was just gray. Howling wind, a torrential, blinding rain like needles on your skin. The waves… they weren't waves anymore. They were just moving mountains of water, steep and black and furious, coming at us from all directions. The boat was too small. Leo was at the helm, fighting it, his knuckles white, but he was out of his league. I took over. I was the captain."

The title, the one Iris used so playfully, now felt like an accusation branded into my skin. She was completely still, watching me with rapt, fearful attention.

"I tried to keep the bow pointed into the waves, but it was impossible. The boat was being tossed around like a damn toy. I remember Caitlin screaming, her hands clamped onto my arm, her knuckles white. Beth was crying in the stern, Leo shouting something at me that was ripped away by the wind. I was just trying to survive. Trying to get us through the next thirty seconds. The next wave."

I had to stop, my throat closing up. I took another ragged breath, the sound loud in the silent cabin. Iris's hand was still on my arm, her grip firm, grounding. So similar to Caitlin's long-ago grip, yet so very different. I focused on it and drew strength.

"And then a huge wave came out of nowhere, a sheer wall of black water. It caught us broadside. I remember the sickening lurch as the boat moved sideways, the world tilting at an impossible angle. The fiberglass screamed as it surrendered to the pressure. And then… just cold. The shock of the violent, churning water closing over my head."

Iris gasped, her mouth forming an *O*.

"I was thrown clear. I don't know how. I surfaced, sputtering and choking on saltwater, the rain still blinding me. The boat was gone. Sunk. I saw a bench cushion floating nearby and grabbed onto it. Held on with everything in me, my body already shaking so bad I could hardly grip."

"And I just screamed. Screamed their names into the void, into the howling wind. Over and over. But there was nothing. Just the roar of the storm."

"No…" Iris's denial was a soft whisper.

"Then I saw him for a second. Leo's head, bobbing on the crest of a wave about fifty yards away. He had one arm in the air, waving. I screamed his name again. When the wave passed, he was gone."

The finality of that word, even after thirteen years, was a fresh knife in my soul.

"The storm passed as quickly as it came. The rain stopped. The wind died down. And I was alone. Floating in an empty, debris-strewn sea. Holding onto a cushion. The silence was almost worse than the storm had been."

At last, I looked at Iris. Her face was white as paper, her eyes wide with horrified compassion. A tear rolled from her eye.

"The Coast Guard found me hours later, half-delirious and hypothermic. They continued the search for three days. Found pieces of the boat. A cooler. But they never found them." I let out an endless, shuddering breath, the confession finally, brutally, complete. "They never recovered the bodies."

The story hung in the still cabin between us, heavy and suffocating. The ghosts of Leo, Beth, and Caitlin were here now, their presence as real and tangible as the gentle rocking of *Line Dancer* in its slip. I had opened the door to that locked room in my mind, and the pain that had flooded out was nearly as raw and sharp as it had been thirteen years ago.

"It was my fault, Iris. I knew the signs. I didn't listen to what the ocean was telling me. And three people paid for my mistake with their lives. My punishment was to go on living."

Silent tears traced paths down Iris's cheeks. My first instinct was to look away, to shut down, to retreat from the naked empathy on her face. But I didn't. I just watched her feel it with me.

"Oh, Austin," she murmured, her voice thick. She reached down, her hand covering my white-knuckled fist on the blanket. "That's terrible. I am so, so sorry. But you must realize it was an accident. A horrible, tragic accident. You were all just kids. Maybe you shouldn't have gone out, but you didn't twist anyone's arm, did you? You didn't force them to go."

Her words were meant to be a comfort, an absolution I'd never allowed myself. But they bounced off the calloused walls of my guilt.

"Doesn't matter." I pulled my hand out from under hers, the loss of her touch like a sudden chill. "It doesn't matter if they wanted to go. I was the one who knew better. I should have shut the whole damn thing down before it ever started."

"No." Her voice was gentle yet firm. She refused to let me retreat into that cold, lonely place. "It was a tragedy,

Austin. A terrible, senseless tragedy. But it's not something you should punish yourself over for the rest of your life. You survived. That's not a punishment. It's just what happened."

I whipped my head back and forth, pulling away from the gentle logic of her words. "No. You don't get it. It's not just about punishment. It's about the... the wrongness of it. I was the one who was supposed to know better. Yet I was the only one who walked away."

I met her gaze and let her see all of it—the ugly, unending loop of my failure. "Why, Iris? That's the question that never stops. Why did I get to live when they didn't? It doesn't make sense. It's a debt I can never repay."

My words hung in the dim air. I waited for her pity, for her to tell me I was being irrational. Instead, her expression hardened into a look of fierce, protective anger. She leaned forward, her hands gripping my arm again. "Then don't try to repay it. Instead, you live. That's how you honor them. Your survival wasn't a debt. It was a miracle. And you are a good man who has been carrying an impossible burden for far too long."

Her words battered against the walls I'd spent thirteen years reinforcing. I shook my head, a small, defeated movement. "You can't know that."

"You're right. I can't." Her anger dissolved, replaced by a look of such patient acceptance it stole the air from my lungs. Her grip softened, and she slowly stroked my arm. "No one can. And you don't have to believe it right now. Maybe you won't believe it a year from now. But that crack in the door you just opened? The fact that you're even questioning it after all this time? That's a start, Austin. That's a huge, scary, very promising start."

I stared at the fierce sincerity in her eyes. She wasn't

offering cheap platitudes or trying to fix me. She was offering me a different perspective. A hand in the darkness. Maybe even a lifeline. For the first time, I didn't immediately slap it away. I held her gaze, a thirteen-year war raging inside me.

A slow, heavy breath shuddered out of me. "It's not gonna be fast."

A beautiful smile touched her lips. "Perhaps not. But you'll get there. I know it."

"I'm glad you're here." The admission was momentous, torn from a place deep inside me. "Being with you has made me realize that maybe life can be good. Not just... surviving."

Her hand came up, and she brushed a stray tear from her cheek before resting her cool fingers against my rough, stubbled one. This time I let it be.

"Your life can be fulfilling, Austin. You deserve to be happy."

The simple, soft conviction in her voice made something clench hard inside me. I had to focus on a scuff mark on the cabin floor to anchor myself.

"Were you and Caitlin serious?"

I nodded, still not looking at her. "Yeah. We'd been together a couple of years. Since high school. We always just figured... you know. We'd end up together. We thought we had all the time in the world, so what was the rush?"

"I'm so sorry, Austin. For everything you lost. If you ever need to talk about it... or if you don't. Whatever you need. I'm here for you."

"Thank you, sweetness." Her support and her gentle strength were the final push I needed to tell her the rest. I met her gaze. "That's what the argument with Eli and Braden was about. At the brewpub."

Confusion clouded her eyes.

"They were worried." The words came out slowly, reluctantly, each one a stone in my mouth. "They think you look like her. Like Caitlin."

I saw it then. The subtle shift. The way her eyes went from pure empathy to something else. Uncertainty. A flicker of doubt.

"Blonde, blue eyes. Similar personality. They were worried about what I was doing."

I rushed on, desperate to fix it, to explain before the doubt could take root. "Iris, I told them they were wrong. I told them in no uncertain terms that I never once compared you two. That I care about you. For who you are. The sunny, noisy, amazing woman who has completely turned my life upside down."

I reached for her and pulled her tightly against my chest as if I could physically shield her from the poison of the thought I had just planted. I wanted her to feel my sincerity, to believe me. I had just taken an enormous leap of faith, sharing the source of my deepest pain.

The tragedy that had defined my entire adult existence.

And in the same breath—in an attempt to be honest—I had handed her a perfectly valid reason to doubt everything.

To doubt me.

To doubt us.

A frigid, sinking sensation washed over me as I held her. I had finally opened the door to that bolted room in my mind, hoping to let in the light. I had an awful feeling that in doing so, I might have just plunged us both into a whole new kind of darkness.

Chapter Twenty-Five

IRIS

AT LAST, the Sand Dollar Suite was starting to look like a suite. One that a guest might enjoy staying in. The new drywall was up and textured, waiting for its first coat of primer. The elegant lines of the future en-suite bathroom were framed in, a promise of claw-foot tubs and gleaming tile. Sunlight, no longer choked by dust, streamed through the newly installed hurricane-resistant windows and illuminated the space with a clean, hopeful light. A week ago, this progress would have filled me with a giddy, triumphant joy.

Today, I was just numb.

I stood in the center of the room, but my mind was a million miles away. In the tiny cabin of *Line Dancer*, listening to the story that had reshaped my entire understanding of the man next door.

Three days had passed since Austin laid his soul bare. Three days where he had been… carefully tender. We'd talked about it more, of course, in quiet, halting conversations that were both heavy and hopeful. This wasn't something to be solved in a single night. It was a wound that would need time, patience, and air to heal. So he'd show up at my porch in the evenings, his presence a quiet promise. We'd share a meal, the conversation carefully skirting the rawest edges of what he had exposed, giving us both room to breathe. He'd hold me secure in his arms while we watched the sun set into the distant horizon.

And every time he looked at me, every time he touched me, my heart would break a little. For the twenty-one-year-old boy who had survived when his world had been ripped apart. For the thirty-four-year-old man who was still paying the price. My love for him, a feeling I could no longer deny, was a fierce, protective ache in my chest.

But beneath the love, beneath the profound empathy, a new and insidious fear had taken root. A cold, slick tendril of doubt had wrapped itself around my heart.

"They think you look like her. Like Caitlin."

I believed him. That was the honest, terrible truth. I believed with every fiber of my being that when Austin looked at me, he saw me. I believed he thought his feelings were genuine. That his desire was for Iris Holloway, the chaotic, pastry-peddling woman who had blown into his life. I didn't think for a second that he was consciously deceiving me.

But what if he was deceiving himself?

That question was the poison that seeped into still moments, the one that cast a long shadow over the warmth of his body next to mine in the dark. What if, after thirteen years of lonely, tortured grief, his wounded heart had simply seen a ghost and latched on? What if this intense connection we shared wasn't a new beginning for us, but just his subconscious attempt to write a happier ending to the saddest story I had ever heard?

The thought made me feel hollow. It cheapened every-thing we had built, and the knot in my stomach tightened. I couldn't untangle it on my own. I needed another sounding board besides Austin. And I couldn't talk to Liv, as much as I'd come to value her friendship. This was a Coleridge issue. A deep, complicated, family-sized wound.

There was only one person who knew him, loved him, and had welcomed me with an open heart.

I pulled out my phone, my thumb hovering over Bren-na's contact. She had said the story was Austin's to tell me, and he had. But now I was left with the reaction. The fear and doubt were a living thing inside me, and if I didn't find some perspective, they might eat me alive. I typed out a message, my words clumsy and inadequate.

Iris: Are you free for a bit this afternoon? Could really use a friend.

The reply came almost instantly.

Brenna: Always. Bookshop. Tea. 30 minutes?

Iris: Thank you. See you then.

I put the phone back in my pocket. I didn't know what I was hoping to hear from Brenna, but I desperately needed her perspective.

Bookshop in Paradise was an oasis of calm as I stepped inside. A quick glance revealed the store was empty except for us, and Brenna casually flipped the sign on the door to Be Back Soon.

"Let's head back to my office."

The room was as cozy and eclectic as the rest of the shop. The walls were lined with overflowing bookshelves, along with a cluttered desk and two comfortable armchairs that looked like they had seen a thousand stories. She closed the door behind us and put a kettle on the hot plate she had tucked in a corner.

"Earl Grey or Chamomile?" she asked, her back to me as she pulled two mugs from a shelf.

"Chamomile, please." I sank into an armchair, my hands twisting together in my lap.

Brenna didn't press. She just moved with quiet efficiency as she prepared the tea, her silence a patient space that invited confidence rather than demanding it. She handed me a steaming mug before settling into the other armchair with her tea cradled in her hands. "What's on your mind, Iris?"

I took a sip of the tea, the fragrant steam doing little to calm the butterflies in my stomach. My words, when they came, were halting at first, a clumsy, tangled mess. "It's… it's about Austin. Something happened a few days ago." I looked up and met her gaze. "He told me. About the accident. About all of it."

Surprise flashed through Brenna's eyes, followed quickly by a deep, profound sadness that seemed to dim the light in the room. She put her mug down and gave me her undivided attention. "What did he say?"

A fresh wave of tears pricked at my eyes as I remembered the raw, broken look on his face. "He told me about his friend, Leo. And Leo's girlfriend, Beth. The storm and the sinking… And Caitlin."

Brenna closed her eyes for a moment, pinching her delicate brows together. "Oh, Iris. I'm so sorry you had to hear that. I'm even sorrier Austin had to tell it."

"He needed to. And I'm glad he trusted me enough to do it." I took a shaky breath, forcing myself to get to the real heart of the matter, the real reason I was here. I explained his argument in the back room of Tidal Hops with Eli and Braden. "The thing is, Brenna… I believe him. I believe every word he said when he told me his feelings for me are real, that they're separate from what happened. I don't think he's lying to me."

"But?" Brenna prompted gently.

"But what if he's wrong?" The question burst out of me, a torrent of fear and doubt I couldn't hold back any longer. "What if he's not being honest with himself?" I shook my head, the knot in my stomach tightening. "What if he saw a woman trying to fix up an old house, a woman who reminded him of a life he lost? A… I don't know. A do-over? How can I ever really know if he wants me, or if he just wants a happier ending at last? And who could blame him?"

The raw, vulnerable words hung in the office between us. I was stripped bare, my deepest, most terrifying insecurity laid out on her cluttered desk.

Brenna listened to my entire rambling confession without interrupting, her expression full of deep, unwavering compassion. "Those are very fair and intelligent questions to be asking, Iris. And they show how much you truly care about him. That you're worried about him, not just about your own feelings." She tilted her head and darted her eyes over my head. "There is sort of a superficial resemblance. From what I can remember, anyway. It was so long ago."

She took a sip of her tea, her gaze thoughtful. "You have to understand something about my brother. We, his family, have been living with the effects of that day for thirteen years. After the first few months, when Austin was still pretty shell-shocked, he never talked about it. Not to me, not to Braden, not to Eli. He said that was his coping mechanism." When her eyes met mine, they were filled with conviction. "For him to willingly walk back into that storm and show you the most painful part of his soul… He wouldn't risk that kind of agony for a do-over. He only would have done that because it's you."

The certainty in her voice was a lifeline, and I clung to it. "That's what I try to tell myself."

"Then keep saying it. Is it possible you reminded him of Caitlin at first?" she asked with a shrug. "Maybe. On some deep, subconscious level that none of us can understand. Who knows how grief and trauma work? They don't follow rules." She leaned forward, her gaze sharpening. "But Iris, you have to look at the evidence. He has made more progress and let more light into his life in the past couple of months than he has in the entire thirteen years before. That's not about the past. That is entirely about the present. Austin discussing the accident at last is solely about the effect you are having on him."

A single, hot tear escaped and traced a path down my cheek. I wiped it away.

"But you're right," Brenna conceded, her voice gentle again. "The only person who can truly answer that question, for himself and for you, is Austin. And knowing my brother, he's just now starting to process everything he unleashed by telling you. The door is open now, and he's terrified of what's lurking behind it. He's going to need some time. And some patience."

"I know," I whispered. "I just… I'm scared."

"Of course you are," she said, her voice full of kindness that made me want to cry all over again. "But Iris? He is too. Probably more than you can imagine. Because he's scared of losing you."

The weight of Brenna's words settled over me, a strange mixture of profound relief and sobering reality. Everything she said resonated with a deep, intuitive truth. Austin had chosen to let me in, to show me the deepest parts of himself. That had to mean something.

"Thank you, Brenna." What I felt wasn't just gratitude. It was a feeling of being seen, of being understood. "I really needed to hear that. From you."

"Of course." She reached across the desk and gave my hand another reassuring squeeze. "Austin is a good man, Iris. He's been lost for a long time. It looks like he might be finding his way home."

She leaned back in her chair, her professional bookstore-owner demeanor returning, though her eyes were still full of a sisterly warmth. "Now are you going to tell me what you really thought of our book for this month, or are we just going to sit here and psychoanalyze my brother all afternoon?"

I let out a laugh, a watery, relieved sound. The offer of normalcy, of a simple book discussion after such a heavy conversation, was a gift. "Oh, it was terrible. The hero was a complete idiot until at least page two hundred. I almost threw it across the room."

"Right?" Brenna grinned. "That's exactly what I said! But the ending was worth it, wasn't it?"

"The ending was perfect," I agreed, and the double meaning of the words hung in the air between us.

I left Bookshop in Paradise a few minutes later, clutching a new book Brenna had insisted I take. My heart was lighter and my path forward clearer, if not easier. I walked the few blocks back to Heron House under the late-afternoon sun, the usual cheerful sounds of Dove Key now brighter.

When I got home, Gus's crew working on the second floor was a steady, reassuring rhythm. I stood on my new, sturdy porch and looked across the yard at Austin's quiet, orderly house. The sun glinted off his windows, making them look like fiery, unblinking eyes.

My fear was still there, a low hum beneath the surface.

But it was no longer a paralyzing fear. It was a clarifying one. Brenna was right. I couldn't push him, and I couldn't demand answers to questions he likely didn't have for himself yet. But I also couldn't just wait, letting this doubt poison everything we were building.

I had to talk to him. Not to interrogate him about Caitlin, but to talk to him about us. I had to tell him that I was here for him, but that I was also scared. I needed to tell him that for this to work, I needed him to be sure. Sure that he saw me and not a memory. I would give him time and patience to find that answer for himself. But he had to know the question was on the table.

He was worth the risk.

And I was worth fighting for too.

Chapter Twenty-Six

AUSTIN

A FRAGILE CAREFULNESS had settled over Iris's and my little corner of Dove Key, a stillness that was more like the dead calm before a hurricane than any kind of real peace. I'd detonated a thirteen-year-old bomb in the middle of our budding relationship. Now she was walking through the wreckage, trying to figure out what was real and what was just shrapnel from the past.

Tonight, we were sitting on her new porch swing, a gentle breeze rustling the leaves of the massive magnolia tree in her yard. The air was soft and fragrant with night-blooming jasmine, the perfect night for airing truths.

"You've been quiet," I said.

Her gaze was fixed on the fireflies blinking in the twilight of her overgrown garden. "Just thinking."

"About what I told you, I imagine."

She turned to me, her eyes dark and serious in the dim light. "Yes. First, I want you to know I'm so incredibly sorry for what you went through. For what you're still going through. And I am honored that you trusted me enough to tell me."

I just nodded, unable to speak, my throat suddenly tight.

She paused for a moment, her fingers pleating the fabric of her shorts. "One thing has been running through my mind. Well, more than one. But, after all you went through, how can you still do what you do? Spend your life on the water? I think it would have made me hate the ocean."

I stared out past the porch railing toward the dark line where water met sky. "The ocean's just the ocean. It doesn't take sides. People make the mistakes. Not the water." I looked at her, needing her to understand this part. "I stay out there because I love it. Because it makes sense to me. Also so it doesn't happen again. Not on my boat. Not on my watch."

The understanding in her eyes was more comforting than any words could have been. She reached out and rested her hand on my knee. "So you took the worst thing that has ever happened to you and turned it into your life's purpose."

I lifted one shoulder in an uncomfortable shrug. "I guess you could say that. More likely, it's just my stubbornness and obsessiveness coming through. Maybe it was also a way to honor their memories."

"And you should honor them." She turned more toward me, setting the swing in gentle motion. "I also want you to know that I believe you care about me. I don't think for a second that you are intentionally trying to deceive me, or that you're consciously comparing me to… to her."

Relief, so potent it was almost painful, washed through me. "I'm not, Iris. I swear."

"I know you believe that." She paused, choosing her

words with a careful precision that caused that relief to vanish. My muscles went rigid. "My fear is… what if you're not being honest with yourself?"

Her words, so logical and so utterly plausible, chased my relief right off the porch. Iris was expressing the same doubt my brothers had thrown at me. Words filled not with concern, but with genuine, heartbreaking fear.

"I need to know, Austin." Her voice dropped, raw with vulnerability. "For this to work, I need to know that you want me. Not a second chance at a different ending. The messy, loud, scone-baking Iris who almost took out your prize-winning hibiscus."

"I know that's a huge, maybe impossible, thing to ask. And I understand you need time and space to process everything you just unearthed. And I want to give you that." She took a shaky breath. "But I can't just float in this uncertainty. My heart's not built for it. Before I give all of it to you, I need to know you're not just giving me the pieces of you that are left over from someone else."

I examined her, the strength, fear, and deep empathy in her beautiful face. She wasn't giving me an ultimatum. She wasn't running away. She was laying her heart bare and trusting me with her own vulnerability.

Something fierce and protective surged in me, a desperate need to soothe the fear I had put in her eyes. I reached out and rested my hand on the side of her face.

"Iris." I waited until she met my gaze. "When I'm with you, there are no ghosts. There are no other pieces. There's just you. Only you."

I could see her processing the words, a flicker of hope battling with doubt in her eyes.

"I know I've got a lot of crap to sort through," I continued. "And I don't have all the answers. I don't know how to prove it to you, other than to keep being here.

Whenever you need me. Because what I feel for you, it's not left over. It's new. And it's all yours."

It was the most I'd ever said about my feelings to anyone. Clumsy and inadequate maybe, but it was the truest thing I had to offer. I couldn't bring myself to say those three words. Why? I had no idea. I just couldn't.

But somehow, my halting, stumbling sentences were enough. With a faint smile, she leaned forward and brushed her lips over mine. Though I wanted to grab her and deepen the contact, hold her close and keep her safe, I accepted what she offered me.

She pressed her forehead to mine. "I know it's not easy for you to say all that. And it's enough for now."

The last two words hung in the air between us, a quiet acknowledgment that this wasn't over. It was a truce, not a surrender. The doubt was still there. And as I held her, the weight of needing to prove myself, to be the man she could trust without reservation, felt heavier than ever.

THE NEXT DAY, my charter was a nice, easygoing couple from Michigan who were more interested in enjoying the breeze and getting some sun than they were in serious fishing. It should have been a relaxing day. Instead, my mind was a churning mess. I went through the motions, finding them a few small snappers and pointing out a pod of dolphins. But my voice and actions were on autopilot while my thoughts were back on that porch with Iris.

Her words echoed in my head, a gentle, insistent refrain. Her soft sincerity had been more devastating than any angry accusation. She wasn't blaming me for my past. She was asking me if we had a future. And though I tried, I had no damn idea how to answer her.

When I got back to the dock, I went through my usual routine of cleaning the boat. I retreated to the cabin, the place that had been my ultimate sanctuary, but even here, Iris's presence now lingered. I sat at the cramped desk and stared at the scarred wood, not seeing any of it.

How do I prove it to her? How do I make her see that my feelings for her, this all-consuming thing that has taken over my life, have nothing to do with a ghost?

I sat up and sighed, stating the inevitable conclusion out loud. "How can I convince her when my own brothers don't even believe me?"

They were the ones who had planted this seed of doubt. They were the ones who had looked at Iris and seen the past. And if I couldn't make them understand, how could I hope to convince her?

The anger I'd felt in the back room of Tidal Hops resurfaced. But beneath it, a new, cool resolve began to form. I couldn't sit here and let this fester. I couldn't solve this alone in my head. I had to talk to one of them and make him see.

So I could figure out how to make Iris see.

Not Eli. Eli was a great brother, but he approached every problem with the well-meaning but sometimes over-bearing authority of a big brother. He'd try to fix it, to manage it.

But Braden was different. He had a way of cutting through the bullshit, of seeing the real heart of the matter, a skill honed by years of listening to drunks and tourists tell their life stories over his bar. He was the one I could talk to, the one who knew how to listen without trying to steer the boat.

I stood up, the decision made.

Tidal Hops was quiet for a weekday evening, just a few regulars nursing their beers at the far end of the bar and a couple of tourists picking at a plate of conch fritters. Braden was smiling behind the bar, polishing glasses with a clean white towel.

He looked up as I approached, his smile faltering as he took in my expression. He put down the glass and towel. "Why do I get the feeling you're not here for a beer?"

I shook my head and slid onto a stool in the corner, away from the other patrons. "No. I need to talk."

Braden's expression shifted, the bartender facade replaced by the concerned brother. He nodded once, then called out to a server. "Can you cover for a few minutes?" Then he poured two glasses of water and led me back to his office.

It was his command center, a crammed, windowless room that was pure Braden—functional, overflowing with ideas, and smelling faintly of malt and opportunity. A whiteboard covered one wall, a scribbled roadmap of his plans for the future. He didn't offer me one of the seats at his desk. He pointed to one of two simple chairs in the corner. The door clicked shut behind us, and the familiar sounds of Tidal Hops faded into a low, distant thrum.

After handing me one of the glasses, he sat across from me and steepled his fingers. "What's up?"

I stared at my water for a long moment, trying to gather the right words, words I wasn't even sure I possessed. "You and Eli's comments. The other day in the back room. About Caitlin." Just saying her name was like swallowing broken glass. "It's… it's caused a problem."

Braden didn't flinch. He just nodded slowly, his gaze steady. "I was afraid it might. I'm sorry if we upset you, Austin. We were just worried. We still are."

"I know," I bit out, the anger still a simmering ember. "I told Iris about it. All of it. And now she's worried. She's scared that I don't see her, that I just see a memory." The admission was humiliating, a confession of a failure I didn't know how to fix. "She wonders if I'm trying to rewrite the past with her."

"Are you?" Braden asked, his question direct, with no trace of judgment.

"No!" The denial was explosive, torn from somewhere deep inside me. "I've never once… when I'm with her, it's just her. She's nothing like Caitlin. She's Iris. She's quirky and messy and she bakes things that are way too good. And she has these ridiculous sayings… She's a disaster. But she's my disaster."

I stopped, horrified at my outburst, at the raw, unfiltered honesty of it.

Braden didn't crack a joke. He didn't smirk. He just watched me for a long moment, his usual teasing gone. He let out a slow breath, a soft whistle of air as he leaned forward. "Okay. 'My disaster.' I don't think I've ever heard you claim anything, or anyone, like that before. Not even your own boat."

He let that sink in, let me absorb the weight of my own words reflected back at me.

Then a flicker of his old self returned, but it was softer now, more knowing. He offered a crooked smile. "You know, I'd be a pretty shitty bartender if I wasn't a good listener. You talk about her a lot differently than you did about Caitlin."

I stared at him. "What's that supposed to mean?"

"I might have only been a teenager at the time, but I saw you two together. With Caitlin, it was easy. Comfortable. You two were inevitable, like the tide. Everyone knew you'd end up together." He met my gaze, his eyes full of surprising wisdom. "With Iris, nothing has been easy. You fought it. And now, you look at her like you're half terrified and half starved. Eli and I both saw it. This isn't the same, man. Not even close." He shrugged. "It's the difference between being a boy and a man."

His words hit me like a punch, a truth so sharp and unexpected it knocked the wind out of me. He was right.

"But what do I do?" My question came out as a raw plea. "How do I convince her of that?"

"The similarities between the two women are there. Anyone with eyes can see them. Eli and I just said the hard part out loud. And maybe that's a good thing." He paused, his index finger tapping his thigh. "Let me ask you a question. And I want a real answer, not your usual grumpy bullshit. What are you actually scared of here? Are you scared your feelings for Iris aren't real?"

"No," I answered immediately. "They're real. Too damn real."

"Okay." He nodded, accepting it. "So, what is it then? What's the real fear, Austin?"

His question landed in the air between us. Suddenly, the impenetrable wall I'd built around that dark, terrible day—the wall I'd shown to Iris—wasn't the real issue.

It was just a symptom.

The real fear, the one I'd never admitted even to myself, was what came after.

"I'm scared of it happening again." My words were low and ragged. The confession felt like peeling back a layer of skin to expose the raw nerve beneath. "I'm scared of being that happy again. Because I've seen how fast it can be snatched away. How a perfect day can turn into the worst day of your life in the blink of an eye."

I looked down at my hands, at the calluses and scars from years of work, but all I could see was that empty, debris-strewn water. When I glanced back up, Braden nodded at me to continue.

"The accident... yeah, the guilt is a big part of it. I

survived. They didn't. I've been carrying that for thirteen years. But the real reason I keep everyone at arm's length… it's because I'm a coward. I'm so damn scared of losing someone else I love. I feel like I'm a lightning rod for tragedy. Like if I let myself love Iris, I'd just be sentencing her to some awful fate. And punishing myself by having to watch it happen all over again. A just punishment for being the one who got to live."

The whole ugly, twisted, irrational truth of it was out, hanging in the quiet air of the brewpub.

Braden was silent for a long time, just letting the words settle. He didn't offer cheap reassurances. He didn't tell me I was being ridiculous.

"Yeah," he said, his voice thick with compassion. He took a long swallow of his water, his gaze distant. "Life can change on a dime, man. You know that better than most. But it doesn't only change for the worse. Sometimes it changes for the better. You're anything but a coward, brother. Let me tell you what I see right now. You're a complete wreck. Tormented. But you know what? You're more alive than you've been in thirteen years. You're feeling something again. Even if it's scaring the living hell out of you. Maybe this painful shit you're going through right now is the change you need. To finally start living again instead of just going through the motions and calling it a life."

His words landed in the quiet office not like an accusation, but like a life ring thrown to a man who hadn't realized he was drowning.

More alive.

The phrase echoed in my head, stark and undeniable. He was right. The last few months I'd known Iris had been a special kind of hell, a constant battle against myself. But they had also been… vibrant. Filled with color and passion and taste and a raw, humming energy I hadn't experienced since I was a stupid, invincible kid.

Before Iris, my life was a flat gray line of routine and control. Work, eat, sleep, repeat. A carefully constructed existence designed to keep the past at bay. It wasn't living. Braden was right. It was surviving. And Iris, with her sweet, hopeful energy and her eyes that saw too much, had lit up that grayness like a perfect tropical sunrise.

I studied my brother, the unexpected, profound wisdom in his gaze. Braden wasn't just the joking brewmaster. He was a man who saw things, who understood more than I ever gave him credit for.

"How'd you get so damn smart?" I asked.

Braden let out a short, surprised laugh, the tension in the room breaking. He shrugged, his usual easy grin returning. "I listen to people's problems all day for a living. Some of it's bound to sink in." He sobered again, his gaze steady. "I just want to see you happy, okay? For real, happy."

"Yeah," I said, the single word thick with a meaning I couldn't fully articulate. I looked down at my hands, then back at him, the truth of my situation, the real core of my fear, finally clear in my mind. "I don't know how to fix this with her, Braden. But I think you're right. I have to try."

"That's all any of us can do," he said quietly. Then he pushed to his feet. "Come on. I'll walk you out."

I finished my water, the glass making a soft clink as I set it on his desk. "Thanks."

"Anytime," he said as he rested an arm over my shoulders. "I mean it. Anytime."

I clapped him once on the shoulder, and then I left him to his polished glasses and unexpected wisdom.

"Hey, Austin?" he asked, and I turned to look at him

over my shoulder. "Just because the truth is complicated doesn't mean it's wrong."

I gave him an acknowledging nod, then stepped out into the humid air.

As I got into my truck, Braden's words echoed in my head, unsettling and strangely comforting all at once.

"You're more alive than you've been in thirteen years."

The thought was a double-edged sword. I'd made progress with Braden, and more importantly, with myself. I had, after all these years, articulated the true shape of my fear.

It wasn't a ghost I was chasing. It was a ghost I was running from.

And it was time to stop.

But that realization also made things more complicated. How could I explain it? That I was terrified of loving Iris, not because of who she was, but because of what could happen to her. Because of a cosmic punishment I felt I still deserved.

How did you tell the person making you feel alive again that you were terrified your very presence might be a curse?

IRIS

THE THIRD-FLOOR SEA TURTLE SUITE was a study in beautiful contradictions. The walls, now a serene, calming seafoam green, provided a modern backdrop for the original, ornate plaster medallions on the ceiling, which Gus's crew had painstakingly restored. Wires coiled neatly from junction boxes, waiting for the elegant, contemporary light fixtures I'd chosen—a promise of new light for an old space.

And the floors... the floors were my favorite part.

"I can't believe these are the same boards." I ran my bare foot over the original mahogany. Gus and his crew had painstakingly sanded away decades of grime, neglect, and questionable varnish. The deep, reddish-brown wood now gleamed with a lustrous, almost liquid sheen that spoke of old money and bygone eras, of times when things were built to last.

Gus stood beside me, his hands on his hips and quiet satisfaction on his dark face. He nodded toward the elegant, framed-in doorway that would soon lead to the ensuite bathroom. "You made the right call here, Iris. A Jack-and-Jill bathroom between two suites always feels like a compromise, like you're telling your guests they aren't quite important enough for their own private space. This," he gestured to the generous dimensions of the future bathroom, "this feels like luxury."

"I'm so glad you suggested we sacrifice that small ninth bedroom." It had been a difficult decision, giving up a potential source of revenue, but Gus had been firm in his professional opinion. "You were right. It's given us the space to do this properly."

"Well, when you bring a place like this back to life, you do it right," he said with a reassuring smile. "We brought the house up to modern standards but kept its soul. That's what matters. The custom vanities should be delivered by the end of the week."

"I can't wait to see them." For the first time since I'd inherited this glorious, terrifying money pit, the vision in my head was starting to match the reality in front of me.

"Well, I'll leave you to it," Gus said, giving me a nod. "I'm going to go check on the boys out on the porch. Make sure those new support posts are going in correctly."

"Thanks."

As he left, a feeling of profound gratitude washed over me. He and his crew were worth every single penny. They were competent, they were professional, and most importantly, they treated Heron House with the same reverence I did.

I thought of the letter, safely tucked away in its drawer under the window seat. "Aunt Constance, I hope I'm doing you proud. I'm sure trying."

I moved to the expansive, newly installed window and looked out over the backyard. It was no longer the untamed jungle I'd first encountered. Gus's crew had cleared away the years of overgrown brush and invasive pepper trees, revealing the true, graceful lines of the property. It was still mostly just trees, dirt, and potential, but I could already see a lush green lawn, winding stone paths, and overflowing beds of fragrant gardenias and bougainvillea shaded by stately trees.

A sanctuary.

My gaze drifted to the property line, to the vibrant red hibiscus hedge that bloomed like a crimson ribbon laid neatly between my chaos and his order. The hedge was full and lush, dotted with those spectacular crimson blooms. We'd worked on it together one afternoon last week. He'd shown me the proper way to prune and fertilize, his large, capable hands guiding mine.

A wistful smile touched my lips. That was the new Austin. Or maybe the old Austin—the one who lurked beneath the layers of grumpy, solitary sea captain. The one who made me coffee in the mornings and grilled fresh fish for me at night. The one whose rare, quiet smiles could make my heart soar nearly out of my body.

He was still guarded. He still held a part of himself back, a part that was locked away in a room marked *Do Not Enter*. I knew that. After his devastating confession and our tentative adjustment to the new reality, I understood the shape of his ghosts. I understood that his walls were built of something far more substantial than simple grumpiness. They were built of grief. Of guilt.

But as he held me, as his actions spoke a language of fierce possession and surprising tenderness, three small words remained unspoken between us. And my foolish, hopeful heart was beginning to ache for the sound of them.

I love you. incredible.

The physical side of our relationship was incredible—deeper and more intimate than anything I had ever known. He was a surprisingly tender, attentive lover, his earlier frantic desperation replaced by a slow, confident exploration that left me breathless and aching for more. He could communicate more with a single touch, with the look in his gray eyes in the hushed moments after, than most men could with a thousand flowery words. I believed his actions. I believed his tenderness. I believed, in my soul, that what he felt for me was real.

But I still wanted the words.

I still needed the words.

And maybe that was selfish. I knew, after everything he'd told me, that those words were likely the hardest, most terrifying things in the world for him to say. I couldn't force it. Austin had to get there on his own. He had to be the one to decide that a future with me was worth the risk of confronting his past.

But oh, how I wished he would let me be the key to that last, stubbornly bolted door.

A soft chime from my phone in my back pocket pulled me back to reality. I glanced at the screen, a jolt of professional excitement chasing away the wistful thoughts of Austin. The email was from Suzanne, the sharp owner of the marketing and PR firm on Main Street I'd hired two weeks ago. After getting to know her at our Sips and Pages meetings, she was my best and only choice. The email's subject line read: Initial Vision Board for Heron House Website.

My heart did a different kind of flutter kick.

I tapped it open immediately and was presented with a beautiful, professional mock-up of my dream. The logo was perfect—a simple, elegant line drawing of a great blue heron in profile, its long neck curved gracefully. Beneath it,

Heron House was written in a classic, flowing script, with *Dove Key, Florida* in a clean, modern font below.

The color palette was exactly what I'd hoped for—soft, sandy whites, the deep green of mangrove leaves, and that specific, perfect shade of Heron Blue I'd chosen for the exterior shutters. Placeholder images of stunning sunsets and charming Keys architecture were arranged around sample text that made my breath catch.

Discover the soul of Old Florida... A historic haven, meticulously restored... Your sanctuary in the heart of Dove Key...

A wide, thrilled smile spread across my face. This wasn't just a chaotic construction site or a flight of fancy in my head anymore. It was a brand. A business. Seeing it laid out so professionally was incredibly validating. It made all the stress, the Mick Riley debacle, and the moments of absolute panic feel utterly worth it.

When I put my phone away, a fresh surge of energy and motivation hummed through me. My usual sunny practicality, now bolstered by this tangible proof of my future, reasserted itself.

"Okay, proprietress," I said with a new sense of purpose. "Stop admiring your future website and contribute to the actual house." Turning from the window, my gaze landed on the fireplace. The ornate wooden trim still needed its final coat of white paint, a small, satisfying job I could claim as my own.

An hour later, I was putting the final, perfect brush-stroke on the mantelpiece. My hand had been steady, my focus complete. Each careful stroke was a victory against the old narrative, the one that whispered I was better at starting things than seeing them through. Stepping back to admire my work, the crisp white trim looked stunning against the serene seafoam walls. For the first time, I didn't just hope I would succeed. I was confident I would.

After a firm nod at my creation, I sealed the paint can, then gathered the painter's tape and the drop cloth I'd used. My arms were full, but I balanced the small paint pail on top of the can.

"I can get all this in one trip," I muttered to the empty room, propping my chin on the can to hold the whole shebang steady.

I padded out of the suite and started down the grand, sweeping staircase. The steps, like the floors in the suite, were bare, gleaming mahogany, sanded to a smooth finish awaiting the topcoat.

I was halfway down, thinking about what Austin and I might have for dinner, when the drop cloth draped over my arm slipped—just a little. But it was enough for the canvas to slide under my bare left toes.

My foot shot out from under me.

A jolt of icy terror vaporized my peaceful contentment. My carefully balanced world tilted at a dizzying, sickening angle.

The paint can clattered away, clanging as it bounced down the stairs. Letting go of everything in my arms, I flailed. My hands flew out, trying to grab the banister, the wall, anything to stop the inevitable.

But I was already falling.

The next moments were a horrifying, tumbling blur. My shoulder hit the wall with a jarring thud. My hip slammed against a step. The world was a chaotic scene of spinning wood and light. As my body twisted in a desperate, uncontrolled cartwheel down the stairs, I heard a distinct, sickening crunch from my lower leg as it snapped over the edge of a step, the bone giving way under the violent, unnatural force.

A bolt of blinding pain, so sharp and absolute it rushed the air from my lungs in a scream, followed right after.

My momentum carried me onward, downward, until I reached the second-floor landing. The beautifully carved newel post rushed up to meet me. My head smacked against the unyielding, beautifully sanded mahogany floorboards with a horrifying, hollow thud.

And the world, only moments ago so full of light and color and promise, went utterly black.

Chapter Twenty-Eight

AUSTIN

"THIS IS THE LIFE, MAN," Dave said with a contented sigh before taking a large bite of his breakfast sandwich.

Across from him, his friend and the other half of my morning's charter saluted with another sandwich. "Sure beats sitting in traffic on the Kennedy Expressway."

"No argument here," I said, then sipped from my coffee mug.

The sea was a flat, turquoise calm, the mid-morning sun a warm, benevolent weight on my shoulders. It was one of those easy days on the water that tourists dreamed of and paid good money for. An easy trip, requiring little more from me than finding a decent patch of water and baiting a few hooks. We were on a break, the boat rocking gently in the calm swell. The only sound was the low murmur of my clients' conversation while we took a break and ate the breakfast I'd picked up from Driftwood Grill that morning.

Half an hour later, I was in the cabin rinsing out my

coffee mug in the tiny galley sink when my phone buzzed against the wooden desktop. I glanced at the screen, expecting it to be one of my siblings or maybe Iris.

But the name on the screen made me frown.

Gus Davis.

It wasn't a text. It was a call. There was absolutely no reason on God's green earth for Iris's contractor to be calling me on a Friday morning while I was out on the water.

Unless something was wrong.

I snatched up the phone, my heart thudding painfully against my ribs, and swiped to answer.

"Austin? Thank God. I wasn't sure if you'd have a signal out there." Gus's voice was tight with stress. "Listen, I'm at the hospital in Marathon. There's been an accident at the house. It's Iris."

The gentle rocking of the boat, the sunlight streaming through the cabin porthole, the distant laughter of my clients—it all stopped. My vision narrowed to a single, tight point, the universe collapsing into the sound of Gus's voice. My blood didn't just run cold.

It turned to solid ice in my veins.

"What kind of accident?" My voice was strangled. "Is she okay? Gus, talk to me, damn it!"

"She fell down the stairs. She's got a bad break in her leg. And a concussion. She was unconscious when we found her."

Unconscious.

The word knocked the air from my lungs. I gripped the edge of the desk, the image of her lying broken a horrifying slash of red against the canvas of my mind.

"They're taking her into surgery now," Gus continued. "For the leg."

My training, the part of my brain forged by years of

dealing with emergencies on the water, kicked in, overriding the raw, screaming panic. "Okay. I'm on my way. I'm turning the boat around now. Tell them… tell them her family is on the way." The word *family* sounded both like a lie and the most honest thing I had ever said. "I'll be there as soon as I can."

"I'll tell them," Gus promised. "Drive safe, son."

I hung up, my hand shaking so badly I almost dropped the phone. For a terrifying second, I just stood there with the cabin swaying around me and the specter of a thirteen-year-old memory rising up to choke me.

Then I shoved it down, hard. There was no time for the past. Only Iris mattered.

When I burst out of the cabin, the sun was blinding after the dim interior. My clients looked up from their coffees, their easygoing smiles faltering as they took in my face.

"What's wrong?" Dave asked, his brow furrowing.

"Family emergency." My voice was clipped, leaving no room for questions. "We have to head back. Now. I'm sorry."

"Hey, of course," the other guy said immediately, already cleaning up. "Don't worry about us. Is everything okay?"

I didn't answer. I was already at the helm, my hands moving with almost violent efficiency. I fired up the engines, the powerful diesels roaring to life, and spun the wheel hard. The boat leaned into a sharp, aggressive turn that sent a spray of white water over the bow. I pushed the throttles all the way forward.

Line Dancer leaped ahead, the bow rising from the water like a startled animal. The usual satisfying roar of her engines was a soundtrack to my terror, each pulse a frantic beat matching the hammering of my heart. The run back to the resort was an exercise in white-knuckled agony. My mind was a churning, chaotic sea of its own.

It's my fault.

The thought was a relentless, punishing rhythm.

I shouldn't have left this morning. I should have known better than to leave her alone in that death trap of a house. That damn huge staircase. Just like the ladder. I'd seen her on that other rickety piece of crap, so determined, so reckless. The staircase was no different. Dangerous.

Please let her be okay. I'll do anything. I'll be better. I'll stop being such a damn hermit. I'll even go to family dinners without complaining. Just let her be okay. Please.

My asshole of a father had shown me how a person could just choose to walk away, to leave a hole in your life where a foundation was supposed to be. That was one kind of loss. But the ocean had taught me a crueler lesson—that the universe could just snatch people away without warning. I didn't know which was worse, but I knew I couldn't survive a third lesson.

Which brought that day back, the same way I saw it in my nightmares. The debris field. The empty water. The terrifying silence after the storm. The ghost of that day, the one I kept chained in the deepest, darkest part of my soul, was rattling its chains, threatening to break free.

No.

I squeezed my eyes shut for a second, gripping the wheel so hard my knuckles hurt. This was not that day. This was not the same. Gus said she was alive. But the reassurance was a thin, flimsy shield against the onslaught of fear.

I docked the boat with a speed and precision born of undiluted adrenaline, the hull bumping against the pilings with a force that would normally make me cringe. I barely secured the lines, shouting a gruff, "Thanks for your understanding" to my clients before sprinting down the pier toward my truck.

I didn't look back.

I didn't care about the boat.

I didn't care about anything but getting to her.

The drive to Marathon was a blur of aquamarine water, sun-drenched asphalt, and green scrub. I pushed my truck, weaving through the slower-moving tourist traffic with reckless impatience, earning more than one angry honk. I didn't care. The cold dread from the boat cabin had now settled deep in my gut, a sickening weight.

I screeched into a parking spot at the hospital in Marathon, not even bothering to see if I was between the lines. I just killed the engine and ran. The automatic doors of the emergency entrance hissed open and swallowed me into a world of jarringly bright fluorescent lights and a low, humming tension that was a world away from the open sea.

The waiting room was a grim space populated by a handful of people in various states of distress or boredom. I spotted Gus immediately in a hard plastic chair, his large frame looking out of place.

He glanced up as I approached, his face a mask of weariness and relief. "Austin. You made good time."

"How is she?" The words were a raw burst, no room for pleasantries. "Have you heard anything?"

"They took her up to surgery about half an hour ago. The orthopedic surgeon met with me before she went in. Said it's a bad break of the tibia. Needs a rod, maybe some plates and screws. But he was confident. Said she's young and healthy."

A rod. Plates. Screws. The words were clinical, brutal. I pictured her leg, so strong and tanned, now broken, needing to be pieced back together with metal. A wave of nausea washed over me.

"And the concussion?" I asked, my voice tight.

"They did a CT scan," Gus replied, his tone reassuring. "Said there's no bleed, thank God. Just a nasty knock. They'll be monitoring her closely."

I ran a hand over my face, the rasp of my stubble a harsh, grounding sound. "Thank you, Gus. For being here. For calling me." The words were ridiculously inadequate.

"Of course." He clapped a heavy, comforting hand on my shoulder. "She's a good kid, that Iris. Got a lot of grit. I heard the thump and her holler when she fell, and I knew something was wrong. I'll head back to Heron House, make sure everything is locked up tight and the crew knows what's going on. You call me if you hear anything, you understand?"

"I will," I promised. "Thanks again."

He gave my shoulder one last squeeze before leaving me alone in the waiting room. I approached the admissions desk, a formidable barrier of beige laminate.

"I'm here for Iris Holloway," I said to the woman behind the glass, trying to keep my voice steady.

She typed something into her computer. "Are you family?"

The question hung in the air. What was I? Her neighbor? The guy she'd been sleeping with? The man who was in love with her but too much of a coward to say it?

"Yes," I said, the word coming out with a surprising, fierce conviction. "Her mother has passed, so I'm her family."

"She's in surgery, sir. The orthopedic floor is on the third level. You can wait in the surgical waiting area up there. Someone will be out to speak with you when they have an update."

The surgical waiting room was even more soulless than the one downstairs. A few rows of uncomfortable-looking chairs, a television bolted to the wall playing some inane talk show with the volume muted, and several sad-looking fake plants. I sank into one of the chairs in the corner. The adrenaline that had been fueling me for the last hour drained away, leaving me hollowed out yet filled with a familiar, low-grade panic.

A crawling dread filled with silence.

Waiting.

Not knowing.

My mind, free from the urgent tasks of driving the boat and the truck, was now a playground for my darkest fears. I imagined the surgeon's face, grim. I imagined a world without Iris's bright energy, without her G-rated exclamations, without her laughter. The thought was a black, bottomless abyss.

I couldn't do this again. Not alone.

A desperate, clawing need for someone who understood rose in me, and one name came through immediately. The one person I knew would understand not just my fear, but my connection to Iris.

Brenna.

My hand was shaking as I pulled out my phone and found her number. The act of reaching out, of admitting I couldn't handle this on my own, went against every instinct I had. But the memory of that empty water, of that soul-crushing loneliness and grief, was stronger than my pride. I placed the call.

She answered on the second ring. "Austin? Hello? What's wrong?"

She could hear it in my silence, in the breath I couldn't quite catch.

"It's Iris," I finally said, my voice cracking. "There was

an accident. At the house. We're at the hospital in Marathon. She's… she's in surgery."

"Oh my God. Will she be okay?"

"I don't have all the details," I said. "She's got a broken leg. A concussion. But Brenna… I… I can't…" I couldn't finish the sentence. Couldn't admit that I was terrified, that I was falling apart.

But I didn't have to.

"I'm on my way." Her voice was firm and steady, a lifeline in the swirling chaos of my terror. "I'll be there as soon as I can."

The forty-five minutes it took for Brenna to get there felt like forty-five years. The muted television droned on, a flickering nightmare of smiling faces and bright colors that were a personal insult.

A soft hand on my shoulder made me jump, a strangled sound escaping my throat.

"I'm here." Brenna's face was etched with concern, her green eyes clouded with worry. But she was here. A solid, comforting presence in the sterile, chilling emptiness of the waiting room.

"Hey," I managed, my voice a rough croak.

She didn't offer cheap platitudes or ask a barrage of questions. She just dropped into the chair next to mine and laid her hand gently on my arm. We sat in silence for a long time, her presence a steady anchor in the storm of my swirling emotions.

Finally, in our corner of the waiting room, away from the other family huddled in their own private bubble of worry, the words I'd held locked inside me for so long began to break free.

"What if she's not okay, Bren?" I murmured. "I just found her. And now… what if I lose her?"

"She's strong," Brenna said softly, her grip on my arm

tightening. "And she's in the best possible hands right now."

"I should have been there," I continued, the guilt a familiar, bitter taste in my mouth. "I should have done something. It's happening again. I can't… I can't lose someone else, Brenna. I can't do it."

"Oh, Austin." Her voice was thick with love and pain that mirrored my own. She scooted her chair closer. "This is not the same. You are not the same twenty-one-year-old boy you were then. You are not a monster. You are a good man who has been through a terrible trauma." She looked me straight in the eye, her gaze fierce, compelling. "And you are falling in love with her. She knows that. She feels it. You just need to be here for her. That's all that matters. That's all you can do."

Her simple, direct words cut through the fog of my panic. *Be here for her now.*

Just as I was about to respond, the double doors at the end of the room swung open. A man in blue scrubs walked toward us, his expression calm, professional. My heart stopped.

"Family of Iris Holloway?" he asked.

I stood, my legs feeling unsteady. "Yes. I'm Austin. How is she?"

The surgeon, a man with kind, tired eyes, approached our quiet corner and gave us a reassuring smile. "The surgery went very well. The breaks were clean, a spiral fracture of the tibia in a couple of places. We were able to set them with a rod and a few plates. She'll have a recovery ahead of her and some physical therapy, but I expect her to heal completely."

Relief, so potent it made me dizzy, washed through me. I reached out and grabbed the back of a chair to steady myself.

"What about the concussion?" Brenna asked, her voice steady beside me.

"We'll need to monitor her, of course," the surgeon said. "But her vitals are strong, and the initial scans showed no signs of intracranial bleeding. She has a significant contusion on the back of her head—a real goose egg—so she'll have a nasty headache when she wakes up. But right now, her brain activity looks normal. She's in recovery now and about to go up to a private room." He gave a small shrug. "She'll wake up when she's ready."

"Thank you, Doctor," I said.

He gave a nod and walked away, leaving Brenna and me in the sudden, echoing silence.

We found Iris's room a short while later. Through the narrow window in the door, I saw her. She was lying in the hospital bed, looking small and so fragile against the stark white sheets. An IV line was taped to the back of her hand, and her leg was encased in a thick wrapping of bandages, propped up on a pillow.

But she was breathing.

Her chest rose and fell in a slow, steady rhythm. She looked peaceful.

As I studied her, a fierce, protective wave of emotion washed over me, so powerful it almost knocked me off my feet.

"She's going to be okay," Brenna whispered beside me.

"Yeah," I said, my voice hoarse. I turned to my sister, my heart full of gratitude I didn't know how to express. "Thank you for coming, Bren. I mean it. I… I couldn't have done this alone."

She gave my arm a squeeze. "You're never alone, Austin. Ever."

I took a deep breath. "I need to be here when she wakes up. By myself now."

Brenna looked at me, a question in her eyes. She was hesitant, worried about leaving me in this raw, vulnerable state. But she also saw the iron-clad resolve in my expression.

"Okay," she said, and gave a nod of understanding. She stood on her tiptoes and gave me a fierce, tight hug. "You call me after she wakes up. Or if you just need to hear a voice. I don't care if it's three in the morning."

"I will," I promised.

She gave my arm one last squeeze, then turned and walked down the hallway.

I pushed Iris's door open and stepped inside. The room was silent, save for the soft, rhythmic beep of a monitor. As I pulled the worn, vinyl-padded visitor's chair close to her bed, the legs scraped softly against the tile. I sat down and reached for her hand, the one without the IV, and carefully laced my fingers through hers. Her skin was warm, her hand soft and limp in my own.

I watched the steady rise and fall of her chest, my thumb stroking the back of her knuckles. My fear was still there, a frozen stone in my gut, but it was different now. It was the sharp, focused fear of a man who had something precious to lose.

And who knew, with a certainty that had settled deep in his bones, that he would do whatever it took to protect it. A man in love.

I was prepared to wait. No matter how long it took.

Chapter Twenty-Nine

IRIS

A STEADY, somehow reassuring beeping cut through the thick fog in my head. *Beep. Beep. Beep.* It was the only landmark in a formless world. I tried to lift a hand, but my limbs were disconnected and weighted down with wet sand. My head thumped with a dull, distant ache, like a bad hangover that was still miles away. And my left leg…

My left leg felt nothing.

It was a heavy, numb weight at the end of my body, a foreign object I was vaguely aware of but couldn't feel. The disconnect was deeply unsettling.

The memories came back then, not in a rush, but in a series of sharp, jagged flashes. The smooth, newly painted trim of the fireplace. The satisfied turn toward the staircase. The sickening lurch of my stomach as my balance gave way. The horrifying, final thud.

I snapped my eyes open.

My world swam into focus, a disorienting collage of an acoustic-tiled ceiling, the metallic gleam of an IV stand,

and the scratchy, unfamiliar texture of a gown against my skin. And a low, rhythmic sound that was different from the monitor. A soft, ragged breathing.

I turned my head, the movement sending a fresh wave of throbbing pain through my skull, and my breath caught in my throat.

Austin.

He was asleep in a vinyl-padded chair, pulled against the side of my hospital bed. He wasn't just sitting in it. He was collapsed, his tall frame folded into the uncomfortable space as if he'd simply run out of energy. His head was slumped forward, his dark, unruly hair falling over his fore-head. His large hand was holding mine, his fingers laced loosely through my own even in sleep.

Dark circles smudged the skin under his eyes. His face, usually so guarded and stoic, was etched with lines of worry and exhaustion that made him look older, more vulnerable.

Just as I was trying to process the heartbreaking sight of him, a soft knock sounded at the door before it swung open. A doctor, a woman with kind brown eyes and a warmly professional smile, stepped inside.

"Ms. Holloway. Iris. Good to see you're awake," she said, her voice calm and reassuring. "I'm Dr. Sharma, the hospitalist on duty this evening."

Her voice startled Austin awake. He jerked upright in his chair, his eyes flying open, wide and full of a raw, panicked confusion for a split second before they landed on me. The relief that washed over his face was a physical thing, a palpable wave that seemed to ease the tension in the entire room.

"You're awake." His voice was a deep, rough rasp. He squeezed my hand, his grip tight and grounding. I offered him a confirmatory smile that was a bit shaky.

Dr. Sharma moved to the other side of my bed. She did an efficient check of my pupils with a penlight, took my pulse, and asked me a series of questions. Did I know where I was? What was the last thing I remembered? My answers came out a little fuzzy, my tongue thick, but they seemed to satisfy her.

She smiled after tapping on a tablet in her hand. "You gave us all quite a scare. You have a moderate concussion, so you'll likely be dealing with a headache and some dizziness for a few days. We'll need to keep a close eye on that." She patted my uninjured leg gently. "But the main event was your other leg. You have some pretty significant fractures of your tibia. Dr. Starling, the orthopedic surgeon, was able to set it with a titanium rod and a few screws. The surgery went well. You'll have a long road of physical therapy ahead, but we expect a full and complete recovery."

A rod. Screws. The words sounded clinical, foreign, like they belonged to someone else's story.

I tried to wiggle the toes on my left leg, to connect my brain to the heavy, bandaged limb propped on the pillows. Nothing happened. It was like trying to send a message down a disconnected phone line.

"That's the nerve block working its magic," Dr. Sharma explained with a reassuring smile. "It numbs the nerves from the knee down. The block will last for another six to eight hours, most likely. It will wear off gradually."

She looked at me, her expression turning serious. "Now, when it starts to wear off, you will start to feel it. It's very important that you press that call button and ask for pain medication before it gets bad. Understand?"

"Yes," I said, the word a little hoarse. "Stay ahead of the pain."

"Exactly." She gave my uninjured foot a gentle pat.

"For now, just rest. Press the call button if you need anything."

She left, the door clicking softly shut behind her, leaving Austin and me in a new kind of silence. The clinical, professional buffer was gone. The air in the quiet hospital room became thick with unspoken emotions, with the weight of his vigil and the reality of what had happened. He was still holding my hand, his thumb stroking the back of my knuckles. I watched him, my heart aching.

He looked… broken.

The usual guardedness in his expression was gone, replaced by a raw, naked fear that he was clearly fighting, and failing, to control. A muscle in his jaw twitched relentlessly. His shoulders were rigid with tension that appeared to go soul-deep.

"Austin," I said softly, my voice still a little hoarse. "What's going on in that head of yours?"

He shook his head, a jerky, tight movement, his eyes fixed on our hands. "Nothing. You're safe, and that's all that matters. You need to rest."

"No," I said, my grip on his hand tightening. "Look at me."

Slowly, reluctantly, as if it took every ounce of his considerable strength, he lifted his head and met my gaze. What I saw in his eyes stole my breath. It was a maelstrom of anguish, of terror, of pain so old and deep I could feel the chill of it. A surge of adrenaline cut through the last of my grogginess.

"Talk to me," I said gently.

"When Gus called… When he said you fell, I thought…" His voice was low and frayed. He squeezed his eyes shut. "I thought it was happening all over again."

A single tear escaped from the corner of his closed eye

and traced a slow, solitary path down his tanned, stubbled cheek.

The sight of it—of this strong, solitary man at the end of his tether—shattered something inside me.

He opened his eyes, and they were swimming with unshed grief. "I can't... I can't lose you."

He leaned forward, burying his face in the scratchy hospital blanket that covered my stomach, his broad shoulders beginning to shake with silent, wracking sobs. My tears, which had been threatening, began to fall freely. Not for my pain, but for his.

The dam was breaking.

Thirteen years of walled-off grief, of suffocating guilt, of soul-crushing loneliness were all pouring out of him, right here in this sterile hospital room. I threaded my fingers through his thick, dark hair, holding him, my heart breaking for the sheer weight of the pain he had carried for so long.

"This is my fault," he finally said, his voice a muffled, broken sound against the blanket. "It's what I do. I let people get close, and then something bad happens. Iris, I love you. I was too much of a goddamn coward to say it, but that didn't make a difference. It should be me in this bed. Hell, it should have been me thirteen years ago. This is what happens when I let myself care about someone. The universe takes them away. To punish me."

The last remnants of the fog enveloping me vanished, along with the dull pain at the back of my head. I barely registered that he told me he loved me because of everything else he'd said. His last word was a choked, broken thing. But I couldn't respond—

Because the dam didn't just crack.

It disintegrated.

A sound tore from his throat, a low, guttural sound of

such raw, animal anguish it could have been ripped from the center of the earth. It was the sound of a soul that had been holding its breath for a decade and was only now just remembering how to scream.

His broad shoulders, the ones I'd admired for their strength and steadiness, shook. Not with small tremors, but with violent, uncontrollable shudders, as if his body was trying to expel a poison. I felt the vibrations through the mattress, through the thin hospital blanket. A silent earthquake of pent-up agony.

My hand moved from his hair to the back of his strong, shaking neck, my thumb stroking the tense cords there. I wrapped my other arm over his rigid, shuddering back and held him tightly against me. I became a gentle, steadfast anchor in the violent storm of his grief and let him break. My tears fell silently onto his hair in a shared baptism of sorrow and long-overdue relief.

I'm not sure how long it took, but the quakes racking Austin's body gradually subsided. His jagged breaths began to even out, though they were still punctuated by the occasional, hitching sob that seemed to tear through him. He didn't move for a long time, his head buried against me in a solid weight of pure grief. I continued to stroke his hair, his back, my tears drying on my cheeks, my heart aching with a love so fierce it was a physical force.

At last, he stirred. He pushed himself up slowly, his movements heavy, exhausted. He wouldn't look at me. His gaze was fixed on our joined hands on the white hospital blanket, his face a ruin of raw emotion. His eyes were red-rimmed, his strong jaw tight with what looked like shame. He looked like a man who had just revealed a mortal wound and was waiting for the final, killing blow of judgment or pity.

I wouldn't give him either.

"Austin," I said, my voice low but firm. "Look at me."

Reluctantly, he lifted his head. The anguish was still there, but now it was mixed with raw, naked vulnerability.

I squeezed his hand. "Listen to me. Look at where we are. In this room. Right now." I gestured with my free hand to my leg, a massive, numb lump under the thin blanket. "Something bad did happen. I fell down the stairs. I broke my leg in two places. It was scary, it's going to hurt like hell, and I'm going to be laid up for a while."

He flinched at my stark, unvarnished words. A fresh wave of guilt washed over his face. But I pressed on. This was exactly what he needed to hear, what he needed to see.

"The thing you've been terrified of for thirteen years, a random accident happening to someone you care about… it happened." I held his gaze, refusing to let him look away. "And look. Here I am. I'm not a ghost. I'm not a memory. I'm right here, and I'm okay. The doctor said my leg will heal. We're still here. Together."

He stared at me, his brow furrowed in deep, painful confusion. He was so used to seeing tragedy as an ending, he didn't know how to recognize it as simply a part of the story.

"Don't you see?" My voice was filled with urgency to offer him the lifeline he'd been too afraid to grasp. "That's what loving someone is. It's not about finding a way to build walls high enough to guarantee they'll never get hurt. That's impossible. Life is messy and dangerous and beautiful, and it doesn't come with any guarantees."

Tears welled in my eyes again, but these were different. They were tears of fierce, protective love for this fragile, courageous, beautiful man.

"Loving someone means risking everything, Austin," I murmured, the truth of it settling deep in my soul. "It means facing down that terror of loss every single day—

that voice that tells you the worst is going to happen—and choosing that person anyway. Choosing to be happy now. Loving them harder because of it. Because the time we have is all we have. That's what makes it real. That's what makes it worth anything at all."

Something flickered in his eyes, a dawning light in the storm. The rigid, defensive lines around his mouth began to soften.

"I'm scared too. I'm scared of this." I gestured to my bandaged leg. "I'm scared of a thousand other things that could go wrong with Heron House, with my life. And after what you told me, I'm scared of whatever demons you're still fighting." I brought his hand to my lips and pressed a soft kiss to his knuckles. "But so much more, I'm scared of a life without you in it. So let's be scared together. We'll figure it out together. Because that's what being a partner means."

He studied me as if seeing me for the first time. The years of haunted guilt—the stormy, self-inflicted torment in his gray eyes—began to recede. It was like watching the sun burn through a dense morning fog to reveal the clear sky behind. The stronghold he had built around his heart wouldn't fall after a single conversation. But it was beginning to, right here in front of us.

A single, shuddering breath escaped him. His shoulders dropped a fraction. His hands relaxed.

"Iris." My name was a raw, beautiful sound on his lips. He leaned forward, his forehead coming to rest gently against mine, his eyes closing. "How do you know all that?"

"I'm not sure," I whispered back, my voice thick. "I just… I look at you. And I know."

He was silent for a long moment, just breathing with our foreheads pressed together. Then he pulled back, just enough to look at me again. "Just tell me what I have to do.

Tell me, and I'll do it. To prove to you that you're what matters to me. That I love you. Not a ghost."

My heart soared, so full it might burst. The last, tiny, cold stone of doubt that had been lodged there vanished, incinerated in the pure, honest light of his surrender. He wasn't just offering me words. He was offering me his beautiful, battered heart and trusting me to help him put it back together. I smiled, a real, teary, triumphant smile.

"Austin," I said softly, my hand tightening on his. "You just did."

He frowned. "Did what?"

"You hung on through the storm. You let me see you. All of you." I took a shaky breath. "And I love you too. So much."

He squeezed his eyes shut, a fresh tear escaping and tracing a path down his cheek, but this time, it wasn't a tear of grief. It was something else entirely. He held me in an exhausted embrace. There were no more specters between us, only the challenging but hopeful road ahead.

The crisis had passed.

The storm had broken.

And we had chosen each other, fully and completely.

After a long, peaceful moment, I gave a little wince as a sharp twinge throbbed in my head. The knot had reasserted itself. I adjusted myself slightly in the bed, the movement awkward and cumbersome.

Austin pulled back immediately, his face etched with concern. "You okay? Do you need the nurse? Pain meds?"

"Probably a good idea," I said, offering him a slightly mischievous grin. "It's just… wow. That was a pretty heavy conversation for someone who just woke up from surgery. You know, after all that, you definitely owe me some serious chocolate. Artisan, not some Pennsylvania shit—I mean nonsense!"

A sound rumbled deep in his chest. It was a dull, rusty sound at first, as if the mechanism was long out of use. But it grew, and for the first time since I'd met him, Austin Coleridge threw his head back and laughed. A real, full, unguarded laugh that filled the hospital room with the most beautiful sound I'd ever heard.

It was the sound of hope.

The sound of healing.

The sound of home.

Chapter Thirty

AUSTIN

THE HOSPITAL ROOM smelled like antiseptic and wilted flowers, a scent I was already desperate to leave behind. After two days in the hospital, Iris was dressed in real clothes—a soft, yellow sundress Brenna had bought for her —and was sitting in a wheelchair by the window, looking pale but stubborn. Her left leg, encased in a thick, bulky dressing of gauze and wrapped bandage, was propped up on the leg rests, fully non-weight-bearing. The headache from her concussion was mostly gone, and her team of doctors pronounced her good enough for home.

Which was more than good enough for me.

A nurse with a no-nonsense ponytail was firing off a list of instructions, pointing to a small pharmacy bag of prescription bottles on the bedside table that I'd picked up. "The anticoagulant pill is once a day. Make sure you take it at the same time each morning. Set an alarm on your phone if you have to. It's important." She tapped the other bottle. "Now, for the pain medication. This is for when you need it. The key is to stay ahead of the pain. It's much easier to keep it at a manageable level than to chase it down after it's roaring. Don't try to be a hero. Listen to your body."

Iris was nodding, but her attention was clearly elsewhere. Her gaze kept drifting to the window, to the slice of blue sky visible beyond the parking lot. I, on the other hand, was laser-focused, committing every word the nurse said to memory.

Anticoagulants, same time daily. Pain meds, stay ahead of it. Keep the leg elevated.

The instructions were a new set of nautical charts I had to learn, and I'd be damned if I was going to run us aground.

"And a follow-up with Dr. Starling in ten days," the nurse finished, handing me a slip of paper with the appointment details. "He'll check the incision and likely get you fitted for a proper walking boot then. But be patient, okay?"

"So what you're saying is I'm officially a professional lounger for the next six weeks?" Iris asked, trying for a bright, breezy tone that didn't quite hide the frustration in her eyes.

"That's exactly what I'm saying," the nurse said with a firm, not-unkind smile.

I took the bag of medications and the appointment slip. "What I'm hearing is no weight on that leg. At all." I leveled a hard stare at Iris. "We've got it."

She met my gaze, her defiant expression softening into a small, weary smile. "Got it, Captain."

Navigating the hospital hallways with Iris in the wheelchair was an exercise in slow, deliberate torture. I just focused on getting her out, my hand a steady weight on her shoulder as a hospital worker guided the wheelchair.

When we made it out into the blinding Florida sun and the soupy air of the parking lot, the real logistical challenge presented itself. My truck, which had always been only transportation, now looked like a damn monster truck. Its passenger seat was a sheer cliff face.

"Okay," Iris said, taking the crutches from me and maneuvering them under her arms only a little awkwardly. "I can do this. Just give me a second to figure out the geometry."

She wobbled, trying to find her balance on one foot while preparing to heave herself up into the cab. It was a disaster waiting to happen. Another fall. Another hollow thud.

No.

I took the crutches from her and tossed them into the back seat without a word.

"Hey!" she protested, one hand on her hip while the other held onto the doorframe, a flash of her old, stubborn fire in her eyes. "I'm not helpless, Austin. It's just a truck, not Mount Everest."

"Nope." Before she could argue further, I bent down, slid one arm under her knees and the other around her back, and scooped her up into my arms.

She let out a soft, surprised "oof," her arms instinctively wrapping around my neck. "Austin! You can't just—"

"Already did," I grunted, carefully maneuvering her through the open passenger door. I was intensely aware of her, of the warm, solid weight of her in my arms, of the different, hospital scent of her hair. I bumped her splinted leg lightly against the doorframe, and a low curse rumbled in my chest.

"Easy, big guy," she murmured against my neck, her voice a mix of exasperation and something else… something soft and trusting.

I managed to get her settled in the seat, her injured leg propped awkwardly across the bench. I buckled her in, my knuckles brushing against the soft fabric of her dress. It was so different from the last time I'd held her like this, when our embrace was all frantic heat and desperate need. This was something else entirely. Quieter. Deeper.

And a hundred times more real.

I wasn't just her lover. I was her partner. I closed her door and walked around to my side, the full weight of that realization settling over me like a perfectly weighted blanket.

I backed the truck out of the parking spot with more care than I used navigating a shallow channel in low tide. The usual rumble of the engine was a soothing, familiar sound. I glanced over at Iris. Her eyes were closed, her head leaned back against the headrest, a faint line of pain etched between her brows. Without thinking, I reached over and took her hand, lacing my fingers through hers where they rested in her lap.

She opened her eyes, a soft, questioning look on her face. I didn't say anything. I just squeezed her hand once, a silent promise, before turning my attention back to the road. She squeezed back, and a few minutes later, the tense line between her brows smoothed out, her breathing deepening into the slow, even rhythm of sleep.

I drove in a comfortable silence, the radio off, the only sounds the hum of the tires on the asphalt and her soft breathing. I kept my hand linked with hers over Seven Mile Bridge, the entire way back to Dove Key. I peeked at her sleeping face, at the pale exhaustion that lay just beneath her tan, the stubborn set of her mouth, even in sleep. The full, steadying weight of what she meant to me settled in my chest, solid as a lead sinker.

My fear in that hospital waiting room had been the old

fear—the terror of a sudden, violent loss. But as I glanced at her now, so fragile and so damn strong all at once, a new understanding began to settle in me. Her fall wasn't a punishment from the universe. It wasn't the other shoe dropping.

It was just… life.

Messy, unpredictable, and sometimes very painful. It was the first storm we had to navigate together. My job wasn't to try and stop the storms from coming. It was to be her anchor when they hit.

The thought wasn't a burden.

It was a purpose.

When I pulled into my driveway, she was still sleeping. I killed the engine and just sat there for a minute, watching her in the quiet of my carport. I didn't want to wake her, but I also knew letting her sleep in the truck wasn't an option.

"Iris," I said softly, giving her hand a gentle squeeze. "We're home."

Her eyes fluttered open, groggy and disoriented. "Oh. Okay."

"Stay put," I commanded before getting out of the truck. I retrieved her crutches from the back, then rounded to her side and opened her door.

"I can try it this time." Her voice was still thick with sleep, but that familiar spark of independence was already returning.

I shook my head. "Soon. But not today."

I helped her swing her legs around, and then, once again, I lifted her into my arms. This time she didn't protest. She just sighed and rested her head on my shoulder as I carried her toward my front door. I nudged it open with my foot and stepped across the threshold. I bypassed the living room, heading straight down the short hall to my bedroom. My sanctuary. The place that had once been my fortress to keep the world out.

I'd spent the morning getting it ready. The bed was made with fresh, clean sheets that smelled of sunshine and sea breeze. I'd moved the small TV from the guest room onto my dresser and placed a stack of books Brenna had dropped off on the nightstand, next to a thermal bottle of ice water.

The sense of rightness, of her belonging here in my space, was an anchoring force. This wasn't an invasion. It was a completion.

I laid her down gently on the bed. Her sigh of relief was a soft, breathy sound in the quiet room. Her eyes drifted around, taking in the preparations, and when they landed on mine, they were full of a sleepy, trusting gratitude that made my chest ache.

With movements that were both unfamiliar and deeply instinctual, I propped her injured leg up on a careful arrangement of pillows, making sure the angle was just right. Her good foot nudged my hip as I worked, a small, unconscious touch that sent a jolt of warmth through me.

"You thought of everything," she murmured, her voice already starting to slur with exhaustion.

"Just trying to stay ahead of the pain."

She gave a weak, lopsided smile. "Bossy, but effective, Captain."

I pulled the blanket up over her, tucking it in around her shoulders. She was already drifting off again, her eyelids heavy.

"Just rest," I said softly.

"Austin?" she whispered, her eyes already closed.

"Yeah?"

"Thank you."

"You're welcome. I love you, Iris." I smiled as her head

drifted to the side. I didn't need her to say the words back. I already knew.

I stood in the doorway for a long time after that, just watching the slow, even rise and fall of her chest. The harsh afternoon sun was softened by the blinds, striping the floor with familiar bars of light. But the room wasn't the same. It wasn't just my solitary space anymore. It was fuller. Quieter, somehow, despite her presence.

The ghosts were silent. The old, familiar ache of guilt and fear was gone, replaced by the solid, grounding weight of this new reality. I'd help however I could.

Iris was here.

She was safe.

She was mine to care for.

I was no longer running from the past. I was actively building a future, one pillow, one bottle of water, one quiet moment at a time.

Chapter Thirty-One

AUSTIN

THE BONFIRE on the beach in front of Mom's house—now Harper and Chase's—roared, spitting sparks into the darkening sky. It was a familiar scene, one I'd been a part of my entire life, but tonight was different. Sharper. Brighter. The scent of burning driftwood and salt was cleaner, the sound of my family's overlapping laughter a warm, welcome hum instead of noise.

I leaned back in my beach chair, the sand cool beneath my bare feet, and took a long swallow of beer. Beside me, Iris shifted, adjusting the bulky walking boot on her propped-up leg. Without thinking, I reached over and draped my arm around her, pulling her closer to my side. She leaned her head against my shoulder with a contented sigh, her hair smelling of the orange-scented shampoo she used.

It had been a month since she'd fallen, a month since my personal true north had recalibrated itself to her in that hospital room. In that time, something had settled in me. A calm I hadn't known in thirteen years. Iris had recently graduated from crutches to the walking boot. After bringing her home from the hospital, we'd negotiated that she would spend the first three weeks at my place. I flat-out refused to let her negotiate stairs. Frustration at her immobility and the fact that wounds healed at their own pace had caused some of her tame curses to venture into more adult territory. I understood her need to prove herself. Once she could hobble on two relatively solid feet, I relented. She needed to be a part of Heron House.

My gaze drifted across the firelight. Harper and Chase were huddled together with tightly swaddled bundles in their arms. They looked exhausted, overwhelmed, and totally besotted with the two tiny humans sleeping within. Cameron and Claire. My new nephew and niece. They'd arrived via a C-section three weeks ago, both small but healthy, and had already turned the entire Coleridge clan into a puddle of cooing, sentimental fools.

Even me, a little.

Mom had returned home temporarily to meet her new grandchildren, and every line in her brow had gone slack when I introduced her to Iris. After a long conversation where I assured her I was overcoming my past at last, she fussed about missing the important parts of our lives. My siblings and I tried to convince her she had been there when it counted and that she'd earned some time to kick up her heels. She went back to Italy a few days ago, but I wasn't sure she'd stay away now.

Big brother Finn was proudly demonstrating the proper technique for toasting a marshmallow to the two sleeping infants, his voice a serious, instructional whisper. On a log by the coolers, Eli and Jules were engaged in what looked like a heated, playful debate about the correct ratio of lime to tequila in a margarita.

This was the chaotic, noisy mess of my family. For the first time in ages, I didn't feel like a stranger at the feast. I felt part of it. With Iris tucked securely against my side, the feeling of being a solitary stone in a rushing river was gone. I wasn't just watching the current anymore. I was in it.

Braden sauntered over, a fresh beer in each hand, and handed one to me with a shit-eating grin that was all too familiar.

"Look at you." He plopped down in the sand at my feet. "Arms around each other. Looking all content. It's deeply unsettling, Austin. Pretty soon you'll be asking for a wine spritzer and talking about your feelings."

"Shut up, Braden," I said mildly, taking a sip of the beer. A few months ago, the comment would have sent a spike of irritation through me. Tonight, it just felt like… Braden.

"Leave your brother alone," Iris said, her voice full of laughter as she playfully swatted at Braden's shoulder. "He's allowed to be content. And for the record, he has excellent taste in wine."

Braden's eyebrows shot up. "He does? Since when?"

"Since I introduced him to it," she said with a wink in my direction that made my stomach do a slow, lazy flip.

I smiled as she and Braden fell into an easy, teasing banter. She fit with my unruly family. She wasn't intimidated by them, and they, in turn, had accepted her completely. Brenna, sitting on the other side of the fire with Hunter, caught my eye and gave me a warm, knowing smile that said, *See? I told you so.*

I placed a soft kiss on Iris's temple. The gesture was simple, public, and more natural than anything I'd done in years.

"So, this is interesting," Eli announced to the group at

large, gesturing with his beer bottle. "My lovely wife sent me on an emergency run to Island Market today for a very specific type of key lime. Apparently, my margarita-making skills are under intense scrutiny."

Jules swatted his arm. "Your skills are fine. However, your ingredient procurement needs work."

Eli laughed, then his attention focused on Braden. "Whatever. But I was over by the produce section, trying to tell the difference between a key lime and a regular one, and I swear I saw Tessa Donovan. Is she back on the island?"

The easy laughter died on Braden's lips. The s'more he was about to take a bite of stopped halfway to his mouth. For a split second, the charming, unflappable bartender vanished, replaced by a younger, more vulnerable man caught off guard. He recovered quickly, but not before a brief, sharp flicker of pain flashed in his eyes.

"Tessa?" Braden's voice was a little too casual, a little too tight. He lowered the s'more and tossed it in the fire. "Couldn't have been. She left Dove Key behind after high school and never looked back. Doubt that's changed in twelve years. You probably saw a tourist who looked like her."

He stood up abruptly, brushing sticky marshmallow from his fingers onto his shorts. "I've slacked off enough. Time to get back to work."

He offered a tight, unconvincing smile to the group at large, his gaze pointedly avoiding Eli's. Then he was gone, his back rigid as he marched into the darkness toward Tidal Hops, leaving a heavy, awkward silence in his wake.

Harper and Brenna exchanged a worried look across the fire. Eli winced, clearly regretting his casual comment.

Iris panned her gaze around the circle. "What was that all about?"

I sighed and pulled her a little closer. Beside us, Harper fielded the question, her voice low and full of a quiet, sisterly sympathy.

"Tessa was Braden's first girlfriend. High school sweethearts." She poked a stick into the fire, watching the embers glow. "Her parents had bigger plans for her than Dove Key. She got a scholarship to a fancy university and left."

Brenna nodded from her spot on the other side of the fire. "Braden always insisted they were too different, and it was for the best. But he's good at hiding what he really feels."

Iris elbowed me. "Sounds like he learned from this one."

"Well," Eli said, his usual levity gone, "looks like I just stomped all over a landmine I didn't know was still active. Didn't think it would be that big of a deal."

The conversation shifted after that, getting back to safer subjects. Soon we were back amidst the happy chaos of Finn recounting a dramatic story about a sand crab and Eli trying to convince Jules that salt on the rim made all the difference.

I brushed my lips close to Iris's ear. "I've had about as much of this wholesome family fun as I can stomach for one night. Let me get you out of here."

An answering spark ignited in her blue eyes, a flash of heat and promise just for me. "Is that so, Captain? And where exactly are you planning on taking me and my boot?"

"Home," I said, the word simple but holding a world of meaning.

She smiled, a slow, sultry curve of her lips. "Lead the way."

Getting away from a Coleridge family bonfire was a

strategic operation, one that required careful timing and firm resolve. I stood and pulled Iris gently to her feet, my hand going instinctively to her waist to steady her as she found her balance with the walking boot in the soft sand.

"We're heading out," I announced to the group, my tone leaving no room for argument.

Of course, that didn't stop Chase.

"Leaving so soon?" he called out, his grin illuminated by the firelight. "The night is young! We haven't even gotten to the part where Eli breaks out his terrible guitar playing yet."

"I'm pretty much dead on my feet, and don't tell me you're not," Harper added as she shifted Cameron in her arms to elbow her husband. "We need to get home too."

I steadied Iris as she turned back with a wave. "Good night."

"Don't do anything I wouldn't do!" Eli and Jules shouted in perfect unison, and they both burst into laughter.

"That leaves the field wide open," I muttered, shaking my head. I leaned down to give Harper a light pat on the shoulder. "Get some rest."

"I will." Her eyes were soft and full of happy understanding. "It's good to see you like this, Austin."

I didn't have a response for that. I just gave her shoulder a squeeze, then focused on navigating Iris back toward the path.

The short drive home was quiet, the windows of my truck down, the cool night air a welcome relief after the heat of the fire. When I pulled into her driveway, the house was a welcoming sight. Gus's crew had finished the exterior last week, and the fresh coat of paint—a soft, warm white with trim the color of a stormy sea—looked beautiful under the glow of the new porch lights Iris had picked out.

The place no longer looked like a haunted shipwreck. It looked like a home.

I helped her out of the truck, my hands lingering at her waist. "You okay? Leg not hurting too much?"

"It's a little sore, but it's a good kind of sore. A healing kind." She smiled up at me, her face illuminated by the porch light. "Thank you for taking me tonight."

"You're part of the circus now. Might as well get used to the clowns."

She laughed, which brought an answering smile to my face. We walked up the new, sturdy porch steps to the front door. A beautiful, solid teak door had replaced the monstrous, screeching beast that had previously guarded the house.

She unlocked it, and together we stepped inside the grand foyer. The air inside was cool and smelled of fresh paint and her unique mix of sugar and sunshine. She turned to me, a soft, happy smile on her face.

A sudden, undeniable impulse seized me. "Wait. Close your eyes."

A question entered her blue eyes, then they fluttered closed, her lips curling up. Before she could get too curious, I scooped her into my arms.

She let out a soft gasp of surprise as her eyes flew open, her arms instinctively going around my neck. "Austin! What are you doing?"

"Carrying you. Saving you that awkward trip up the stairs." The excuse was flimsy, but the action was monumentally right. I turned and started up the wide, grand staircase.

Her head was tucked into the curve of my neck, her warm breath a tickle against my skin. She was light in my arms, a warm bundle of chaotic, wonderful Iris. As I carried her upstairs and past walls that were no longer crumbling, I thought about the first time I'd seen her, a vague, annoying whirlwind of noise next door. Now, the thought of this house, this life, without her was unimaginable.

When I reached the third floor, I didn't stop until I reached the doorway of her master suite at the end of the hall, now fully remodeled. The walls were a soft, calming shade of blue. The teak floors gleamed. A comfortable king-sized bed, piled high with pillows, stood against the far wall. Through the wide glass doors that led to her private balcony, the moon cast a silvery path across the calm, dark surface of the Gulf.

It was a reflection of her. Peaceful. Beautiful. Full of gentle strength.

I set her down next to the bed, her hands still linked around my neck. The air was cool and still, a hushed sanctuary after the lively noise of the bonfire. She looked up at me, her blue eyes dark and luminous, full of a deep, trusting love that made my heart ache in the best possible way.

This was the peace I had spent all those years searching for, a peace I'd thought could only be found in solitude. I had been so wrong. True peace wasn't the absence of chaos.

It was finding your anchor in the middle of it.

And Iris was my anchor.

I leaned in and kissed her, a slow, deep kiss full of all the things I still had trouble saying. Full of gratitude, of reverence, of a love so profound it still scared the hell out of me.

She sighed into my mouth, her body melting against mine in total surrender that was also a claiming. This wasn't the frantic, desperate coupling of our first time, nor the playful, exploratory passion of our night on the boat. This was something else entirely.

This was worship.

My hands moved to the buttons of her soft cotton shirt, and I unfastened them slowly, deliberately. I kissed the warm skin of her shoulder, the hollow of her throat, the perfect swell of her breast above the lace of her bra, savoring her taste, her scent. She arched into me with a soft moan escaping her lips.

After crouching to the floor, I opened the Velcro straps of her boot and gently lifted her leg out. Brushing my fingers over her scar, I pressed a kiss to it. Returning to my feet, I framed her face in my hands and kissed her fiercely.

She undid the button of my shorts, her fingers sure and steady, her touch sending a familiar, welcome fire through my veins. We moved with the easy, practiced rhythm of two people who had memorized the language of each other's bodies. Clothes were shed not with frantic haste, but with a slow, sensual purpose, until we were skin to skin on the cool, soft sheets of her bed, the moonlight painting silvery patterns across her body.

I took my time, exploring her with my hands, my mouth, loving every curve, every plane, every secret, sensitive spot. I loved the way she trembled under my touch, the way she gasped out my name, the way she gave herself over to the pleasure. There were no shadows of the past.

There was only Iris.

When I moved over her, positioning myself between her legs, she looked up at me. Her eyes were full of a love so open and unconditional it was like a benediction.

"I love you, Austin," she whispered, the words a soft, perfect caress.

And this time, the answering words didn't feel stuck,

didn't feel terrifying. They were inevitable. "I love you too. So much."

I entered her slowly, a deep joining that was both a promise and a vow. This was a homecoming, a final clicking into place of a piece of my soul. Her hot, slick body welcomed me, and she let out a soft, breathy sigh of pure contentment.

I stayed there for a long moment, buried deep inside her, my forehead pressed to hers, just breathing her in. I wanted to memorize the feel of her around me, the scent of her skin, the look of unguarded trust in her eyes.

I began to move in a slow, deliberate rhythm. She met me with an answering passion, her legs wrapping around my waist, pulling me deeper. Her hands roamed my back, her nails scraping with a confident, possessive touch that sent fire through me.

Our pace quickened, the slow burn building into a roaring fire. Her soft moans became sharp, breathy gasps, each one driving me on. Tension coiled in her body, and the tremors started deep inside her.

The pressure built inside me in a rushing, unstoppable tide. I drove into her one last time, deep and hard, my control shattering as her body convulsed around mine. A raw, guttural groan tore from my throat, my release a shuddering wave inextricably linked with hers. We crashed over the edge together, two parts of a whole, complete.

Afterward, we lay with her head on my chest, my hand stroking her hair. The rhythm of our breathing was the only sound in the room. I knew a sense of peace unlike anything I had ever known.

She propped herself on an elbow to stare at me, a contented smile on her face. Her gaze swept around the beautiful, finished room, at the moonlight streaming in, at the comfortable sofa in the corner, at the wide, inviting bed we were currently occupying.

"You know," her voice was a low, teasing murmur, "it's almost a pity to have this be my private bedroom. It's the best room in the house. I could add it to the booking engine and make a fortune. Maybe I'll just remodel an old broom closet downstairs for myself."

That made me laugh. A real, free, hearty sound that filled the air. "Don't you dare get any ideas, Holloway. Gus will have you committed, and I'll have to bail you out." I hooked an elbow around her neck to pull her down for a kiss.

She giggled against my lips. I pulled back to take in the absolute joy on her face, and a thought settled in my mind. My smile subsided, my expression turning serious. "Then again, if you ever did want to rent out your bedroom…" I paused, brushing a stray strand of blonde hair from her forehead, my gaze locked on hers. "You could always move into my place."

Surprise lit her eyes, followed by that familiar, teasing glint. She arched an eyebrow. "Captain Grumpy? Willingly giving up his sacred, solitary fortress for good?"

I smiled, an easy expression that held no shadows. Then I leaned in and kissed her again, a deep kiss full of a promise I had every intention of keeping.

"I thought that was what I wanted. But I was wrong." I looked directly into her wide, beautiful blue eyes and said the truest thing I knew. "I found something so much better."

Epilogue

IRIS

SIX MONTHS LATER

THE MORNING RUSH at Heron House was a scene of controlled bustling, and I was its director. The air in my beautiful, functional kitchen hummed with the cheerful clatter of plates, the rich aroma of locally roasted coffee, and the scent of my signature lemon-lavender scones, fresh from the oven. Through the wide pass-through window I'd had Gus install, I could see the veranda was full. A couple from Chicago, here for their tenth anniversary, were laughing at something one of their kids said. A trio of women on a girls' getaway were planning their morning of diving with Eli, followed by shopping. A quiet, older gentleman was reading a book, a contented smile on his face as he sipped his coffee.

This. This was the dream. Not a hazy vision on a Pinterest board, but a living, breathing reality. A reality filled with happy guests, the scent of baking, and the steady hum of a business I had built from the ground up.

A monumental project I had started and finished.

My gaze swept across the sunlit room and landed on the magnificent potted Bird of Paradise in the corner. Its wide, glossy green leaves unfurled toward the light in a vibrant splash of life against the calm blue walls. Brenna and Liv had lugged it in on opening day, their joint gift to celebrate Heron House B&B's launch. They had been a lifeline during those first weeks after my fall, a constant stream of smuggled pastries from Liv and new paperbacks from Brenna. They'd sat with me on Austin's porch, letting me vent about physical therapy and celebrating every construction milestone Gus reported. Second only to the rock-solid presence of Austin, they had been the anchor that kept me from drifting into frustration. They, too, were part of the foundation of this new life.

Gus and his incredible crew had finished the last of the major renovations nearly two months ago. The grand Victorian lady was no longer decaying. She was resurrected, a perfect blend of historic soul and modern comfort. We'd been open for six weeks, and I was booked at ninety percent capacity. The reality and the sheer, wonderful success of it still hit me at odd moments.

I moved with confident, pain-free grace, plating scones, refilling coffee mugs, chatting with my guests about the best places to rent a kayak or see the sunset. The frantic, overwhelmed woman who had once battled a rogue sprinkler and a rickety piece of siding was like a character from a different story.

My gaze drifted past the veranda to the lush green lawn that sloped gently toward the sea. The magnificent magnolia tree stood tall and proud, its waxy green leaves gleaming in the morning sun. Its branches were dotted with creamy white blossoms that filled the air with their sweet, intoxicating perfume. Austin had taken over its care with his usual reserved, obsessive competence, and the tree looked blissfully healthy. It was our tree now, a silent, beautiful symbol of our shared life.

Our shared homes.

The thought still sent a thrill through me. I'd been living with him, in his peaceful, meticulously ordered conch house, for five months. Five months of waking up to the steady rhythm of his breathing, of sharing cups of coffee on his patio before the rest of the world woke up, and of falling asleep tangled in his arms. Feeling absolutely safe.

My idea of renting Heron House's master suite had blossomed into a very lucrative revenue stream. And as Austin informed me, even a successful proprietress needed some privacy.

By late morning, my guests had headed out for their day's adventures. I was in the kitchen, stacking plates into the commercial-grade dishwasher—a luxury I thanked my lucky stars for every single day—feeling profoundly happy. The kitchen door opened with a soft click, and I turned to find Austin there. He'd showered after his early morning charter, and the fresh, intoxicating scent of him cut through the lingering sweetness of the scones. He was wearing a button-down shirt and new jeans, and he looked so impossibly handsome that the air stuttered in my lungs.

"Morning." His gaze swept around my beautiful kitchen, then landed on me, his eyes soft with an emotion I was no longer afraid to name. After gentle prodding from me and several of his siblings, he was seeing a counselor in Marathon to help him process that long-suppressed grief and guilt. As a result, the tight lines around his eyes were fainter these days, his walk more relaxed.

"It's closer to noon now, Captain." I smiled, wiping my hands on my apron. "You're just in time. The last scone has your name on it."

"I've already had breakfast." But he walked over, stealing a crumb from the plate anyway. He popped it into his mouth. "Just came to see you."

My heart melted into a happy, ridiculous puddle when he leaned in and gave me a slow, lingering kiss. Even after all these months, his simple, quiet affection still had the power to make my knees wobbly.

"I'm glad you did," I said when he pulled away.

He seemed a little on edge this morning, a purposeful intensity humming just beneath his calm surface. He took my hand. "Come with me for a minute. There's something I want to show you."

Intrigued, I let him lead me from the kitchen, through the now bright and airy living room, to the quiet nook I had come to love most in the entire house: the window seat. The place where I'd found Aunt Constance's letter. The sun streamed through the wide window as we sat on the cushioned seat. Austin's large frame filled the intimate space. He still held my hand, his thumb stroking the back of my knuckles.

"I brought you something," he said.

After letting go, he reached into the back pocket of his jeans and pulled out a flat, small, and neatly tied canvas pouch. It was the kind of bag he used for holding spare parts or special lures, practical and well-worn. He pressed it into my palm.

"Ooh, a present!" I exclaimed. "Maybe a shell you found on a remote flat? Or perhaps a piece of sea glass worn smooth by the ocean?"

I cocked my head, but he remained silent and just

smiled faintly. I carefully untied the drawstring and tipped the contents into my hand.

It wasn't a shell.

Several perfect, intricate loops of thin rope—twine that looked like he'd used it a time or two—were coiled in my hand. Smiling, I gently separated the loops, then froze. My heart stopped.

A ring lay in the center.

It was simple, elegant. A band of shining white gold holding a single, square-cut diamond that sparkled with a hint of blue.

Remembering its job, my heart pounded a frantic rhythm against my ribs. I jerked my head up, my eyes wide with a question.

Austin rubbed both palms on his jeans, but when he met my eyes, his gaze was unwavering, so full of raw, powerful emotion that made my eyes begin to sting.

"That's a fisherman's knot." His voice was low, steady, as he gestured to the coil of rope still resting in my palm. "It's a variation of a uni knot. It's the one you use when you want to make sure the line never, ever slips, no matter how hard the fight is, no matter what storm hits. You tie it right," his eyes held mine, "and it holds forever."

He took my other hand, his grip firm, grounding. "Heron House was your new beginning, Iris. A place where you put down roots and built something lasting." He took a deep, shaky breath. "And you were my new start. I spent thirteen years thinking my life was over, that all the good parts were just memories. You taught me how to live again, not just survive."

His voice was thick with emotion he no longer tried to hide. He took the loop of rope from my palm and expertly slipped the ring free. He didn't get down on one knee. He didn't need to. All he had to do was meet my gaze—his vulnerability his greatest strength, his heart in his eyes.

"I want to be your anchor, Iris. And I want you to be mine. For all the storms to come." He held up the ring, the beautiful gem catching the morning light. "Please marry me."

I couldn't speak. I could only nod, a frantic, jerky motion, my throat too tight with joy.

He took that as the answer it was. A slow, beautiful smile bloomed on his face. He took my left hand and slid the ring onto my finger.

"Yes," I managed to choke out, my voice a watery, triumphant whisper. "Oh, Austin. Of course, yes."

I threw my arms around his neck, burying my face in the warm, solid curve of his shoulder, breathing in the scent of him. Of home. He held me tightly, his strong arms a promise of forever.

Eventually, we broke apart. He picked up the coils of rope, turning them in his hands. "I set it up first with fishing line since you usually make this knot in line, but I thought it looked stupid for a proposal. The rope has more weight to it, more meaning."

"It was perfect. All of it. Completely you."

We sat there for a long time, in that sunlit, meaningful spot, surrounded by the hum of the life and love we had built together, my new ring a cool, solid weight on my finger.

Our future was secure.

One knot, tied forever.

THANK you for reading BETTER THAN SUNSHINE! Grumpy-sunshine is such a great trope, and add in a wounded hero, and you've got what I hope was an unput-downable read!

If you'd like a glimpse into **Austin and Iris's happy future**, scan or click below to sign up for my newsletter:

Beach Read Update
(www.erinbrockus.com/sunshine)

As a thank you, I'll send you a **bonus scene** which peeks into their lives several years in the future.

If you're already on my list, I've got you covered! At the bottom of each newsletter is a link to all my free content for subscribers. Just find your last email from me to read this bonus, as well as any others you might have missed. Or you can simply sign up again—you'll have your bonus in a flash.

Keep reading to discover what's next in the Sunset Siesta series...

BRADEN

The back door of Tidal Hops slammed shut behind me, the sound a punctuation mark on my hasty retreat. The cheerful noise of the bonfire—my family's laughter, the crackle of burning wood—faded, replaced by the familiar, steadying chaos of my kingdom. The brewpub was humming with its usual night energy, but I bypassed the front of the house. My usual charming-host persona was currently locked away somewhere deep and inaccessible.

I pushed through the swinging doors into the kitchen, the blast of heat and the sharp scent of onions and sizzling meat a welcome assault. Andy, my best line cook, was bent over the grill, his movements practiced and efficient.

"Hey, boss. Back so soon?" he asked without looking up.

"Had enough of the family bonfire circus for one night. A little bit of Eli goes an extremely long way." I forced a smile and made my voice soften. "I'll take over here. You can get a jump on the prep for the weekend rush."

Andy straightened, his brow lowered with a question he was too smart to ask. "You got it."

He moved away and left me at the grill. I grabbed the heavy metal spatula, its familiar weight a comfort in my hand. Order tickets were lined up on the rail, a neat row of demands I could meet. A burger, well-done. Fish tacos, no cilantro. A blackened wahoo sandwich.

Simple.

Solvable.

Unlike the mess I'd just walked away from. The night had started out fine, better than fine. At the bonfire, seeing Iris propped up and laughing with that bulky walking boot on her leg had felt like a win. Austin had his arm slung around her like he'd been doing it his whole life. The rest of us gave them a respectable amount of shit for it, the way Coleridges do when one of us actually looks happy.

Then Eli, with the casual grace of a man dropping a lit match into a puddle of gasoline, had to open his big mouth. Of course it was Eli. Who else?

Tessa.

The name had landed in the middle of our easy family circle and exploded.

I slapped a burger patty onto the hot grill, damn near squishing it to death with the spatula as the hiss of searing meat made a satisfying roar. I focused on the task, on the physical reality of it. The heat on my face. The precise timing needed to get that perfect char without overcooking the center. This was the empire I had built from a half-baked idea and a whole lot of debt. A place where I was in complete control.

Not her. Couldn't be. The thought was a frantic, repeating loop.

Eli was an idiot. A lovable, sometimes infuriatingly shrewd one, but an idiot nonetheless. He saw a tourist with red hair and made a leap. He didn't know what he was talking about.

I flipped the burger aggressively, the sound a sharp smack against the metal. Another ticket came up. Two more burgers, one with Swiss, one with cheddar. I worked with a focused fury, my movements almost violent. I was a machine. Toast the buns, melt the cheese, plate it with a side of fries.

Next.

The kitchen door swung open, and a server called out, "Hey, Cade! Can you run another keg out? We're out of Hopical Storm!"

From the bar, I heard a woman's laugh. Bright, clear, full-throated. A sound that was nothing and yet everything like Tessa's laugh.

I faltered for a second. The spatula paused. My breath halted. The sizzle of the grill faded to a distant hum.

Stop it, I commanded myself, my internal voice yelling. *You're imagining things!*

But the damage was done. The castle had been breached. The memories came rushing back in.

The hot, greasy air of the kitchen vanished, replaced by the sharp scent rising off the Gulf. I wasn't thirty anymore. I was eighteen, standing on the north shore beach with Tessa Donovan, the world new and tasting of possibility.

The memory was so potent it was physical. The sand was damp and cool under my bare feet, the humid breeze whipping her fiery hair across her face. It was the summer after graduation, the sky full of clouds and the air charged with electricity. She wasn't just talking about the future.

She was inhaling it, her dark-green eyes blazing with intelligence and drive.

"My parents worry that you'll never be able to get a *real job* in Dove Key." Her voice was full of fierce, youthful frustration as she gestured out at the churning water. "They don't get that you could build something amazing right here."

A knot formed in my gut, the familiar shame of my family name. "Yeah, well, to them, Coleridge is just another way to say 'going nowhere fast.'"

It was the truth I'd been running from my whole life.

But she turned to me, her expression full of belief in me I hadn't yet found in myself. She grabbed my hand. "They're wrong. You're going to accomplish whatever you set your mind to, Braden. I know it."

We were so damn young, standing on the edge of everything. I'd just started diving after being taught by Eli. I'd talk to Tessa for hours about it, about the silent, beautiful world beneath the waves. A world apart from the noise of my family. She understood. The ocean was a part of her, like it was with Eli and Austin. And I had this half-formed, impossible dream of a place of my own, a real business that would prove I was more than just another Coleridge.

She squeezed my hand. "And whatever happens with college, we'll figure it out, right? We'll make it work."

The promise had been as real and solid as the driftwood near our feet. We both believed it. Two kids against the world, convinced that love and ambition were enough to conquer distance. I told myself I was being noble, letting her fly without trying to cage her. The truth was, I was afraid she'd eventually realize she was meant for the sky, and I was stuck on the ground. I was just a Coleridge from

Dove Key. Tessa was destined for greatness, a full-ride scholarship waiting for her. We kissed then, a desperate, salty goodbye that already tasted like the end.

She left and never looked back. I never tried to fight for her. The end.

A sharp, acrid smell—the scent of burning fat and ruined meat—yanked me back to the searing heat of the kitchen.

"Boss, that burger's a hockey puck." Andy's worried voice cut through the memory.

I looked down. A blackened, smoking circle of what used to be a burger sat on the grill, a perfect monument to my distraction.

"Goddammit," I snarled. "Son-of-a-bitch burger."

I scraped it off with a sharp, angry motion and tossed it into the trash. The memory of Tessa's kiss lingered on my lips, a phantom taste of salt and rain and a future that never happened.

All these years, every success with Tidal Hops, every new beer I brewed... in some quiet, unacknowledged corner of my heart, it had all been for her. A silent, one-sided conversation with a memory. A decade-long effort to prove to a girl who was long gone that her parents had been wrong about me.

And now?

The central, agonizing question, the one Eli had so carelessly unearthed, knocked the air from my lungs.

What if he was right?

What if, after all these years, Tessa was back? Not just as a presence in my head, but as a real, breathing woman who had built her own life, her own world, far away?

The thought was a terrifying, exhilarating jolt to my system. The persona I'd built, the easy charm and professional success, was like a sandcastle about to be washed away by the incoming tide.

And I didn't know if I wanted to run for higher ground or stand my ground and let the water take me.

Click to grab your copy of book four in the Sunset Siesta series, BETTER THAN YESTERDAY!

Also by Erin Brockus

SUNSET SIESTA SERIES:

Sunset Charade: A Sunset Siesta Novella

*Available free to subscribers

Better than Never: A Small Town Enemies to Lovers Romance

Better than Home: A Small Town Brother's Best Friend Romance

Better than Sunshine: A Small Town Grumpy-Sunshine Romance!

Better than Yesterday: Book Four coming mid-2026!

CALYPSO KEY SERIES:

Main Novels:

Visions of You: A Small Town Single Dad Romance

Because of You: A Small Town Fake Relationship Romance

Memories of You: A Small Town Second Chance Romance

Shades of You: A Small Town Forbidden Romance

Associated Short Stories and Novellas:

Traces of You: A Small Town Rivals to Lovers Romance*

* Subscriber exclusive

ISLAND ESCAPES SERIES:

Betting on Paradise: A Fake Relationship Billionaire Romance

Clock Strikes Paradise: A Billionaire Cinderella-Retelling Romance

In Too Deep: A Second Chance Romance

Beached in Bali: A Friends to Lovers Romance

HALF MOON BAY SERIES:

About the Author

Erin Brockus writes steamy small-town romance with a tropical twist. Her tight-knit island communities have all the charm and heat of your favorite small town, plus an ocean right outside the door. Her characters are smart, grounded women and the irresistible men who can't stay away from them—the kind of people you actually want to grab a drink with.

What sets Erin apart? Her stories go underwater. Drawing on her real-life passion for scuba diving and international travel, she builds worlds that feel like a vacation you never want to end. Her stories are full of salt air, adventure, and steamy tension that finally ignites.

She lives in Washington wine country with her

husband, who is also a scuba instructor. When she's not sending her characters on island adventures, she's running, mountain biking, or enjoying a good book with a cup of coffee.

Erin Brockus—where passion meets paradise.

www.ingramcontent.com/pod-product-compliance
Lightning Source LLC
Chambersburg PA
CBHW032147050726
47591CB00001B/122